Meeting the Dog Girls

stories

Gay Partington Terry

nonstop press • new york

MEETING THE DOG GIRLS
Stories

By Gay Partington Terry

Copyright © 2011 Gay Partington Terry

First Edition:
2011

Editor: Luis Ortiz
Production by Nonstop Ink

ISBN 978-1-933065-30-4 Trade Paperback

PRINTED IN THE UNITED STATES OF AMERICA

www.nonstop-press.com

 Nonstop Press

Contents

Introduction

 I've been writing off and on since grade school. Here's a very early example:

Where

Where is the mountain?
Where is the hill?
Where is the tree and the whippoorwill?
Where is the fish?
Where is the bear?
I think they're around here somewhere.

I had a long way to go and it got a lot worse before it got better and still has a ways to go.

I say "off and on" because periodically, I'd give up writing and do things like: play jacks, read unrequired books in college, watch Sesame Street with my children, or perfect my pie crust. I gave it up for reasons like: persistent frustration; the need to see that my small children didn't kill each other; and because I read things by Marquez and Millhouse, listened to Bob Dylan and Steve Earle, and concluded that I'd never be remotely close to that good. I tried to channel my writing urge into diaries but I don't have a firm grasp of reality. So the diaries aren't diaries, they're ... well, I don't exactly know what they are. I gave that up too. ("The Goddess of Outen," "The Backward Man," and "The Tale of the Glass Man" are all part of an illustrated autobiographical novel [unpublished]. You can see how that goes.)

I always went back to writing.

I'd start making up stories in my head and eventually put them on paper. Or I'd take a class from someone I really admired thinking they'd tell me I was wasting my time. But they didn't. Shawna McCarthy, Thad Rutkowsky, and especially Patricia Eakins and Carol Emshwiller — when people like that encourage you, you develop hope. Now I'm in a writing group with some really smart skillful writers and they haven't thrown me out so I keep plugging.

In terms of process, I don't mean to imply that I have voices in my head but it almost always starts with a character. They say something, do something. I try not to push them too hard. Sometimes they push me around. (Mostly they push me around.) The ones that have a story go out into the world (and sometimes come back).

Some of them don't have a story. They have a place, maybe some friends or acquaintances and a small life. They might putter around but it doesn't amount to anything. I cram them into envelopes and drawers (and occasionally the trash). I feel really bad about this because I'm strongly attached to some of them, but what can I do? I don't understand it — they insist on coming out and then they just sit on the porch and talk, or walk around aimlessly, or take bus rides. I suppose I'm so attached because these are the characters that are most like me — or would be if I had a porch.

I get a lot of inspiration from the F train, sitting in Madison Square Park before Tai Chi class, from middle-of-the-night muses, the children in my life (not necessarily all young in age), and from an abundance of slacker moments that I'm loathe to admit to.

Is this the part where I mention people I want to thank? Here goes: M & Pop, Howie, Travis, Zoe, Becky, Mike, Adriana, Evan, Landon, Miss Thompson (fourth grade), Miss Roland (HS), Shawna, Patricia, Thad, Bob, Gabriel, Patti & Patti, Bert, Linda, Sophia, Master Chen, Alex, Margaret, Ada, Barbara, Maria, Florence, Gabriella, Luis, and Carol Carol Carol.

Gay Partington Terry
Brooklyn NY

The Line

▣ There is no beginning, no end to the line, just women waiting. The women are beautiful in a disheveled sort of way. A slick of sweat illuminates skin in sunlight and moon glow whether the complexion is dark or pale; the powdery dust adds glistening texture. We don't look around much; we wait. Though there are many of us, we're all too exhausted to be companions to each other. Once in a while we move forward ever so slightly. The children do not play; they're much too lethargic from hunger. They stare out from behind mothers and strangers or weep quietly.

It does no good to worry. We stare into space. We attempt to patch our ragged garments. We wait enshrouded in our own thoughts. Yesterday there was a great storm so we're feeling cleansed. We're lucky to have warm weather and sun now. When the rainy season comes, we'll have to dig out our old tarps and endure the smell of mold.

The woman ahead of me picks nits out of a small girl's hair; perhaps it's her daughter. Like the line, there is no end to the nits. She crushes them in her fingers and eats them or feeds them to the girl. Both are so thin that you can see bones through the skin, but their faces are beautiful. Their dark watery eyes are deep-set, and chapped lips perfectly rounded. In front of them an old woman sits like a stone reliquary, lines of dignity set into her face and pendulous breasts resting beneath her thin dress. The woman behind me never looks up. Her sad eyes are intent upon the earth, her head intricately wrapped in yards of faded muslin. I asked where she came from, but her answer was unintelligible. It's possible that none of us really know what we're moving toward. At least we're not being shot at and the KEEP workers come by occasionally with water and a little food.

Mornings go quickly. Afternoons are intolerably long, hot, and dull. Evenings we eat the hard biscuits and bruised fruit we've horded all day. At night there are stars to watch, some shoot across the sky from above; some rise up from the ground. The expanse of sky makes our brief lives and hardships seem small. In the relative coolness of night, we sleep. Somehow, mornings are hopeful – even without promising expectations.

I sit on my bundle of belongings when I'm tired, curl up around it at night. There isn't anything in it but rags, a cup, and a dish or two. I wrap myself in the tapestry my great grandmother wove. It was kept in the ancestor chest at my mother's house, only brought out on special occasions. It's all I have left of a life that may have been a dream or a dream that may have been a life. Like me, it has begun to fade and unravel. During the day I attempt to patch it, but it wears faster than I can sew. I've run out of scraps with which to piece it back together and my fingers are becoming stiff and unresponsive.

I keep three photos in the pocket of my dress. One is a smiling child with parents, one a street in a small town, the other is so worn that I can no longer make it out. I pretend that these are familiar. The truth is that I only remember the line and the tunnels …

Our men are all dead or at war, even many of the boys have gone. There are bodies in the fields and on the road, too many for the animals to take, animals that have grown fat and lazy from overeating. Blood has made the ground so fertile that the bush grows thickly, covering them. The river is polluted with blood and body parts. Many of the men have been in tunnels for months. I myself was in one for several days. There's little air in the tunnels and some very bad odors come from the wounded that hide there. The husband who protected me has been gone for a long time. I can no longer remember his face but I see images in the clouds and the dry earth about me, of the child we lost.

Occasionally a truck passes by and sometimes they stop and take a woman or two with them. I smile, though never right at them, and try to stand straight. I'm hoping one of them will take me. Though the men in the trucks carry weapons and seem rough, I would be happy to go with them. I don't mind a little roughness. Sometimes they sing and shoot their guns in the air. The women in the line never sing, though I may have heard someone humming once.

I hope that we're waiting for transport though I'm not sure the people on the trucks know their destination any more than those of us on the line. But at least there's movement, wind in your hair and singing.

Last night a boy came and pretended to be my son. I shared a biscuit with him, but this morning he was gone. Men and boys don't have patience for the line; they'd rather take their chances on the road or fight.

It's easy to believe that the gods have abandoned this place, but sometimes at night the distant thrum of gunfire becomes a low-pitched note that vibrates inside the body and resonates with the peace of the line and the mercy of picking nits from someone's head or sharing a biscuit. I have learned enough to know that there's always been lines, and there's always been war.

I would leave the line if I had any place to go or anyone to go to. I'm trying to remember … Perhaps I'll go anyway, just for the walk. I could look at the bodies, those in reasonable condition, to see if any look familiar. Perhaps I could find more pictures or some useful items. But then what would I do with them? I couldn't sell them even if they were useful, because no one has money to buy with or goods to trade. And I can't carry any more in my bundle; as small as it is, it's still a burden in the heat. I don't want to end up in the tunnels again. Perhaps someone in front of me will get tired of waiting or get picked up by a truck and I'll be able to move forward. I could join the fight, but what good would that do? What side would I fight on? I know nothing of sides.

I only know waiting …

The Promise

Outside, babies float gently down from the sky. All traffic has stopped; people watch in awe. The blind mother stands on her hands in a red cubical positioning her legs in a protective mudra to keep the babies from crashing down recklessly. She wears only grey undergarments and high heels.

The babies fall like feathers, rocking to and fro on wind currents; they never cry. In the town square, their soft naked bodies land and are cradled in bushes and tree branches safely. People approach; the babies smile and coo. There are many: twelve or fifteen, similar but not exactly alike. The attendant has watched from the tower. He tip-toes down the winding stairs to the blind mother's cubical and opens the door quietly so as not to disturb her.

"It is finished," she whispers.

"All is well. I shall fetch your robes," he answers.

He brings robes from across the hall and helps her dress. There are three layers of the finest silk; yellow, orange and ruby. Because she's spent so much time upside down, nothing can be done with her startling yellow hair which stands one hand high in unruly waves. More attendants emerge from hall doors to follow her down to the square. The crowd parts for them.

The blind mother approaches each baby, lifts it from its cradle of foliage and sniffs. She smiles and hands it to an attendant who wraps it in an apron and carries it back to the stone tower.

Two babies are rejected. They are sniffed, assessed by touch and intuition, and replaced in their trees. When all the babies have been checked, the mother is led back to the tower. The babies won't be seen again until they can walk.

After they're gone, the crowd lingers. A young woman approaches one of the babies left behind. She reaches out for it and the baby grabs her finger, smiles up at her. She hums quietly and the baby turns its head toward her. She reaches up, lifts it, wraps it in her over-skirt, and turns to leave. She is followed by a young man.

A slightly older woman steps up to the other child, removes her ragged shawl, wraps it about the baby and walks away hastily. She is followed by the eyes of the crowd but no one dares interfere.

These are the women blessed by babies without having to perform the acrobatic mudra. These are the women who take on the anomalies.

The crowd disperses. No one looks up at the sky as they go about their day.

In three years the babies emerge from the tower. Dressed in colorful jumpers and soft fur slippers, they walk in two lines, led by five attendants. The young mother and father appear with their well-behaved child. Each proud parent holds one of its hands. They lift it over curbs and puddles.

There is no sign of the other mother and her child, and the children and towns people converge on the square where a celebration ensues. There are carnival rides and games, booths of sweet smelling food, antique vehicles for the adults to peruse. Each attendant supervises four or five children. The blind mother sits at the tower window listening to the sounds of contentment and smelling the sweetness of holiday food.

The king and queen, who've been watching the festivities from a castle window across the way, call their attendants to them. With a nod of her head, the queen commands them to follow behind with packages wrapped in azure-colored tissue paper. In the packages are finely carved spoons, one for each of the blind woman's children.

The king and queen lead the procession to the square. The queen is wearing her finest jewels and carrying a delicate fan which she uses to avoid directly breathing in the air of common people. The king is dressed in military fashion with all the appropriate insignias. He carries a cane of ebony and gold. The children of the blind woman line up to receive their spoons, even the child raised by the young couple. As the attendant places the packages in their hands, they bow to the king and queen, one child at a time and retreat to open their packages.

But there is one missing …

Suddenly the sky darkens with birds. All is silent, for these are not a species of bird that must flap wings to fly. These are birds that ride currents of air, birds that exploit the wind. These are the birds belonging to the second mother who chose to raise a child rejected by the blind woman.

The birds continue to swirl and swoop as the woman and her child enter the square. It's obvious that they've dressed up for the occasion, though their clothes are more worn than the others, softer and looser, the girl's dress a smaller version of the mother's. The king and queen study the pair and look at each other. The queen calls an attendant over and whispers something to him. He runs off in the direction of the castle. The mother and child whisper back and forth and the mother makes a half-hearted attempt to tuck the child's shirt in. Everyone waits.

Above, in her tower, the blind woman smells paradox.

The Queen's attendant returns with a package wrapped in red velvet and with a nod from the queen, he offers it to the child. The girl opens it to find a jewel encrusted dagger. The crowd gasps. Her eyes light up and she looks to the mother who nods in approval and whispers something. The child makes an exaggerated bow to the queen who smiles back at her.

Then the child hands the dagger to her mother and runs off to the pony ride. The queen is guarded, the crowd horrified. The mother smiles. Soon the other children drop their spoons and run off to join in. There's laughter and shouting. The peace of the afternoon is disrupted; attendants run in circles trying to catch children; the mother of the other rejected child cries in her husband's arms while holding her child closely.

The blind woman jumps from the window of her aerie. She catches a drain pipe and slides down, summersaults to the square in her grey underwear and stockings. The crowd parts for her. She wrinkles her nose and strains her neck; she sniffs them. When she finds the king and queen, she snorts.

"Whoock!" She squeaks.

"Whoock!" She hasn't spoken aloud for a long time and she has to stop and swallow several times to moisten her vocal chords.

"Who awk gave you the right awk to give an instrument of death awk, awk to a child of this age, to awk anyone?"

The crowd gasps. The Queen scowls. The last mother puts her hand gently on the arm of the blind woman. "It's alright," she whispers. "I'll save it for her; she'll need it when she's grown – to cut bread and skin fruit."

The queen turns and stomps off, followed by the confused king and their attendants. The blind woman falls to the mother's feet and cries hysterically. The mother wraps her own tattered apron about the blind woman's shoulders and wipes her tears with the hem of her skirt.

"Awk," she sobs. "They think awk it's all so easy, so awk foolproof."

"But we know better," the mother assures her.

People turn away; many hurry out of the park. But some loiter, wistfully watching the children play. The mother takes the blind woman to a bench.

One of the children's attendants follows them. "The children are getting dirty," he says.

"But don't they sound awk happy," the blind woman says.

The mother sighs; "Too bad it won't last."

"Promise me one thing," the blind woman says.

"I can only try … "

"That's all I ask … "

The Holy Sisters of Shedir

Each tiny stitch the holy sisters embroider bares a prayer. They are committed to a lifetime of devotion through the eye of a needle. A baby blanket might have millions of stitches, enough prayers to protect a child through puberty. A house banner with a similar amount of stitches protects a family from certain categories of pestilence and infringement by lesser demonic creatures. But it's a rare person that could hope to obtain such a valuable piece. A lucky woman might acquire a mantilla to cover her hair or wrap around her throat for refuge. It was more common for both men and women to obtain socks stitched with prayers for mobility, stability, and steadfastness. But few peasants could afford even these treasures. They were fortunate if they could procure a wee pouch in which to keep a "lucky coin."

The price of these needlework masterpieces was, not only gold and gems, but good deeds, high ideals, modest sentiments and temperance. Of course, there were always worthy people who fell into dire circumstances that compelled them to relinquish a precious prayer piece in charity. And an unknown number of these treasures fell into lesser hands by fraudulent means. Sometimes the prayer-stitches worked to save the illicit beneficiaries from their base affectations, and better their lives. Others, the more vulgar or evil recipients, often had strong physical reactions to the objects and if they were not discarded, the torment they produced incited them to new and more fervent acts of maliciousness and vice. For it is known that people can not be protected from their own malevolent natures if they're not willing to participate in the process of benevolence.

On the morning of the seventh day of the sixth lunar month of the 1,018th year of the Era of Sand, the Sixteenth Holy Mother called the sisters together.

"We've been offered a formidable commission," she told them. "The new High Chancellor asked us to create a work to cover his Royal Divan, the seat of power."

Astonished whisperings swept through the room.

The Sixteenth Holy Mother waited for it to stop. "As you can imagine, the High Chancellor is not our ideal patron but I sense a vein of posibility in him, albeit overlaid by frustration and disappointment. I'll want volunteers to prepare a ritual supper for us tonight." She sighed, "the Chancellor believes we fast on such occasions."

The sisters chuckled.

"I'll collect the dream threads in the morning. That will be all for now."

The Sisters ate their fine meal of sweet rice, leaves of the feathered palm steeped in exotic herbs, curry sea lily, juju figs in cream, and cardamom taffy.

They all slept soundly except for one novice who'd joined the order after her lover was killed in battle. Sister Glory Grace tossed and turned sweating beads of grief as she did every night. In the morning she laid her bedding on the low bushes outside her window in the hope that wind would blow the night's remorse out of them. She'd done this every morning for fifteen months. She purified herself and her belongings often, humbled herself with hard work, sat in meditation, and chanted ritual prayers endlessly. But she still heard the sound of his boots on the stones of the old hallway at night, felt his hand on her shoulder at vespers, and caught the scent of him on her pillow (even though this was the eighteenth new pillow she'd acquired).

When she went before the Sixteenth Holy Mother to receive her assigned task for the day, the Holy Mother told her, "Everyone must work on the High Chancellor's commission, at least for part of the day."

"Please, Mother, I don't feel I'm proficient or virtuous enough to work on such a project."

"Nonsense. I've seen your samplers. Your stitches are as tiny and uniform as Sister Violaceae. It's time you involve yourself in a communal project." The Holy Mother put her arm about the girl in a tender gesture. "It'll do you good, dear."

So Glory Grace joined the other Sisters in the sunroom to work on the piece for the High Chancellor. The sun was so bright as to be nearly blinding, the better to see every tiny stitch. The Sisters were busy untangling the dream threads and winding them on spools when Glory Grace added her meager thread to the cache. Because the sun was so bright, no one noticed the slight discolor of her dream fiber and it was wound on the spool set for the embroidered clouds, along with pearly grays, alabasters, whites and silvers. No one noticed the slightly grizzled tone of her thin strands.

This alone, however, would not have had a formidable affect the design except to temper the light it emitted and moderate it's effect slightly.

What did alter the work's intention was an incident that occurred on the fifteenth month and fourth day of work in the last hours of peak afternoon sun. The sisters were intent on their work when a peasant woman who was carrying pea beans for the Sisters' supper, was stung by a bode wasp. Father Icilius, who was taking a meditative walk in the garden on the other side of the nunnery in order to mentally prepare for evening prayer, was the first to reach her. The cry of agony he emitted when he found her dead was … indescribable. For he'd seen her fall and was there in seconds, unable to offer nostrum or solace.

Perhaps Sister Glory Grace was aware that the agonized cry had precipitated thoughts of her dead lover. Perhaps she even realized that she'd dropped a stitch. But the sight of the poor village girl ashen and shriveled, her pupils snapped in agony, the site of the sting on her ankle black and swollen, emitting a rank odor and oily discharge, drove out all rational thinking.

The Sisters spread bane nettles about the ground to kill off the bode wasps (for where there's one bode wasp, there's always a mate). They washed and wrapped the poor village girl and called her family for burial. Afterward, they were in such a state of emotional exhaustion, no one noticed the dropped stitch.

Six days later, after the funeral and after the bodies of two bode wasps had been collected and burned, the Sisters partook of cleansing rituals and went back to work on the Chancellor's project with pure hearts, unaware of the dropped stitch.

The divan cover took another twelve years to complete which was amazingly swift for such a project, as the larger and more complex pieces often took a lifetime to finish. But all other projects had been put on hold and every Sister and Novice worked long hours deferring all but the most necessary tasks for survival.

Sister Glory Grace found her calling with the Chancellor's project. She worked tirelessly and perfected her stitches until they were the finest, most even points of subtle prayer. She wore out hundreds of needles and dispelled her grief with the prick of each stitch.

The Sixteenth Holy Mother had chosen a design that mirrored the enchanted realm of the Great Mother of All, the magnificent Kingdom of Deep. The nun's delicate stitches would depict an ornate landscape bursting with pristine streams, exotic flowers, fantastical trees dripping with chilli-berries, and the enchanted creatures that serve The Mother, thousands of details set to invoke the perfection of a higher world. It was a task so awesome that it couldn't be contemplated as a whole. Each small unit was it's own ideal, worked on as a separate entity, refined to a precise archetype. Sister Glory Grace's assignment was to make the small knots and spiraling stitches that depict the flowers of the sacred gem fruit.

When they finished the project, the nunnery was in ruins, the once lush gardens a tangle of dead vegetation and weeds. The roof leaked, the plumbing had failed, and mice overran the empty larder. The nuns, especially the older ones, were decrepit; many had become delirious in the last year of frantic work. But the aging Sixteenth Holy Mother was certain that with the commission they made from the Chancellor, they would be able to restore the nunnery and its gardens to it's former quiet elegance and nurse the nuns back to health and spiritual well-being.

The High Chancellor was informed and royal upholsterers set to finish the divan. A great unveiling, to be held in the castle's rotunda, was hurriedly announced and the nuns assembled on the appointed day.

The nuns had had very little contact with the world for the last fourteen years so they were astonished at the change in the countryside on the way to the palace grounds. Farmlands had declined and streams were choked and filthy. Smoke from factories wafted through the air and mountains were scared and collapsed. The people, however, were better dressed and many were plump, a sure sign of abundance.

In contrast to the sister's dull disheveled appearance, the palace was a splendor, reflected a hundred fold in the pools surrounding it and the mirrored ceilings of the interior. Some of the nuns were embarrassed at their ragged habits but the Sixteenth Holy Mother told them, "It's no matter. We are aesthetics not court figures."

The Sixteenth Holy Mother was still vigorous and had become more animated in her eagerness to collect the appalling sum promised them and reestablish their peaceful pious life. But she was visibly shaken by the overly warm anterooms choked with a cloying mix of perfumes, an annoying murmur of derisive whispers and the rustle of silk taffeta.

"Stay close, my dears," she said. "We're in a house of impure spirits."

Sister Glory Grace was especially appalled by the vast expanse of the town cemetery and the pile of unclaimed bones at the west gate.

Lord Ashberry called for quiet and the High Chancellor addressed the company. The Sixteenth Holy Mother accepted payment and thanked him for the commission. Father Icilius delivered a brief blessing over the divan and the retinue passed by to marvel at the fine needlework, brilliant colors and intricate design of the cover, as well as the delicate carving of the spalted bloodwood frame.

Then the High Chancellor sat, heavy with authority.

He rested his elbow on the padded armrest.

He leaned back and the crowd applauded. Attendants brought trays of cream fruit and mandrake wine. Musicians played and costumed dancers swirled through the room. No one noticed the High Chancellor's fists curl.

When the Sixteenth Holy Mother came before the Chancellor to repeat her gratitude and take leave, she observed that the light of fulfillment had gone from his eyes, but she didn't say anything. The rest passed by one by one. Only Sister Glory Grace recognized the aspect of regret and realized he was encountering his lost moments, sinking.

Later that night, as the lights flickered dreamily and the lavish company chattered, the High Chancellor fell through the dropped stitch.

Perhaps he landed in the Kingdom of Deep, in the presence of the Mother of All, though this is doubtful as he did not possess the exemplar qualities necessary for access to that place. Perhaps he still hovers between that world and this. Perhaps he resides in some other realm or in the darkness of oblivion. No one knows and it's of little consequence to all but him.

With his disappearance, the position of High Chancellor went to his son, a quiet peaceful boy. But before all his treaties were in place, he fell through the dropped stitch and disappeared forever. The office passed to his brother, well-meaning but dull-witted, then to a cousin more interested in the arts than the welfare of his people, the brother of that cousin who was untutored and insane; all disappeared mysteriously by way of the divan. Three more distant cousins fled rather than accept the position, and an unscrupulous merchant who bought the office sat on his own throne, but was killed by a mob. Power was seized by an evil dictator who decreed himself divine. He divested the kingdom of all things beautiful and frivolous. The divan was placed on a bonfire along with elegant and coveted objects from all corners of the kingdom. The Holy Sisters of Shedir were nearly thrown on to the fire also had it not been for the pleading of the crowd and the promise that they would give all their assets to the state, remain isolated in their nunnery, and never work their needles again.

This was agreed.

But the Sisters stitched prayers of hope and justice in secret and after many years, a hero arose and set about overthrowing the dictator. Then came an era of violence that lasted only months but seemed to last a very long time, as all such eras seem. The season of death and destruction brought memories crashing back to Sister Glory Grace, memories of her lost love, of the Sixteenth Holy Mother, Sister Violaceae, the High Chancellor's kind son, and others long gone. Sister Glory Grace was an old woman but she had a nagging sensation of guilt. She'd spent her whole life doing needlework; it was all she knew. So she commenced stitching a mantle of guilt. Some of the other Sisters joined in and when word of it spread, men and women from all over came to add to it.

Soon the Mantle of Guilt was so heavy it couldn't be moved and many citizens believed they could do whatever they pleased, stitch their guilt into the Mantle, and be rid of it. Lines of people formed at the entrance of the nunnery. The kingdom was in turmoil and many small animals and children were lost and suffocated by the heavy cloak.

It had to be stopped.

On the morning of the first day of the ninth lunar month of the 1,088th year, the Nineteenth Holy Mother turned the line of pilgrims away and called for men with pack animals. It took thirty-one sturdy oxen and forty-seven good men to drag the Mantle of Guilt out to a field where it could be burnt. Smoke spread across the kingdom and blanketed the sun for six days bringing with it dreams of tragedy and turmoil, betrayal and regret. No one was exempt. Nineteenth Holy Mother announced that from that day forward, no disparaging emotions would be stitched into any of their projects. Should such emotions arise, the sisters were to report to the grounds keeper for heavy labor until these sentiments were sweated out into the soil where they might act as fertilizer.

The grounds of the nunnery were transformed to gardens pristine and elaborate, the Sisters grew strong and healthy, their needlework reached a level of perfection greater than the world had ever seen, the citizens resumed responsibility for their own actions, and the kingdom prospered in peace and harmony for a thousand years, though such eras seem all too short. We can only imagine what happened after that thousand years as we know, alas, such perfection isn't meant to last. Sooner or later a stitch is dropped, a tear is shed, a whisper of contempt seeps into the waft of even the finest material.

Should you come upon a sample of the work of the Holy Sisters (which is unlikely in our world but who is to say impossible?) pass it on quickly if you think there is any possibility you might harbor a secret nature that would pervert it, for it could could have a ruinous effect on your life. Take it as a sign that you might become worthy of it one day. Covet your good fortune and say a prayer for the soul of Sister Glory Grace and the talented hands of the Holy Sisters of Shedir.

The Prison Of Kronos

Fragments from the diary of Alber Istott Cretius

Day 4 – The Wing of "Before and After" where time begins anew

I was put behind bars for stealing moments. Time is a most coveted commodity and you dare not take what doesn't belong to you. It was decided that the Time I'd taken was the property of Mgsr. Lockes Enitsu, though some was initially believed to have belonged to Sister Filomena. I was humiliated and defeated by the suggestion that I would have taken something of such value from the good sister when, as everyone knows, had I asked she would have given it to me, steeped in charity as she is. I protested the accusation and was absolved by the Sisters of Almanac.

As for Lockes Enitsu, I admit guilt, resentment, and premeditation. I remain unrepentative, despite the harsh sentence bestowed upon me. I believe he spends his own tenure unwisely, repetitively, and embezzles that of others unjustly. When I'm released, I will be expected to repay Lockes Enitsu, in full plus penalties, for that which I've taken from him even though Enitsu is rich in time. A few moments are nothing to him but my crime is an assault to his image and ego.

My cell is exactly four paces wide and not quite five paces long. It contains a narrow metal cot, one fist wider than my body, with a mattress exactly two-thirds the depth of my index finger. Under the cot I keep my meager belongings: books I've been permitted to borrow from the Unit library, writing materials, two changes of uniform, an extra blanket, a cardboard box of photos, and chamber pot for night relief. I must petition the use of a toilet during the day.

Three days a week I work in the Expansion Practicum. Two days I'm on cleaning detail in the Denial Unit, and two days in the kitchen. I'm not permitted to work outside in the gnomon farm or in the quartz/crystal mines. Because of the nature of my crime, I must remain in sequential spaces where I can be monitored so as not to repeat my offense.

I'm popular with guards as well as inmates since Lockes Enitsu is universally detested. There is a groundroot movement to have me freed but I have little hope of it succeeding. I don't discourage the collaborators as they afford me connection to the Outside as well as a modicum of sympathetic mail.

In the cell next to mine the infamous Duce Mogon resides. It is he who defaced the grotesques in Hagora Square. The priests of Elapse were alarmed when the figure of Father Sinew expanded in girth and musculature. They were incensed that the Great Mother should have had her hump reduced, her nose reworked and her legs straightened. The citizens do not want their deities to approach perfection; they require more identifiable divinities. For this reason, Duce is unpopular and may face execution. The priests have now accused him of endangering celestial motions.

I find him quite personable, albeit a little sad. He yearns for beauty and is unsatisfied with the world as it is. He desires icons more like himself – that is: tall, muscular, even featured. They've provided him with ill-fitting shoes in an attempt to disfigure him from the ground up. They beat him when he attempts to remove them. Already, one knee is twisted and the hip lowered. Soon his body will spiral into a more acceptable form, his gait reduced to a suitable measure. His is a crime of tempo punishable by footwear, incarceration and possibly extinction.

He reminisces a great deal and is generous with his conversation. I, as you can imagine, am a sucker for a good story. We must be cautious though, as talking and especially listening are absolutely against regulations unless directly work related. As I am respected though, Guard Seven ignores our late night musings. It's only on his one night a week off that we must observe silence or incur the wrath of Guard Fourteen.

Day 17

Duce has devised a plan of escape and I've agreed to assist him with the understanding that we might plunder a portion of Guard Fourteen's tenure. He was pleased to agree despite his unfamiliarity with the illicit business of Time theft. For you see, Duce is a simple man, a man of black and white, do or die, "shit or get off the pot" as he colorfully puts it. He's a man of cliches – which is possibly why he was placed in the Wing of Before and After.

I consider myself a simple man also, but apparently my crime is one of devious cunning in these precincts. The injured parties of such misdeeds are considered "innocent" and there are no misdemeanors or insignificant transgressions perpetrated on members of the prevailing classes by those of us who rank lower in the social order.

Day 19? Or 1? Or 137 in the 36th year? (if I was permitted to return to my previous past)

The plan was successful, in its way, and I am "free" and in possession of the totality of Guard Fourteen's unappreciable interval. Duce has set off to live a life of imprudence and I am left a lone fugitive and relative neophyte to the precarious world of chronometric commerce. How I long to return to the finite space and predictable program of Kronos, days without the burden of dissent term. It conflicts and opposes, renders me unable to sustain my identity.

I repent and solicit mercy at the gates. Almighty Winter, give me strength with which to persevere.

Day 3. Or 20 (imprisoned). Or 140 in the year … but that is no longer viable.

I've been placed in the "Absolute/Relative" Wing. Here, those who are accused of the most depraved offenses are housed, those who've committed illegal division, felonious abstraction, lewd simultaneity, timebinding and worse. We sleep on thin floor mats, our meager possessions exposed on one narrow metal shelf. Not all my fellow inmates are in possession of their sanity; the disheveled boy in the cell across from me sits cross-legged in a corner, eyes rolled up into his head, occasionally murmuring. He is accused of transcendental intuition. When his medication wears off he becomes violent. It's said that he isn't the only inmate capable of reducing the stone walls to sand …

Day ???

A flood of contraband has found its way into the Unit, isochronons, telltales, pendulums. The hallways vibrate with whispers. Several of the guards have gone missing. The word "eternity" inscribed on the yard wall, has been filed down, painted over, replaced by "TRANSIENCE" in painted scrawl. My sympathizers, and those of others, picket the prison relentlessly and nosily. Their chants and movements are calculated to disturb The Continuum. Their placards denounce malpractice and insist that there is "No Time Without Change."

The incarcerated commit supportive transgressions and discount reprimands. I've resigned myself to persistent disturbances of the Hereafter. We await the uprising which has been given the code name "Meanwhile." The prison walls have begun to fall like sand through a glass.

Spirit Gobs

None of the four people I killed deserved to die.

The first one, Alfie, was just in my way. I didn't realize how slippery life was before I took Alfie's life. A little poke, a crack on the head, some blood, and ... gone.

The second one, AmberLynn, really riled me. Everything about her was as stupid as her name: her stupid hair, her stupid laugh, those jeans with holes that she made on purpose with a screwdriver. AmberLynn. She didn't do nothing wrong but she made a nuisance of herself to everyone, even though they all pretended to be shocked by her passing.

The last two, I barely remember. One was paid for. What he done was to fuck some guy's wife, a real mean guy with money to spend. My Aunt Fran needed to get her gall bladder took out and didn't have no insurance. It was kinda like cooking – I did the deed and this other guy cleaned up after. The last guy had some money on him but not enough to make me rich.

You probably wonder what I did with the lives I took. Most folks with my temperament don't do anything with them; they just let em fritter away. There's no excuse for this:

"I don't have anywhere to store them."

What do you need to store a life? It's not like you was gonna to store the actual flesh – that, you put in the woods for the critters to eat up. A jar with a good stopper or tight lid isn't hard to find. A fridge?

As long as the lid's tight, a life'll keep in most temperatures. Light, no light, it don't matter much. I have a fine cool root cellar where I keep mine.

Or: "I wouldn't know what to do with em."

Come on, who can't use a little pick-me-up? A drop or two in your Mountain Dew, or you can zap em for a quick snack. You don't have to be one a them gourmet cooks to add a pinch to your cereal or mix some with your greens, for god's sake. Maybe you have some friends over and the party's not happening – a few gobs on Ritz crackers with some spray cheese – how hard is that? People make such a fuss ...

A young guy like me ain't about to settle down to wife and family any time soon. My folks died when I was in my teens and left the house, not much else. No, it wasn't me – their lives were taken from them by a trucker who'd done too much crystal that day. The jackass took his own life too and I never did find out where those gobs got to. Folks like that don't bother to preserve what they unloose. I guess that's most folks for you. I got no kin, to speak of, just Aunt Fran and Uncle who live over to Red Sink. They don't come around much.

But this one day I was sitting on the porch when I seen their truck come down the road.

After we was done with "howdy's" and weather talk, Aunt Fran brought out her peach cobbler. "We woulda called if you had a phone."

"Got no use for a phone, too busy to talk. It's fine you stopping by when you've a mind." Aunt Fran and Uncle were always good to me. "I'll fetch some plates and forks."

"You done a real good job keeping this place up all by yourself," Aunt Fran tole me.

"Nothin' to it."

"How's things at the mill?" Uncle asked.

"Laid off twenty last week. I'm good till they close it down. They got no harder worker than me."

Aunt Fran give me a pat. "You was always a good boy, hun. I'll just go wash up these dishes. Al, you go get the preserves out the truck. I brung you some goodies from my garden. We had so much this year."

Uncle and I strolled out to the truck and he handed me a cardboard box with, musta been six jars in it. "I got a little home brew for you too," he said. "But we don't want your aunt to see." He reached under the seat for a jar a White Doggie. "Let's put this stuff away in your cellar and have us a pull."

So we did. Uncle got to lookin' around and asked about my jars.

"Them's spirit gobs."

"Spirit gobs? You grow em?"

"Naw. You jus pluck out when you see em, fry em up in a pan, or not."

"I never seen nothin' like em round abouts Red Sink."

"Here, try one."

Uncle popped a gob in his mouth and chewed. He got a thinkin' look on his face and said, "Not bad. You could sell these."

Got me to thinkin' about how we could use a little more lively around these parts. A shot of "elan vital," what my grandpappy used to call it, might be a good thing, get us some respect from a world that like to forget about the poor folk in these parts.

So Uncle and me had a few pulls and some gobs till Aunt Fran come lookin' fer us.

"What'r you boys up to down here?" She yelled from out in the yard. "You're not givin' that boy licker, are you Al?" Aunt Fran stood in the doorway. A large woman, she wasn't about to come down the creaky cellar stairs without good reason.

Uncle slipped the bottle behind an old lawnmower before she could see and said, "No ma'am. You ever hear a spirit gobs? Jess got the darndest stuff here. Come have a taste."

"You can bring it on up. These steps is too rickety for a woman my size."

I knew Aunt Fran would like the gobs; she liked most anything and if she didn't, she'd put enough salt or ketchup on it to make it tasty enough for her.

After they ate, they commenced to laugh like school kids. I put on the radio and Aunt Fran showed us some steps. Big women is always good dancers but you hardly ever see Aunt Fran move around like that. It was a mighty fine sight. I was happy I got her that gall bladder operation and happy the gobs give her some zip.

They went home in fine spirits and never knowed it was the gobs that give em the livelys. I gave em a jar for later.

The next day the supervisor told us the mill was closin'. It wasn't much of a surprise. All the boys was figurin' how long before they go on Relief and it get me to thinkin' ... I could hold out longer than most – I had a house free and clear and land to grow stuff on. I could hunt, maybe get some odd jobs now and again. I wasn't gonna be no clerk in a grocery or the Walmart. That was chump work, and folks with families to feed needed those jobs anyways. Then Uncle come by on his way to a lodge meetin' after he heard, to bring me one a Aunt Fran's casseroles. "You should sell your gobs," he said. "Them's real tasty and make you frisky too."

I had two shelves, three deep of jars (some from Pappy, Granpappy and some I'd come upon by chance). With no job and all, it wasn't a bad idea. I'd been tuckin' into the stuff too much lately, tryin' too hard at work, thinkin' they'd keep me on at the mill. My head was spinnin'. I could use the rest, live off the government for a spell instead it livin' off a me. I wasn't about to go peddling door to door but there was a county fair comin' up. Folks from all over would be comin' in for it. All I needed was a folding table and one a mama's tablecloths, which I surely had somewheres.

So that's what I did. Sold out the first day. Folks was buzzin' around like flies at a picnic, askin' could I get more and where could they find some themselves. A couple a bartenders made me offers and a fella from Walmart come to the house with papers and hung around till I sent him packin'.

Now here was my quandary, if I was to go into the gob business wholehearted, in order to harvest gobs, I'd have to kill off my customers (or hope they died off in front of me). It was a business doomed to go bust even if, in the long run, I could get rid of some riffraff around here. But folks tend to notice when their neighbors and kin go missing or when there's a odd fella turn up at a body's passin'. Sheriff Willard wasn't likely to take to that kinda goings on in his county. In fact, he'd been around askin' after Alfie and the others, talkin' about cereal killers – had he already figured out what it was that was on folks cornflakes?

I figured that I was bound to end up like everyone else, on Relief, and I wouldn't a chanced it – then ole Mz. Collier give Sheriff Willard a bag a gobs she'd bought at the fair and not ate up, cause he got her cat, Moonie, unstuck from the roof gutter. The old bat.

The sheriff had one of his "feelings" and come round to my house.

He sat on the porch with me, knocked back a Mountain Dew, talked bull crap for a while, then he said, "you make them spirit gobs what Mz. Collier buy at the fair last month?"

"They's already made, I just pluck em."

"You pluck em off a what? A tree? A bush?"

"No sir, I just pluck em."

"Out of the air?"

"Kinda."

"Son, I got a feelin' about these gobs and I got a feelin' nobody's gonna swallow my feelin' this time."

"Why's that sir?"

"Because in my business feelin' don't count. You gotta have proof. And I got a bad feelin' about gettin' proof in this case."

"You're a pretty respected man around here ... "

"And I'd like to hold on to that respect. I don't want nobody thinkin' I'm crazy or that I can't do my job. You see what I'm gettin' at, boy?"

"I think so, sir."

"Good. I'm thinkin' you haven't 'plucked' any more of those gobs lately and I'm hopin' you won't be doin' it again."

"Wasn't plannin' on it. I'm goin' on Relief next day or so."

"That's fine. When you do, there's a social work fella I want you to talk to, name of Cordel Crockett. Will you do that, son?"

"I surely will."

"Fine."

Sheriff Willard is a good man and I was hopin' this Crockett was too, maybe a relative of Davy, what fought in the Alamo. But he surely wasn't. He was a in-your business, know-it-all, paper shuffler with a runny nose and a wimpy handshake. He wanted to put me in a nut house and when Aunt Fran went to speak for me, he called her a name and he called her fat.

It's not for me to say who's deservin' what, and who's not deservin', but there's no call to put upstanding folks away nor call a poor old woman names ... I'll keep my word to Sheriff Willard about not sellin' gobs but I got a real hankering for some myself.

Slowdown In Paxville

A little girl in a white dress was standing in the middle of the sidewalk on a warm cloudless summer day. She might have been lost. She might have run away from home. She might have been looking for her missing puppy. She might have been an angel. Hooper didn't dare pass by or go near her. He had a "thing" about little girls in white dresses. For this reason, he walked up Mrs. Whipkey's driveway and cut through her backyard.

Mrs. Whipkey watched him from her second floor bedroom window, the small bay that faced the back. She wondered if she should call the police – or his mother. For, although Hooper was thirty-eight years old, he'd never gone to high school and was unemployed. He still lived with his "widowed" mother. (Mrs. Whipkey doubted this story as she'd never seen a man around that household, ever.) He disrupted the stones in the driveway as he passed through; he stumbled near the magnolia, grabbed at a branch and pulled down a cluster of petals. He disturbed the lilies and left dusty footprints in the grass.

Mrs. Whipkey decided to call his mother.

"Your boy is roaming."

"Hooper's a good boy. He don't harm nobody," his mother said.

"He doesn't belong in my backyard."

"You tell him to come on home. I can't go out. My legs … "

This was no surprise. Hooper's mother only left the house to go to Kingdom Hall on Sundays and then the Jehovah Witness disabled van picked her up and brought her home.

Mrs. Whipkey had no sympathy. "I may have to call the Sheriff then." After all, wasn't she a widow herself these eighteen years and didn't she manage to keep herself and her home presentable. Had she children, she would most certainly do the same with them.

She hung up.

Vella Carney (Hooper's mother), whose knees were so swollen from arthritis that they looked like grapefruits, got up out of her lounge chair and slipped on her (twenty-six year old) slippers. She fastened the buttons down the middle of her worn housedress, the ones she'd undone after a breakfast of Poptarts and cornchips, and shuffled out the door unsteadily.

It took her 47 minutes to walk the half-mile to Mrs. Whipkey's house, past well-kept Colonials and Ranches with tidy flower gardens and lawns so unlike her peeling clapboard saltbox, even though Hooper kept the crabgrass trimmed. When she saw the little girl in the white dress on the sidewalk ahead of her, she knew why Hooper had cut through Mrs. Whipkey's yard. Surrounding the girl were three transparent moths of the type called Daydreamers. Paxville was commonly beset with these insects in the summer, this summer more than usual. They emitted a pleasing murmur in the summer stillness.

The sun was very bright and Vella Carney was used to sitting in a darkened room with only the glow of the TV as company. To her tired eyes the girl looked like an angel. She had a glow about her, scraggily yellow hair that kissed her shoulders and tiny hands balled into fists. She was just looking down at the sidewalk.

Vella Carney tottered painfully forward hoping that if she pretended she didn't know the girl was an angel and if she was nice enough, the angel would cure her.

"Are you lost, little girl? Where's your momma?"

The girl just stood there looking down at the sidewalk.

"What's the matter, hon?"

Vella waited for an answer but none came. She tried to stoop down and look up at the girls face but she couldn't get very low and didn't see anything but hair and the hint of an up-turned nose. The daydreamers glided about them murmuring quietly.

"Have you seen my boy? My boy, Hooper's out here somewheres. He don't do no harm though. Mz. Whipkey jus like to make trouble." Vella knew right away she'd said the wrong thing. Angels didn't like gossips and, if by chance the girl wasn't an angel, she might be related to Nina Whipkey and take offense.

"You kin to Mz. Whipkey? I suppose she don't mean harm; she just … are you lost, honey?" Just as Vella Carney uttered these words her knees buckled and she fell slowly to the sidewalk. The pavement, where her body landed, was warm and the grass, where her head landed, was soft and cool. It was more comfortable than the lounge chair that had came from the Salvation Army store twenty years ago and who knows where before that. Vella knew she couldn't get up by herself and it didn't seem as if the little girl would help her, so she just lay there. It was comfortably warm with a hint of a breeze, so soothing that Velma closed her eyes and forgot about … everything.

Mrs. Whipkey ate her poached egg and toast, read the Paxville Courier (Martha Beeman elected president of the Garden Club again!), and did the dishes as she did every morning. Then she went into the living room to close the drapes against afternoon sun that would arrive in a couple of hours to fade her green and rose chintz living room suite. From her window she saw the little girl and Velma Carney, both as still as statues. There was rarely anyone on the sidewalk of the small town, only old Mr. Sheetz who took his constitution around the block every day at exactly 11:30 in the morning, Susie Grasso who walked her dog (when not being relentlessly teased about being oblivious to the world around her), and Timmy the paperboy who had three paper routes in order to avoid going home to his drunken parents. Seeing two people at the same time, one of them a stranger, was a shock. (There were no strangers in Paxville.) The fact that they weren't moving at all was extremely upsetting. She opened her front door and shouted from the porch:

"You there! What's going on? Little girl? Velma Carney, is that you?"

There was no answer.

Mrs. Whipkey was incredibly irritated. She didn't have time for this nonsense. It was Tuesday. She had to water her African Violets and dust the livingroom knick knacks before she went to meet her sister at the mall for lunch.

"You there!" She called. "Move along now."

Neither of them budged.

Mrs. Whipkey did not have the patience to deal with a deranged or sick child, let alone a white-trash lunatic like Velma Carney so she dialed Sheriff Miholy.

"Daniel," she said. "You best come out here. Velma Carney is laying on the sidewalk in front of my house and there's a deranged child with her."

"Did she have a heart attack? A stroke, or something?"

"How should I know; I'm not a doctor."

"Whose child is it?"

"I DON'T KNOW."

"Is it the Miller girl? What did she say?"

"She's acting crazy and I'm not going out there to have a conversation with her. You're the sheriff. Come do your job."

"All right, Mz. Whipkey. Take it easy; I'm on my way."

"That retarded Carney boy is roaming around somewhere also." Mrs. Whipkey hung up. What else does he have to do, she thought. It's not like we have any real crime around here. He sits in his office eating beef jerky all day, reading the Paxville Courier, that never had anything of consequence beyond high school sports scores in it, and begging the state police to let him in on a meth lab raid. (They never did.)

Nina Whipkey picked up her keys and pocketbook, locked the back door (something no one in Paxville had ever had to do before 1994 and crystal meth), and backed her Corolla out of the garage slowly. At the end of the driveway, she opened her window and yelled, "This is private property here. The sheriff's on his way."

When there was no acknowledgment, she backed on to Nutmeg Lane and drove away.

When Sheriff Maholey got there, the girl and Velma Carney were in the same position. He asked politely if they could hear him — several times. Then he put his hand on the girl's shoulder but removed it quickly as that was the kind of thing that might be taken wrong if anyone were to pass by or the little girl wished to make a "thing" about it later. Then he knelt down near Velma Carney and gently lifted her eyelids, but he didn't really know what he was looking for. He put two fingers on her neck and was relieved to feel a slow easy pulse. He was so relieved that he sat himself down in the grass next to her. He could hear the robins in Mrs. Whipkey's Japanese Cherry tree and feel the June wind carrying the scent of roses that grew up the side of the garage, roses like his own mother used to grow before she forgot where she lived and how to dress herself – a duty he'd grudgingly taken over. He lay back on the grass thinking that since there was no hurry, he'd just watch the clouds drift overhead for a minute before calling an ambulance …

Stogy, Susie Grasso's dog, stopped to lick Sheriff Maholey's face and curled up under the cherry tree. Susie laid her head on the dog for a little nap … Timmy threw his bag of papers down, sat cross-legged near the driveway and bent his head to look for a four-leaf clover. An out-of-work mechanic passing by pulled his pick-up over to see what the problem was and ended up staring at the roses. Maud and Cleo Mayercheck, the spinster sisters from next door went over to see if Mrs. Whipkey knew what was going on and ended up posed holding hands at the foot of Mrs. Whipkey's porch steps. Sara Mooney (from the house on the other side of Mrs. Whipkey) dropped her grocery bags on the lawn and stood gawking. She read Us magazine and watched Entertainment Tonight faithfully but had no hope of ever getting out of Paxville where nothing ever happened except that she was pregnant again and her husband would not be pleased as he wanted a new car. Her two-year-old daughter, Megan (bored by lack of parental enthusiasm), wrapped herself around her mothers lower leg and closed her eyes.

By the time Mrs. Whipkey got home from the mall there were fourteen adults, four children, a dog, and three squirrels posed motionless in her front yard. Hooper sat on a low branch of an Osage orange tree on the hill across the street alternately waving, shaking his head and mumbling to himself.

Mrs. Whipkey drove up to the front of the house and sat in the car dumbfounded, afraid to pull into the driveway or venture across the lawn to her own house. She heard Hooper call from across the street:

"Hoo, hoo, Mrs. Whipkey! Lookie! Lookie! Mrs. Whipkey, lookie!"

Mrs. Whipkey whipped her head around and gave him an old schoolteacher look that shut him up fast. She got out of her car and slammed the door.

"What the Hell is going on here?" She screamed. "What?"

No one moved or made a sound except Hooper, who began to whine. Mrs. Whipkey shot him another "look." She thought about the game, "statues," that she used to play with her friends in the schoolyard when she was a child. She remembered being a perfect child and excellent at the game of statues in her day – but not this ... this was not a game. Or was it?

"I saw you move," she called out.

No one budged.

She hesitated for a moment, turned her back, then spun around.

"Moved ... you moved. I saw you."

Still, no one flinched and Mrs. Whipkey knew she'd lied. None of them had moved.

She'd always hated being "it" anyway. It was much more fun being a statue. She remembered how comfortable it felt to hold very still and experience a cat's paw of summer air on her exposed skin, like the touch of a lover. Then she thought about Albert, the love of her life, who wouldn't wear a tie when they went to Villa Ramona in Hunker for dinner. She remembered the white dress she'd had as a young girl (the one her mother threw in the rag bag before she was ready to give it up, even though it was too small), and the sister who couldn't stop talking about her daughter's money and weight problems at lunch every Tuesday. It was much better to keep moving and not have to think.

She jumped in her car, drove it into the garage and took her packages in the back door. She noticed a tiny spider on the back stoop; it wasn't moving either. She swung her Val-U Mart bag through the web, stomped on the spider and went inside.

After she put her purchases away, she fixed herself an ice tea and sat in the living room with the "Reader's Digest" for ten minutes before opening the front door and yelling, "this is NOT funny!" Then she sat on the couch with her tea, feeling sorry for herself. When she'd had enough of that she turned the TV on to watch Ophra. Sometime toward the end of the evening news, Jeff Mooney (Sara's husband) pulled in to the driveway next door. Mrs. Whipkey peeked through the side drapes so he wouldn't see her.

"What the hell...," he said when he saw her yard and walked toward his wife and daughter.

Mrs. Whipkey lost sight of him and tiptoed to the living room where she could see better but, by the time she got there, Jeff Mooney was frozen in a ridiculous gaping pose next to his wife and baby. Her mind started to race. Should she call the fire department and wind up with all the firemen stuck in her yard. Should she call the state police? 911? Her sister, maybe? She could call her niece first, just to see her sister's face when she saw her daughter frozen. She stood in her living room, unsure of what to do and wondered if she might be immobilized too. Then she heard a noise in the yard. It was Hooper. He tapped on his mother's shoulder and then began circling the others, mumbling and crying.

Funny, he didn't freeze like the others.

Then he ambled up to her front door and knocked.

"Mz. Whipkey. Mz. Whipkey. Somethin's wrong out here. Mz. Whipkey, open the door. Come look."

At first she thought if she stood real still, he wouldn't see her in the shadows or he'd think she was frozen too. But she'd left the outside door open for some air and he put his hands around his eyes and his face right up to the screen. She had to scratch a terrible itch on her left shoulder. Of course he could see her.

"Go away," she called.

"I'm hungry. It's past supper time."

Lord, she thought. Why doesn't *he* freeze?

"Please, Mz. Whipkey."

Why was it that he didn't freeze up like the others out there? Come to think of it, she hadn't frozen when she got out of the car earlier either. What was it about the two of them that protected them from what ever was happening to everyone else? What could she possibly have in common with Hooper Carney? She looked at the big rubbery face in the screen-door and shivered. What ever it was that they had in common, there was only one way to find out.

"Come round the back," she called. (The front door was off limits to everyone as it opened right into the living room and her four-year-old beige Aubuson from Carpet Emporia.)

She had some hot-house tomatoes and American cheese. She put these between two pieces of white bread, put that with some potato chips on a plate, and handed it out to him with a couple of paper towels.

"You just sit there on that first step and eat now," she told him. "Stay down at the bottom. I don't want a mess up here."

"My momma makes toast," he said.

"We're not having toast tonight."

"Momma gives me milk?"

"Just a minute."

When she got him settled, she made herself a plate of tomato and cheese and sat on the top step.

"What's wrong with my momma?" He asked.

Why, he's just like a child, Mrs. Whipkey thought, a child Vela Carney made 38 years of toast for. "I don't know, dear." She hadn't called anyone dear since Mr. Whipkey died of a stroke eighteen years before. Had she mistaken resoluteness for patience all these years? Could she exercise patience now?

"Can you fix her?"

"I don't believe I can."

"Well, you have to get somebody to fix her."

"Who should I get?"

"A doctor."

But when Doc Porterfield arrived, he froze like the rest of them. Hooper lay down on the grass and cried.

Mrs. Whipkey patted him on the shoulder tentatively. It was getting dark.

She couldn't see that they had anything in common at all. He was a retard-mentally challenged child-man, and she was a capable woman. He was confused and inept, at odds without his mother to care for him whereas she was an intelligent woman who persevered without benefit of aid from husband, friend or relative. (Her sister was an irritant and bother, definitely no help to her.) He wandered through life, useless and feeble. She had a schedule and kept to it. Nothing at all in common …

Slowly, Hooper's sobbing became a low whine, then a hiccup, a sigh and finally, Mrs Whipkey realized he was not moving or making a sound. He was at perfect peace, frozen like the others. Mrs. Whipkey's patting slowed until her hand was resting lightly on his back. She closed her eyes so she could feel the faint warmth of him progress up her arm, through her body and release the strain in her muscles. The light evening breeze swept thoughts and worries out of her head, leaving her with a pleasant fuzziness she'd never experienced before. A transparent Daydreamer moth landed on her arm, just the slightest touch … she hesitated to savor the moment.

The Queen's Instructions

The Queen's instructions to her attendants:

It is your job to thrill me, to lift my mood when I feel hopeless, to see to it that I am comforted, unfettered by stress. I like surprises.

You must open the drapes to sunshine daily so that melancholy can not fester in corners.

You're in charge of music. This is an onerous job; think carefully who you give the instruments to. You must see that the Lords learn to dance.

Report all abnormal odors.

On alternate days you must patrol the tunnels to make sure the way is clear in case there is need of escape. There should be plenty of room for dancers and leopards.

Beware the silvery secretions on the ramparts. They are highly toxic. If any should get on your clothing, remove it before it seeps through skin into the bloodstream.

DO NOT disturb the fine weavings of the old women and DO NOT refer to the King's mother as a "spider" despite her hirsute spindly limbs.

Pay no attention to the writing on the wall.

In case of emergency the kitchen staff is most trustworthy, but make sure they keep pigeons and spider nymphs outside the inner walls at all times.

Beware of skirmishes among the poets; avoid their sharp teeth.

It is your job to tend to the small animals that come each morning to the priestess' chambers. It is your job to speak to the priestess' about their attitude.

It is your job to make the popcorn.

DO NOT enter the red chamber unless you are summoned with secret phrases.

It is your job to whisper encouragement, your job to see that I am kept warm on cold nights and to keep the wereworms at bay.

I rely on your competence and loyalty.

The Tale Of The Glass Man

There was once a man who was made of glass. He was usually very careful to keep his stomach covered for when it was bared, people were hypnotized by its intricate workings, the multihued liquids that churned in its depths, the minute organisms that dwelled in its folds, the kaleidoscopic dance of biomechanical operations. Crowds formed, traffic stopped, mothers dropped the hands of their children, lovers lost each other, and emergencies were forgotten.

The man of glass shed shards when he saw how easily the fleshy ones were distracted from their own lives to look at him. He was surprised that they were not interested in the exposed ankles of their women or the silky hair that blew in the wind. He was distraught that no one considered his feelings or asked about his thoughts, assuming that these were transparent too. They stared at the pulsations of his heart and, in public bathrooms, snickered at the plumbing in his genitals.

The man of glass would never have bared his stomach had he not been offended by their flippant attitude. "Oh, him," they said. "We can see through him." It was as if he wasn't there.

"Really," he'd say. "Well, see through this." He was always sorry after he'd lifted his shirt and everything around him stopped. He wished there was a way to see through the fleshy ones, but he never found one.

It was a lonely life for the man of glass and cracks began to appear.

The grinding in his feet curtailed his mobility. An increasing number of chips caused his clothing to tear and snag. He could no longer wear sweaters and the cold winters caused him to crack more. Still, he kept himself clean with Windex. Even when a woman drove into him with her car and he was shattered, he continued to go about his daily routine in pieces.

Then one day, in the course of building a superhighway, a powerful wrecking machine swept its steel arm at him. With one stroke, he was gone. Tiny pieces of him shone in the sunlight for a while and then were ground into the earth.

Some tales have no moral; they're just stories. What can we learn from a man of glass? None of us are made of such a material ...

The Goddess of Outen

Somewhere in the debris of the Lesser Sunda Islands in the Indian Ocean, lies a tiny, but lush, island known as Outen. The inhabitants are a mixture of Dyak outcasts and lost pirate crews, people that even the outlaws of Australia refused to take in. Through centuries of isolation and inbreeding, they developed their own civilization and racial genre.

They are small and brown. Most have shocking orange hair that seems to grow straight out from the head, a trait inherited from one extremely robust renegade from the pirate contingent. These rogue outcasts, deprived of civilized influence and left to their own devices, flourished on the little island and evolved an extremely good nature as evinced in the gentle eyes of their descendants. They retain the cleverness of pirates and dexterity of the Dyak, and they move about their daily occupations with the languid rhythm of the waves that lick their shore.

Among the residents of Outen, there was once a woman named Anathema; the old ones call her the Goddess of Caducity, and worship at her sacred mountain. This sacred "mountain" in the vernacular of such a small island is little more than a hill, but it seems to attract all the lightening that befalls the area. (Scientists speculate the existence of a metallic vein of some kind.) Anathema's mountain is covered with briar bushes, which accounts for the many tears in her clothing. She is taller than the general population, and bone-thin; a build never prized by the Outen. A missing arm is replaced by a thick briar branch, laden with bits of refuse caught out of the air. One eye is replaced by a button which, when tapped, enhances her brain and stimulates her thought process. In her frazzled gray hair she keeps snacks and writing materials. Despite her appearance, not even the children are frightened of her.

They say that when the Goddess was a young woman, she captained a pirate ship out of Doubtless Bay, that she watched her crew tortured and eaten in Palau Uwi before escaping to Borneo and falling in love with a mortal head hunter possessed of many brave souls. Together they settled in Outen and when her mortal lover died, she went to the mountain to dwell with the lightening.

Because the lightening is drawn to Anathema's mountain, the people believe all lost things are attracted to her; and because the briars hold what is blown by the wind, they believe all that is missed is in her keeping. The women bake bread in the shape of lost people and possessions. They mark it with stones, speak charms over it, and offer it to the Goddess. The men keep the mountain paths cleared so the lost things can make their way to Her. Together, they perform ritual dances in intricate interlacing patterns, and pray at the foot of the mountain.

The Outen do not pray for the return of their lost things, however. That would be heresy in virtue of their history. They pray to the Goddess to respect and care for what has been lost. They ask forgiveness for their attachment to the person or thing that is missing. Then, if the Goddess deems the supplicant truly pious, she will offer something in return. For the Outens believe that loss is necessary to stimulate development, that we gain ten-fold what we lose, that those who lose abundantly are most sacred. They revel in privation, give thanks for bereavement.

In the 250 years since Outen was settled, they have periodically been plagued by developers and pillaged by merchants. The Outens welcomed these vandals with open arms. It is even said that one particularly ruthless merchant was sacrificed to the Goddess, who then butchered and dressed the carcass, grilled the meat, and delivered it to the village in order to stave off the famine that he'd caused.

"Just as the Goddess sustained the loss of her loyal crew and was given the love of the many souls that inhabited the head hunter; just as she lost him and was given the very lightening from the sky; just as her appendages were lost and replaced by more useful contrivances, so shall we gain by our losses. Amen."

Now You See It ...

My greatgreatgreat grandfather was an Ashanti sorcerer, come here on a slave ship to save his brothers. He made a powerful spell and caused war in this country between white men. Many were killed. He didn't kill all because he said they was evil and good in all races. But he was disappointed in men and how they used their power, so he passed his powers on to women. Women, he said, were more trustworthy.

I'm the last in that line – so far. If there's to be more, mama says I'll have to trust a man. I have time for that.

Greatgreat grandmother moved north and settled in the mountains they call the Appalachians. She planted herself in the only state that cut itself in half to protect black folks freedom. In the old days our hollow was the home of self-sufficient and freethinking folk, everyone living how they seen fit and not judging how others lived, folks who wanted to be left alone to live out their lives without bother – so grandmother and great grandmother told it. Now ... it's not the same. Things change. Though there be some fine folks thereabouts, it's not all a them.

No one since has been as powerful as ggggfather and I'm not smart like mama and grandmother. I was hard-put to learn the herbs and the mixing, better at spells when mama put music to the words.

The tune make them stronger anyways. Grandmother said you're always better at what you're keen on and what I was keen on was disappearing. I worked hard and hoped one day to be good at it.

I thought a lot of my shortcomings was from the watering down of my Ashanti blood. Greatgreat grandmother married a Seneca Indian. Grandmother up and married a white man, or didn't marry him but had mama with him anyways. My daddy is a mix like us but look white. Seemed to me that the more kinda folks you were made up of, the more folks looked down on you and sometimes I wondered if they wasn't right.

Mama said it weren't so, that it's a good thing to carry blood from different peoples but by the time I was old enough to go to the county school, it didn't seem to put me in a good light. Which is why learning to disappear was so important to me. Grandmother called the trouble makers "inbreds" and told me not to pay them any mind 'cause they was just scared at what they didn't know. They was so crazy that there wasn't much learnin' goin' on at that school so I up and quit.

I got a job cashering at "Wayne Potts Park and Save." We sold everything the Walmart sold and more, only Walmart was forty miles away and Wayne Potts was here long before it come along. I suppose there was a fella named Wayne Potts but he's been gone or disappeared a long time. Did he know the secret of disappearing? In my time it was run by Mr. Hoag. Mr. Hoag was pretty fair and give us nearly union wages and half toward doctoring. He didn't know what to make of me 'cause he knew mama, daddy and grandmother long time and I'm like them and not.

"Ashie," he'd say. "You're a smart girl. Why don't you finish school?"

"I'm learnin' plenty, Mr. Hoag, more'n they teach at that school."

"I'll bet you are."

I got that job 'cause I pass for white, light skin, mousey white-trash hair. But I got dark Indian eyes and Ashanti spirit. I think Mr. Hoag knew, that from time to time, I "forgot" to add on some a Mz. Pacer's produce 'cause she had nine kids and a husband on disability, and old Mr. Sumer's tobacco when he run out of food stamps. He also knew I'd help unload a truck after I punched out and drive his daughter Macy home when I seen her walking crocked on the side of the road.

How I knew my invisibility was coming along is that Bart Omalacy, who was a stockboy but thought he was in charge when Mr. Hoag was busy, didn't see me much. There's others didn't notice me either. Bart, who was on everybody about something, didn't bother with me. Sometimes I forgot myself in front of him and he look like he never seen me before. Then I'd give him my Ashanti stare and scare him away, make him forget. It's partly in the attitude and what you wear and how you move and your speaking voice help you disappear.

One day grandmother told me she's gonna soon travel to another place, not in this world, and not come back and I should be a good girl.

"But how am I gonna learn to be invisible?"

"Child, you're gonna learn all kinda things without me teachin'. Just keep watchin' and stay open to things around you."

My folks thought she died but I knew better. I seen her spirit rise up. It wink at me, then disappear. When her spirit gone, folks put the body in the ground. Daddy carve a stone hisself even though she be mama's mama. We had us a old dog name of Francie who lay down at the grave till her spirit disappear too.

So I come to feel it was my time to disappear from the hollow only I thought maybe I'll see some a this world before I go off to the other.

Mama give me ggggma's earbob made into a pin for protection. She give me fifty dollars set aside for who knows what and I went off to the big city where it's easy to disappear and where there's folks practicing invisibility without knowing it. There's also a whole lot a folks callin' out to be seen and heard. Lord, what a racket they made. And what most a them wanna be seen and heard for, I couldn't figure for the life of me. I don't think most of them got it figured it out either because when somebody did pay attention, they had nothing to say, nothing to show. Go figure.

I got a job from Mr. Halim Hill who needed someone to watch over his store while he cheated on his wife. The store sold whatever Mr. Hill could buy cheap that week, food, toys, pens and paper, Lottery tickets, Christmas ornaments in June ... it was like a mini "Wayne Potts Park and Save" right there in the city. Mr. Hill seen I had the kinda experience he needed and hired me even though I never finish my schooling. I got a room in the house of Mz. Beatrix Escovedo who paid me to tidy up and read to her. I didn't have to do much at either place so I had plenty of time to work on being invisible.

If yo[ ]folks, you can always get a job and the quiet[ ]er they think you are. Then you disappear, th[ ]and they never know they been hoodwinked. [ ]pay a whit of notice to me but Mz. Escovedo seen through me right off. "I can tell that you know some magic," she said. "I hope you don't think you'll be using any spells on me, young lady, because I'll spell you right back."

"No, ma'am," I said. "I don't do no spellin' on nobody."

"What is it you do then?"

"I'm learning to disappear."

"Whatever for?"

It was the first time anyone asked me that question. "I got a talent for it."

"That's apparent."

"Shouldn't a person develop their god-given natural talent?"

"I'll have to get back to you on that," she said.

Mz. Escovedo and I got along just fine since then. I read to her when she was of a mind to be read to. Once a week Jenny came in to give the house a good cleaning so I just picked clothes up off the floor and washed a few dishes. Mz. Escovedo ordered in food every night and ate the left-overs for lunch the next day. I made her tea and toast for breakfast. The rest of the day she watched the neighborhood out her window.

At my job I practiced disappearing around some folks, some not. I was gettin' better at it. I don't know who folks thought was taking their money, giving them change, bagging their stuff when they didn't see me. City folks don't get riled by that kinda stuff is all I could figure.

One day this kid Cooly come in, pulled a gun and asked for money. I give it to him and disappear but Mr. Moskawitz, there to buy some canned soup, don't have the knack and Cooly shot him. Blood spattered all over the cereal and flowered sheets. Cooly run off. Cops and EMS took their time coming. I never thought a old man had so much blood in him and still live, which he did, but he was in the hospital four months and then use a walker ever since. The night after that was the only time Mz. Escovedo made tea and toast for me.

Cooley went to jail and his little brother, The Worm, started dogging me. He'd watch the store during the day and follow me home sometimes when I'd forget to disappear. He was watching the day

Mrs. Hill came in and asked me where he█████████e day of the robbery. Before I could disappear she █████████now where he was. He was with that hussy. I'll sho█████████what robbery is."

Halim Hill was too smart for her though, and she ended up having to go back to her family in Lebanon, Oklahoma. After that Mr. Hill moved in with "the hussy" and started cheating on her.

The Worm never left me alone and finally one day he came into the store and pretended to go through a pile of mittens for about fifteen minutes before he bought a pack of gum. I thought I'd pretty much faded away but ...

"How do you do it?" he asked.

"Pardon?"

"I've seen you disappear. How do you do it?"

"It ain't easy."

"Can you teach me?"

"You have any Ashanti blood?"

"What's that?"

"Slave blood?"

"I'm black, ain't I? What does that have to do with it?"

"Magic comes form the mother country."

"You're white!"

"Looks is deceiving. Why you want to disappear?"

"I just want to. Can you teach me?"

"I can't if you have evil intent."

"I hate it here," he said. "I hate this neighborhood. I hate this city. I hate my folks and their stinky apartment. I hate being called The Worm."

"What's your name then?"

"Akins."

"OK Akins, I'm not the best at this, but I'll show you what I know."

After that Akins and I started spending time together. First I had to clean him up; if folks can smell you, you're not going to be invisible. His mom wasn't about to do his laundry, so I took it on. I could see why he didn't like living with his folks. They was dirty and loud and mean. He had a pretty nice grandma but she didn't want another mouth to feed so he had to sneak in to her house at night and be as

50

invisible as he could. Mz. Escevodo let me have him over for supper a couple times a week and he got some food from his school. He got to be pretty good at being invisible at school, sneaking into classes and sitting so quiet that nobody noticed him. The two teachers who did notice him, told him he was doing real good. They wanted to see him go to to college and would help him get in and get scholarship money. He let them do it and things was lookin' up for him, then one day he came to see me ...

"I gotta get my brother outta prison," he said.

"Whoa there fella, I don't think you're up to that. Where would you hide him? And anyways, he shot a guy!"

"He didn't do it on purpose."

I looked him in the eye serious.

"Guns go off sometimes by themselves," he said.

"Not where I come from."

"Well they do here − if you don't know what you're doing and you get scared."

"He shouldn't a had no gun. You got no hunting season here. There wasn't nobody after him."

"What do you know?"

"Was there someone after him? Who?"

"A guy ... "

"Then he shoulda told the cops ... "

"Come on!"

"OK, so it's a long story and your brother's a innocent lamb. But you can't get him outta jail. How much more time does he have?"

"Three, four years maybe."

"That's not so long. Tell you what we'll do. We'll teach him how to be invisible and that way nobody'll mess with him while he's in there. He'll do his time quiet and they'll let him out."

I got Akins to agree that this was the best plan and all we had to do was convince Cooley and get him to work at it.

Cooley tried to be invisible but he didn't have the knack. He'd try for a few hours, then get frustrated, get seen and get in trouble.

I wanted to disappear on Akins but the kid was just too pitiful and he needed a good meal now and again.

"Don't give up your schoolin' no matter what." I told him I was sorry I quit, so he worked hard an graduated.

Then of a sudden, he wasn't there. I walked around the neighborhood calling him, waited outside his grandma's building. Three days went by and I had a knot in my gut so I went to see Cooley.

Cooley knew why I was there.

"I don't know how he got in," Cooley said. "The dumb kid thinks he's gonna bust me out; what a joke that is. He hides out in the library, the laundry. I don't know how he hasn't got caught. Who busts into a jail? Only a dummy."

"Don't call him dumb. He wants to help you, ya big asshole!"

Cooley banged his fist and started raving. Guards came and took him away.

"Just get him to call me," I said.

That night Akins called and I taught him a powerful spell I promised grandmother I'd never give out. The next day I rented a car and at midnight waited a mile down the road from the jail. Akins made it out but he brought Cooley with him.

"You shouldn't a brung him," I said.

"Shut up and drive," Cooley said.

At first he wasn't going to let me go back to the city but I talked him into it, not because it was the best thing for him, but I had a job and a place and, hell, I had to get the car back to Mr. Hill. Cooley laughed about shooting Mr. Moskawitz and said he learned a lot a useful stuff in jail. I took him to his friend's building and let him off. Akins had disappeared into the seat next to me and Cooley got out without saying anything or asking after him.

Akins and I returned the car and went up to make Mz. Escavdo breakfast.

"I shouldn't a done it," Akins said. "He's a bad man. I saw it as soon as I got into that jail. I thought he was telling the truth about the gun going off but he lied. I thought jail would make him better but it didn't."

"Well, it's done now," I said. "We gotta undo it before he shoots someone else."

"I ain't gonna call the cops on him."

"It'd just get us in trouble anyways."

"We could disappear for good."

"We could. But why should we leave what we got here? You goin' to college ain't you? Make yourself scarce while I go in to work. We'll both think on it."

Cooley must a been practicing invisibility more'n we knew because he'd be there on the corner, loud and nasty, smoking with what Mz. Escavedo called "the black-hearts," the cops would come roarin' in to question neighbors about him, and ... poof! He was gone. Then he'd turn up at a bar or the luncheonette to threaten folks. He'd pop out of an alley and take your money. He'd stand on a roof pointing a gun at you. He'd walk into a store and take what he wanted. Everybody seen him but nobody knew where he was hiding out. If his folks had known, they woulda told; they didn't care. Only Akins knew but the cops didn't bother him much since he was "a good kid."

Akins came for supper one night and Mz. Escavedo ordered in tacos and pizza. You can get pretty much anything in this city.

"You must turn your brother in before he kills someone," she told Akins (who had thought he was pretty invisible that night).

We was both surprised that she knew about Cooley and we musta looked it 'cause she said, "Magic comes in all colors and cultures. I know what goes on around here."

"He can't do it," I said. "Cooley kill him sure."

"Well, we can't let that happen, can we?" she said.

"Whata we gonna do? Cooley's a fearsome black-heart even he got no magic."

"I'll call in some favors. Go get Hadar Rubinstein, she lives in the Fisk Building, Catlyn McBride, she's at 407, Alek at the newsstand, Diwata at the dry cleaners, Kunthea at Stop and Shop, Mrs. Wu and Lara ..."

"Lara the hussy?"

"Lara the Candomble healer. Tell them to meet here Friday night."

I seen what a real mix look like that night. Folks came to the city from all over and I never realized how many different kinds lived right in my neighborhood. There was Brazilian, Albanian, Gaelic, Hebrew, Latin, Tagalong, Cambodian, Chinese, African ... who knows what all! Everyone of them came with their magic and their gear. There were herbs and candles, exotic oils, crystals, bells, dolls, feathers, books. I never seen the like.

I served snacks and lemonade and then Mz. Escavedo called for quiet. "You all know why we're here," she said.

A wave of anger passed through the crowd. "The bastard's not going to be harassing anyone after we get through with him," someone said.

Akins stood up, as visible as he'd ever be. "Please don't hurt him," he said.

There was moaning and complaining. Someone said, "We want our neighborhood back." And the group agreed. I heard, "he needs to suffer."

"No!" Mz. Escavedo said. "The boy's right. We can't stoop to Cooley's level. We have to set an example of how people, cultures, nations can come together for the good of all."

"What are we, the UN of hoodoo?" someone said.

The discussion went on into the night. I'd never understood why people couldn't just compromise and get along. I had no brothers or sisters and I just disappeared around anyone I didn't like, so I'd never taken part in such a squabble. Some folks argued over differences that didn't matter a whit and some were arguing the same point and didn't know it till I pointed it out.

But come dawn, after we ate each others food and swapped stories, we came to an agreement. It meant three people had to leave and promise not to interfere but it was a mighty unity happened that night.

Everybody went about weaven' their magic with each other. It reminded me of makin' braided rugs out of old clothes, like grandmother used to do. There was smoke and dancing and chanting of spells, a grand spectacle that left everyone spent. Some fell asleep right on Mz. Escavedo's Egyptian rug and some trudged home. Akins took the potion to sprinkle round his brother and came back to say it was done.

Stores didn't open that day, restaurants stayed closed, an unbound stack of newspapers layed in the street. The only thing that moved in the neighborhood was a startled red fox who came out of the shadows in the afternoon. Folks watched from their windows until the Animal Control fellas finally showed up to catch him. They put him, dazed and tranquil, in the back of a truck.

"Where're you taking him?" Akins called out of Mz. Escavedo's window.

"Our vets'll check him out and if he's OK we'll take him back to the mountains, the Catskills, where he came from." I thought about

Francie, a fine loyal dog, and wondered if Cooley would ever be loyal to anyone. He sure wasn't loyal to Akins. Everyone was glad to see him disappear.

The neighborhood was quiet for a while, then the black-hearts started up again and Mz. Escavedo was doing poorly. She tried to convince folks to come together but tryin' made her so sick she had to go to "assisted living." No one else could call up that kind of unity so a lot of the neighbors moved, packed up their magic and left for better neighborhoods or the country. Things change. New folks come and old ways disappear. I seen it happen in country and city now.

Akins went off to college and I watched tension and discord build up as new folks moved in. I don't expect to see the kind of harmony Mz. Escovido called up any time soon but I'm tryin' to find it in myself. I made peace with not being pure Ashanti when I seen what power there was in diversity.

I got me a job on a cruse ship so I'm off to see more a the world before it's time for me to disappear altogether, like grandmother. Maybe I'll even let some of the world see me.

The MacGuffin

My neighbor, Mali, runs for her life, every morning, sometimes before the sun comes up. "Are you training for a race?" I ask.

"Na."

Life is a marathon for Mali.

Mrs. Peabody, on the other side of the building, has neither computer nor cell phone. She has a dishwasher but doesn't use it. "I use so few dishes," she tells me. "It's easier just to wash them out in the sink." It's not like she has a lot to do otherwise. Her husband's been dead fifty years and they had no children. She drinks tea and raises African violets that sit on clean doilies atop tables that are antiques now. Mrs. Pea is the cliché maiden aunt, living in a different era.

I'm the amused insomniac in the middle. Though no one seems inordinately amused with me, least of all my boss Mr. McNeely. Mr. McN is always wondering why I won't go to lunch with him and his clients, show some leg, listen to his Foreigner CD's. I spend more than enough time in the company of Mr. McN and his needy clients. We're in the business of selling insurance, not assurance. I spend as little time as possible at work and thinking about insurance. It's just a job to me and jobs end at five o'clock, then you go home and write your novel.

I'm happiest in my tiny apartment on Second Avenue where I've been since before Al left, two years ago – and none too soon for me. It's a small building, four floors. There are three small apartments on my floor (the second), Mr. Zingether, the super, on the first floor, Mr. Heath and Mr. Varney on the third and the Farthings, with their shockingly ugly baby, on the fourth floor.

Living here is very much like being in a band. On the rare occasions that we get together, we make a kind of strange harmony, all of us different but together on cold water days and not–enough–heat days and what–is–that–disgusting–smell days.

I sit at my window and watch Mali run, thinking I could use a friend, a girlfriend to watch stupid movies with and go shopping and ogle boys. But Mali works, runs and sleeps, period. She rarely stops to talk except for those occasions the whole building comes together to protest something or celebrate new tile in the entry hall.

Mrs Peabody, on the other hand, is always inviting me in for tea and tasteless cookies. I can't be friends with Mrs. Pea because she has a sad life in another era and I always manage to spill something on a doily, which she says she doesn't mind but I know she does. She could use a friend, too.

I'd like to have a boyfriend as long as he had nothing to do with the insurance business and didn't loose all his money betting on football and didn't have a mustache.

This was my life until one Tuesday in October.

That's when I heard something in the hallway about four AM (I told you I was an insomniac). It sounded like someone pacing back and forth, and when I looked out my peephole, there was Mali. So I opened the door and asked if anything was wrong.

"There's … something … in my apartment," she said.

"Mouse?"

She shook her head.

"Rat? Bugs? What?"

"I don't know. Something weird."

"Wait a minute." I went in and got my Asbury Park Souvenir Flyswatter. "OK, let's see."

"I don't think that'll work," she said.

"OK, OK." In the back of my hall closet I had a tennis racket Al left behind. I'd thrown everything else of his out but kept the racket because I knew he loved it and I figured I could get something for it on eBay, but had never gotten around to figuring out how to do that.

When I went back into the hall, Mali was just standing there. It was obvious that she wasn't about to make a move so I turned the knob on her door and pushed it open. Mali was right in back of me; I could feel her breathing. Her arm came from close behind and pointed to the living room. We tiptoed, in sync, toward the light.

There, in the middle of the room, stood … a little shiny man. He cocked his round head and even though his eyes were tiny dots and his mouth a wide slash, he looked pitiful. He held out his little fat hands to show that he had no weapon, and just stood there.

"He looks like a 'Playschool' person," I said.

Mali shook her head. "Otterness."

"Other … ?"

"Otterness," she said. "He's one of the Otterness people from the 14th Street subway station."

Sure enough, he looked exactly like one of those little bronze sculptures that were all over New York, but especially in the 14th Street station. Only, his little round belly was expanding and contracting as if he was breathing. Suddenly, he plopped down on the floor. He tried to remove his stovepipe hat but it was stuck, a part of the sculpture. He leaned his elbows on his knees and put his big round head in his fat hands.

"Can you talk?" I asked. The mouth slit wriggled and twisted but wouldn't open. He shook his head. "Are you hungry?" Mali asked, stepping out from behind me. He looked up at her like he was thinking about what he might eat, then he shook his head and rested it on his hands again. "Do you have a name?" Mali asked him. And he shrugged his shoulders, held his hands out.

I asked, "Would you like one?"

He nodded slightly.

"OK, let's see … Fred, no. Micky? No, there's already a cartoon mouse with hands like yours."

He shook his head violently. Apparently he wasn't a Disney fan.

"Are you crazy?" Mali said. "What are you doing? He's not an abandoned puppy we're taking in. We have to think of what to do with him."

I appreciated the fact that she said "we're" taking in and "we" have to think, like we were friends. She did seem less frightened now that

I was on the scene. "OK, but let's give him a name first. He seems harmless and everybody should have a name."

He nodded enthusiastically.

"Fine," she said. "How about Sandy."

"He doesn't look like a Sandy at all. Sandy's a name for one of those skateboard dudelets. He's bronze, for god's sake." I turned to him. "Aren't you?"

He shrugged his shoulders again and held out his hand. I went toward him with my index finger extended to touch. Mali followed. His skin was smooth like bronze but a little rubbery like skin. Mali touched him too.

"Sandy was my dog when I was a kid," she said.

"I've got it," I said. "We'll call him MacGuffin."

"MacGuffin?"

"Yea, Hitchcock came up with it. It's the thing everybody's looking for in a story, like the Maltese Falcon."

"Or the holy grail."

The little man's mouth slit turned up, into a big grin.

"It seems to me he's the opposite of a MacGuffin since we're trying to get rid of him, but fine." Mali said.

With that settled, Mali pulled some big pillows out and we all sat on the floor and thought about what to do.

"We should call the police," She suggested.

MacGuffin shook his head violently.

"They might accuse us of stealing him."

"Oh, right. Too bad he can't talk." But we could see that he didn't want police involved anyway.

"One of our clients is a lawyer," I said.

MacGuffin's little hands clutched into fists and his face scrunched up.

"He's a public interest lawyer, one of the good guys."

"No lawyers," Mali said. "Is that what you do?"

"I'm a receptionist at an insurance company, but I'm writing a novel about dead people."

"Euwww."

"No, it's funny, a humorous novel about dead people. What do you do?"

"I'm a waitress but I'm going to be a singer."

"Oh, that's you I hear at night. Not bad."

"Thanks."

MacGuffin tapped his metal foot impatiently and the room shook. "You have any ideas, MacGuff?" I asked.

He shook his head and we all sat for a while saying nothing. The sun had started to come up when MacGuffin lifted his leg and pointed the heel of his shoe at us. Written on the bottom was the name of the artist, Tom Otterness.

"Good idea," I said. "We'll call Mr. Otterness."

"Oh really?" Mali said. "The guy's a famous artist. He's not going to talk to us."

"He might. He looks like a good guy. I saw him on TV when they put up that big statue by the Brooklyn Bridge."

"Famous artists don't put their phone numbers in the book, you know."

"He probably has a website or something. They all do. They'll be some way to get a hold of him. I'm pretty good at this."

"And what are we going to say? 'We have your man. Leave a million dollars in the trash can in Union Square?'"

"I could use the money ... "

"You can't be serious."

"If I had a little money, I could quit the insurance business and finish my novel. And how about you? How many demo's have you made?"

"I'm saving up. There's a guy that works with me who plays piano and he knows a guy who knows a guy ... "

"Still, a little funding wouldn't hurt ... " McGuffin held his hands out to us as if he was willing to be tied up. "Let's just try to get in touch with this Otterness guy and see what happens."

"You want to hold his statue for ransom but you're just going to wing it! Call him up without any kind of plan?"

"Maybe you'll change your mind."

"Yea, I guess we should sleep on it. I can call in sick tomorrow."

Tired has a funny way of sneaking up on you when you have insomnia. So I headed for the door.

"Jane, you're not going to leave me alone with him?"

"Come on, look at him. He's a cartoon character, a cartoon character that weighs two hundred pounds. He can barely move. You're not going to tell me you're still afraid?"

MacGuffin gave her a pitiful look and she said, "OK, get back here by ten."

"You got it."

I'd barely gotten to sleep when she started banging on my door. "Jane, let me in."

"What is it?"

"He tried to feel me up."

"What? Who?"

"MacGuffin. He put his hand on my boob."

"How..?"

"I was half asleep, on the couch and I then felt this hand coming up under my shirt."

"You're telling me that the little bronze cartoon man put his hand up your shirt?" Both of our doors were open and I guess we were making pretty much noise. Suddenly, there was Mrs. Peabody in the hall.

"What's going on here?" She asked. "Who's this?"

We stepped out into the hall and saw MacGuffin standing in Mali's doorway, head down, looking all shamefaced. Mrs. Pea was standing over him. "There, there, little boy," she said. "Would you like a cookie?"

He nodded and Mrs. Pea looked at Mali who stood there like a deer in headlights.

"It's Mali's nephew and he shouldn't have cookies before breakfast," I said. "Could you watch him while Mali and I … "

"Check on his mother," Mali said. "She's been sick. That's why he's here."

"Of course, dear. His name?"

"MacGuffin."

"Come on then, MacGuffin."

The little shit waddled into her apartment and Mrs. Pea closed the door.

"Aren't you glad we gave him a name?" I said.

"What if he tries something on Mrs. Peabody?"

We looked at each other and burst out laughing.

"Let's see if we can find Tom Otterness."

Tom Otterness did have a web site with lots of links and finally we hit on a tai chi school he went to. A guy named Max answered the phone. He thought we were friends of somebody called Tiffany and since he was in a hurry to get out and meet his girlfriend he gave us Tom Otterness's phone number.

"Mr. Otterness," I said. "I'm calling about the people in the subway."

"People in the subway?" He didn't sound as if he was awake (it was seven AM).

"Your little statues, in the 14th Street station."

"Oh," he said. "Oh, god. One of them's run off again. Is that it? Listen, there's nothing I can do. You don't have my address, do you? I've moved three times. I can't help you. You have to call the city – no, don't call the city. They just think you're a crazy thief. They'll lock you up. How did it … ? I thought we had them secured."

"He's pretty slow, but he's definitely not secure. He put his hand on my friend's boob."

"Listen, I have a wife and a young daughter. I can't take responsibility. I'm sorry. I'd like to help. I really would but they don't like me. Oh, no, some of them have tried … they want me to fix their mouth's and get them into clubs, and Broadway shows, and find girls … They want me to take them to some restaurant in Hoboken, for god's sake. There's a lot of them … and there's alligators and feral birds, dogs and … oh, those big plants! I can't do anything about them. I can only make them and, oh boy, they want to be made. Maybe you can find a dentist."

"A dentist?"

"Yea, well, they understand the lost wax method at least, how they're made, what might have gone wrong. Maybe you'll find one that can figure out … something. I gotta go. My daughter has to get up for school. Let me know what happens. I mean it; if I could help, I would. I'm sorry. Good luck."

"What'd he say?" Mali asked when I hung up.

"Well, ransom is definitely out. He said we need to find a dentist."

"I think one of the gay guys on the third floor is a dentist. Why do we need a dentist?"

"You mean Heath and Varney? They're gay?" She just looked at me. "Aww, they're so cute; they're so nice."

"No shit, aren't they always."

After I filled Mali in on the conversation, we went out to check up on Mrs. Pea. Her door was unlocked so we peeked in. He had his hand on her boob and they were just sitting on the couch, watching the Today show. They looked very peaceful.

We went up to the third floor and told Larry and Harry (can you believe it?) our story. It turned out that they were both hygienists. They only wanted to know if Mrs. Pea was freaked and when we told them no, it seemed as if she liked it, they had to come down and see for themselves. Mr. Zingether turned up to mop the hall and so now everyone was involved except the Farthings.

"Can you believe that baby?" somebody said.

"Ugliest critter I've ever seen."

"Like out of a Wes Craven movie."

"Why do you think we don't have mice in this building."

"They'd be better off with your MacGuffin."

We all looked at each other.

"Then what would we do with that baby? Even the zoo wouldn't take it."

"Well, now," Mr. Zingether said. "Your little pal is damn heavy and pretty awkward to be carrying around. The Farthings do have a wagon for little Sylvie."

"It's a girl! Good Lord!"

"If we had a place to take him," Zingether said.

"I don't know," Larry chimed in. "He looks pretty content where he is."

"We can't let him abuse Mrs. Peabody," Mali said. "It's not right. And Jane and I don't want him creeping around. And how about little Sylvie?"

"It might be the only chance she gets," Harry, followed by a lot of guilty snickering.

"Can't you send him back where he came from?" asked Larry.

"He won't go back to the subway and Mr. Otterness doesn't want him."

"Maybe we could give him to someone. He is a beautiful work of art," Harry said. "Otterness is a genus with irony. Maybe we should take him."

"Oh, please," Larry snorted. "How would he look with the pewter walls and the Empire side chairs? We'd have to completely redecorate."

"Well … "

"We can't afford it. Do you want to go to Milan this year, or do you want a little bronze pervert in the house. Nothing personal girls."

"I think I know someone," I said. "Someone a lot like MacGuffin."

"Who?" Mali asked.

"My boss. I'll probably loose my job, but I don't like it anyway."

"I can get you a job at the restaurant. The tips are good."

"She works at the French bistro on Tenth Avenue," Harry said to Larry.

"Oooo, I love that place!"

So the five of us put MacGuffin in the Farthings wagon and threw a blanket over him. He struggled but every time it looked like he'd get out, little Sylvie would growl and make a face at him and he'd dive back under the blanket. Mrs. Pea was a little upset at first but the Farthings said she could sit with Sylvie any time she wanted. Sylvie grinned up at her and apparently Mrs. Pea's eyes weren't good enough to register the horror in that look.

Mr. McNeely hated MacGuffin, which pleased Mrs. McNeely no end. She crocheted little covers for his hat and made him purple cotton pants. She pampered him to death. Mr. McNeely was infuriated that she lavished attention on MacGuffin as she'd never done with him and took it out on everyone in the office. I was glad I didn't work there any more. MacGuffin found occasions to fall over onto Mr. McN's feet and finally broke his foot as well as all the Steuben glass and crystal in their house. The McNeely's had no home insurance! Go figure. Ultimately, Mr. McNeely moved out and Mrs. McNeely took him for everything he was worth.

MacGuffin quickly got tired of being fawned over. He hated the clothing Mrs. McN made him wear and the reality TV she watched incessantly. He couldn't stand her snobby friends. After a few months at the McNeely's, he realized there were a lot worse people in the world than Tom Otterness (who is really a nice guy) and even worse places than the 14th Street subway station where, at least, you got to see all kinds of people (who might be in a great hurry but were rarely snobby) and hear street musicians and there was no reality TV. So he spread the word among the "Otterness people" who seemed to have similar experiences out in the world. They apologized to their creator and now they all go to a reunion at the Otterness' once a year on a date I can't divulge, and

Tom invites our whole building. He also convinced Mali and me (who are best friends now) to study Tai Chi with Master Chen. Mali wonders what she was running from all those years when what she really needed was to be grounded, which is what Master Chen teaches. We meet a lot of cute guys in push hands class and I'm working on Master Chen's awesome son Max (who's a little shy but coming around).

Mrs. Pea's dishwasher goes all the time now as she cooks for Sylvie and for Harry and Larry's get-togethers. And little Sylvie ... she's growing fast and turning into a swan. Neighborhood boys are starting to hang out on our stoop hoping she'll talk to them. Go figure.

This Is Not A Pipe

inspired by René Magritte

The old house had the feel of stalled shadows, wispy ghosts of furniture that might be jolted by a flash of errant sunlight, but would never escape the faded order. The house was built by the captain of the brigantine Magree who was lost at sea before inhabiting it. The old captain filled it with charmed treasures and objects fantasque gleaned from his widespread travels. The elaborate vitrine entry was occupied by a midnight glass forever darkened by the reflection of knock-kneed trees and clinging brush. In the glass the faint outline of a woman watched over all with serene dignity. Each day a bird called at the front door, and each day was answered by silence.

Time wielded its ruin.

The captain had left the house and its belongings to his pampered niece. In those years, the house was a haven, a romantic paradise for eccentric society: damsels and dowagers, merchants and friars. Viscounts and baronets from the lands of Mu and Atlantis, Camelot and Lemuria came to call. Immortals, demigods, fairyfolk, sorceresses, wizards, priestesses, magicians, homunculi, Titans, Amazons, Tellem tribesmen, and gypsies feasted on delicacies like basilisk, hamshaw, sunfish, gemfruit, sinroot, jujube wine and ambrosia. The house flourished with great gatherings, light and noise. The servants sought out despair and hung it on fragrant hedges until wind blew great holes in the weave and filled them with dragonfly wings. With prodigal fervency the house enclosed and warmed, it nurtured pure thoughts, inspired poetry.

But such patronage is a formidable undertaking. Eventually the house became weary, overspent; the niece retired to the shadows. Looming guests grew brutish and melancholy and the old house renounced its practiced ambiance. Purged of thankless sycophants, it embraced solitude and settled into gloaming. Somber hinges dangled in fatigue. Stout chimneys were beset with mildew and pokeweed. Shadows and ivy replaced propriety. A hundred years passed and yellowed memories clung wearisome and demanding, years of nullity became untenable. Empty rooms longed for vindication.

More time passed.

One night the mournful salon invoked the dream of life and mothered a young girl.

She named herself Immaculata and the house allowed her one companion, a bird called Mujipor. Mujipor was an uncommon creature. Small of stature but bold as the hoopoe, he was as estranged to the world as the phoenix, an incarnation of an entity that haunted the doomed Magree off the port of Chatrapan. He'd been incubated in the drawer of an Arlesian mangadou.

While the house kept watch, Mujipor entertained Immaculata with transformations. He might be transparent, the melancholy greatroom or faded dining room visible through his plumage. He might change his feathers to lavender, spreading the sweet odor onto an unsuspecting breeze and wafting it through the moldy house. Or he might manifest propriety, mimicing the appearance of a slightly stunted parrot or vivid heron.

In the years after the Magree was lost and before Mujipor belonged to Immaculata, he accompanied a hollow man from the wastelands south of Udza. Mujipor lived inside the man's body and subsisted on perseverance and pollen inhaled by his host. The man traveled by foot, his only possessions were a good sunhat and a walking stick. When he came to the old house he was mesmerized by the boulders that levitated along the front path and unable to continue his journey. Immaculata should not have invited a strange hollow man into the house, but she did.

The man fell asleep for nine days. When he awoke, he approached Immaculata with evil intent. She was not experienced enough to be frightened, so she stood stoically while the man placed his hollow hand on her breast. Mujipor was disgraced by this depraved action. He flew out of the man's throat, flapping his wings wildly, causing the man to loose his balance and fall. Immaculata was terrified until Mujipor transformed himself into a pleasant blue sky in the shape of a bird.

"Do not fear," Mujipor said. "It's only the man who means you harm; I shall protect you."

Immaculata looked down at the hollow man whose body had deflated and shrunk to the size of a sleeping cat without the substance of the bird inside. "What will become of him?" She asked.

"I'll carry him to the mountain where the wind is strong. It will sustain him until he imbibes another entity."

"He won't die, will he?"

Mujipor thought this a strange question. "Not to worry," he answered evasively.

Immaculata thought her companion would never return, but he did, his feathers resplendent in vibrant hues of poppy, chartreuse, azure and amethyst. The frivolous colors cheered her immensely. Mujipor held in his beak a crimson rosebud. Immaculata put the rosebud in ruby water and it grew and grew until it was the size of the room, an auspicious opportunity for a dream of beauty without mortal flaws. The house leaked so much that they never had to water the flower, and when it died Immaculata foraged through the old larder and baked the petals with Laxey mushrooms in Andalusian hens. She wrapped them in night fronds and sent them to feed the peasants.

Mujipor tidied the house, pulled the frayed edges off furnishings and flapped his wings to blow the dust outside. One day he grew so tired that he invited a small cloud in to keep Immaculata company while he rested. Delighted, Immaculata romped through the house with the cloud until it dissipated completely. She slept for three full days afterward and woke with a horrible case of the grippe from eating tainted moonberrys. When the cramps and delirium subsided, she set out to look for Mujipor. He didn't answer her call in the house, so she climbed out onto the widows walk. There she found a nest woven of discarded strands from the furniture and drapery. In it were two tiny opalescent eggs. Mujipor was standing guard.

"Where's the mother?" Immaculata asked.

"I dare not say," Mujipor answered.

She could tell he didn't wish to speak of it, yet she had to ask, "Who is the mother?"

Mujipor did not answer. His feathers mottled camouflage in the same shades as the foliage beyond. For eighteen days he exposed the eggs to the sun during the day, covered them with a warm blanket of tuckahoe and straw at night. He never left them unprotected for more than a few minutes. Immaculata brought him bittersweet grains and mustard tea. She sang Manx lullabies and warmed the eggs gently with her own hands at dawn and twilight.

On the evening of the eighteenth day, a tuft of resentment that had been caught in a corroded spile hole in the old root cellar since the era of the Captain's niece, broke loose. It wafted through a rusted flume and transformed into three black-suited men. The moon was a silver sliver and pale lights from the distant village illuminated the horizon. Immaculata and Mujipor stood on the widows walk in fearful silence and watched the men circle the house like shadows. The eggs began to quiver.

"The fumes will peel the wallpaper and harm the fledglings if we don't do something," Mujipor whispered.

Immaculata did not like the sound of that.

"I dare not leave them," said Mujipor.

"I'll think of something." Immaculata fled down the stairs.

She searched frantically for some weapon with which to frighten them or some treasure to offer as bribery and in desperation grabbed a tin coal scuttle. She doubted that these men would be easily deterred, for they didn't appear to be hollow. When she reached the front hall, she was shocked to see how much the exterior had infringed on the house during her illness and preoccupation with the eggs. Stepping over gnarled roots and through tangled creeper, she came upon the midnight glass and felt a stirring within it. She thought she saw the phantom interred within, smile and nod in recognition. Immaculata put the coal scuttle down.

She grasped the mirror with her small hands and pulled with all her might, but she couldn't lift the ancient glass. It was imbedded in the dusty mold, entwined in a thicket of creeper, merged with the essence of the house. Immaculata did not hesitate.

She flung open the front door and called out. "Mister, Mister, help me please! Could you please help me?"

The men turned to her as one and walked slowly up the derelict stairs and through the creeper in lock-step. They did not speak or smile. They didn't remove their bowler hats to diminish the impenetrable shadow from their pale featureless faces.

"I must get this mirror outside. Help me, please."

The men just looked at her. She regretted that she'd allowed them to gain entrance to the house. Perhaps she'd made a grave mistake with this ruse. Was the phantom of the glass in league with the darkly clad men? She took one side of the glass in her hands and, with great effort, moved it ever so slightly. The men stepped foreword and lifted it; the creeper retreated; the glass slid slowly off of its perch on the copswood. Immaculata thought the men might drop it; their blank faces were crimson with the strain. She attempted to help, but they gestured for her to withdraw.

"Out here! Out here!" Immaculata called, and led them back out into the somber night. "Lean it up against this stone wall," she directed them.

The men settled the glass against the ruined garden wall and stepped back. They stood stock still and looked deep into the glass for a long time, mesmerized by the phantom within. Immaculata moved to one side and watched them. Such men are rarely confronted with the mythical and were frozen in disbelief, spellbound by suspicion.

"What is the meaning of mystery?" she asked.

Immaculata waited, afraid to move. They did not answer.

The stars inched their way across the heavens and a shooting star fell from the sky into the glass.

The men did not flinch.

Immaculata lifted her foot tentatively and took a step. She walked around them. She walked under the floating boulders. She walked up and down the ruined front steps. The men did not move, didn't follow her with their eyes. She walked between them and the glass, but they were irredeemable from the lavish shadows. Their outlines had begun to fade and merge with their reflections. Soon they'd become smudges on the glass to be wiped away by industrious hands.

Immaculata heard a sound from the widows walk. She ran into

the house and up the creaking staircase. There in the nest, two wet birds had squeezed themselves out of broken eggs. Mujipor was gently waving his wings to dry them. As they dried, Immaculata could just barely see the pink hue of dawn through their tenuous forms. She ran inside to retrieve the pomegranate that rested in a bowl in her bedroom. She returned to a strong smell of anise and all three birds had transformed their feathers to leaves.

"They learn quickly," said Mujipor.

"They're surely celestial," said Immaculata.

"More than that," said Mujipor with pride. "They're practically human."

The fledglings allowed Immaculata to feed them the tiny red fruit of the pomegranate, but it was a messy procedure. Crimson pulp splattered her mousseline blouse and brocade pantiloons. After she bathed, she took to her bed for a long rest. Mujipor brought the birds into her room so he could watch over them. They named them Velvalee and Sophronia.

A few days later, an indraft of expectation through a leaded-glass transom produced another man. This one was eminently solid, though he tended to float an inch off the floor when he stood still. Immaculata thought he might be an emissary from the waking world as he wore an overcoat and rubber galoshes (two articles of clothing that she'd never seen before), and carried an umbrella and attache case.

"I'm here for the meeting," he announced.

"I'm not aware of any meeting," said Immaculata. "Perhaps you could entertain the fledglings."

"That would be fine."

He proceeded to balance things on his opened umbrella: glasses and apples and small moon-like knick knacks he collected from the parlor. As time went by, he taught them board games and devised disguises.

Eventually Velvalee and Sophronia left for the Lesser Sunda Islands to establish their purity.

The man hurried off to his next meeting. Immaculata retired to the glass that had been carefully cleaned, purged of the smudge of Resent-Men. Mujipor called at the front door and was answered by a long satisfying silence which, if you're quiet, you might hear …

Barbara Hutton Toujours

"Sad. Empty. Heavyhearted. Even though you watch everyone around you die, you never quite get used to it, even when omens tell you to prepare for it and you spend your teenage years in the city morgue studying bodies under pretext of looking for a runaway cousin, even when you steel yourself for loneliness. First one goes, then another: mother, friend, father, your only uncle and finally, the man you married in order to escape that loneliness. It never gets any easier." Alice wadded up the postcard and dropped it into the wastebasket; it didn't help to write out her feelings and there was no one to send a postcard to anyway.

Marty, her husband, had been very fond of insurance, which left her reasonably well fixed – in at least one aspect. At forty-two, she thought she might go back to school and become a librarian or research assistant, anything solitary and all-consuming. Instead, on a whim, she took a long trip. She sought solitude and peace in the museums of Europe but never quite shook the feeling of restless agitation.

London was a pleasant town but hard on the sinuses; Paris was entirely too intrusive. Rome was glorious with its excellent food and Roman shadows, but the innocent warmth of its inhabitants made it difficult to remain anonymous. Athens frightened her; its ruins so sterile and precise, its population so viscous. Spain's obsession with relics and ritual only served to make her more depressed.

The truth was, with all of this, she hadn't learned to accept death. Not for herself. And not for anyone else. She kept thinking that she recognized someone in a crowd: Marty, her mother. She would run after them but, of course, it was never them. Sometimes she'd loose them in a crowd, but remain certain it had been them. Because of this, she had convinced herself that the dead, or some of them, still walk among us and just don't allow themselves to be found; that those souls possessed of attachments have established parallel lives and persist among the living.

She had begun to think of school again and dusty, seclusive research projects when she was accosted by a gaggle of American tourists at her Malaga hotel – a situation she'd successfully avoided throughout the trip.

"For god's sake don't go to Tangier," they said.

"The stench!"

"The obscene people!"

"Not safe in Arab countries, you know. Especially for women traveling alone."

Not only did she go immediately, but she took the Algeciras ferry. She did, however, book first class, a regrettable decision since she spent the entire voyage standing at the door that separated the classes, watching veiled women and dark men holding chicken and goats. The gamy smells and murmur of voices beyond that door invigorated her as much as any great museum. They captured her entire attention except for the interval she was drawn to the great Rock of Gibraltar which thrust itself up from the water and was only partially claimed by man. Just as the rock had ruptured the province that belonged to water, so the tenuous margin between real and unreal had been weakened beyond that door. It seemed an excellent context to conceal the deception of Death.

The landing was chaos: shimmering heat, dark smells, and heavily draped people. Frightened tourists were accosted by potential guides who were illiterate in eight languages.

"Hashish? Kif?" They called.

"Everyone comes to Tangier seeking something. What is it you seek?"

What indeed, Alice thought. Peace of mind? Peace of spirit? Eradication of the self-imposed myths that give me hope? Release from the ghosts who follow me? No, they were all ghosts now, friends and family; it was fitting that she keep them with her. Maybe she just needed a reason to shave her legs again or wear makeup, or just get up in the morning.

Two smarmy locals fought over her luggage and Alice was barely able to escape into a cab and get to her hotel.

The Hotel Toujours was run by Moroccans, and not Frenchmen as she'd feared, but it had a French menu as well as Moroccan and what they called International, the names of which were as obscure to Alice as the Moroccan specialities. The food, however, was seductive in taste and smell, and the cool, tiled corridors a delightful maze. The hotel was central and although the front overlooked the busy city and entrance to the Medina, the back looked out onto a lush garden with a splendid azure pool. Alice took her mint tea on the back terrace after dinner with vicarious contentment.

"Excuse, Madam," a young waiter bowed.

"Yes, I should love to have a pastry." Alice smiled at the African moon.

"Certainly."

The boy was back in a flash with a silver tray.

"This one, please." She watched as he ceremoniously lifted it onto a clean dish and placed it in front of her.

"Has Madam secured a guide yet?"

Alice thought of the two men fighting over her luggage and the twenty or so other dirty hucksters who had accosted her at the ferry landing.

"No. Is it really necessary?"

"Not if one knows the streets, and can bargain in Arabic, and can protect one's self from the unsavory characters who prey upon tourists."

"Oh." Alice surprised herself by having the first easy conversation with anyone since she'd begun the trip. Surely it signified the end of her reluctance to go home, an unhappy thought in this exotic place, but convenient since she had less than three days left before her return flight. Later, she would not remember this misread omen.

"If it please, Madam, I have a small brother, knowledgeable of the streets and history of the city, trustworthy as the Prophet's word. He is needing money to enter the University in the future, and free for several days."

Alice could not bear to take even a small forkful of her pastry in front of the boy and give evidence of American bad manners, nor could she bear to dismiss him for some reason.

"Very well, but I sleep very badly and I don't know when I will be taking breakfast in the morning or when I shall be about."

"No matter, he will wait at the entrance of the hotel. Many thanks, Madam." And the boy backed into the hotel.

Alice was relieved at the chance to finally take a bite of the delightful pastry in front of her. She was not disappointed in the flavor, which was thick with coconut and honey, nuts and ... was that ginger?

The waiter appeared once more with a plate of macaroons. "Try these, Madam. Barbara Hutton says our cook makes the best *ghoriba* in all of Morocco. She orders thousands for her parties."

Alice smiled and took one. How odd. She knew Barbara Hutton was long dead. So, I'm not the only one who carries around the ghosts of dead acquaintances, she thought as the young waiter disappeared into the kitchen.

She was instantly regretful that she'd forgotten to discuss money. Never mind, I'll hash it out with the child in the morning. Her sense of well-being in this mysterious place made her smile despite the complications.

Alice's nights had become ritual. Ritual cleansing, methodical arrangement of time and possessions, order that was meant to tranquilize but never quite did. The book had to be in a certain spot on the nightstand so that when she woke up in the middle of the night, she could find it easily in order to evade her own thoughts. Tissues. Slippers. Extra blankets. Sometimes it took several to stop the tremors. The dreams were disconnected, unresolved. But each had its own sad song, a song she would hum to herself through the following day.

She rose late and felt no need of hurrying her breakfast for she did not really expect the "small brother" to be waiting for her. As she was not the type to seek company anyway, she was relieved to face the prospect of exploring the city alone. She was dressed in a brown and turquoise rayon skirt and beige cotton sweater, her "travel suit," because, from what she'd seen on the way to the hotel, she could tell that the Moslems were very proper and well mannered. Her figure, once considered "sturdy," had compressed itself with grief.

She stepped out of the hotel and into the clutter of Arab mid-morning. For a moment she panicked despite herself, then a dark, bone-thin boy of about fifteen or sixteen broke away from a huddle of boys across the street and ran up to her. He was wearing a Grateful Dead T-shirt and trousers that barely reached his ankles.

"I am Mohmud, brother to Rashid."

"The waiter?" Alice asked.

He nodded.

Below them by the entrance to the Medina, Alice could see a group of men and women wrapped in bright colors.

"Who are they?" She asked.

"Bedouins. Nomads from the desert. Come to trade."

Perhaps it would be well to have a guide, she thought, to lead her through the peculiarities of this place.

"Where do you wish to go?" His English was quite good and he had an unintrusive smile. When he spoke, he looked away.

"I don't know," said Alice. "Where is there?"

"The Medina, the Grand Socco, the palace of Sidi Hosini which was owned by Barbara Hutton, the Kasbah? Perhaps Madam is looking for something special? I am acquainted with many fine merchants."

"No, nothing special. I would just like to walk, to see the old city."

"Ah, the Medina, a wondrous place," and he led her through the arches, down dark, narrow, pungent streets. The heat was confining but not oppressive. The buildings reminded her of adobe houses built by Native Americans, only more ancient, more enclosed. What color was adobe? She couldn't remember; certainly not the somber ash-grey of these structures.

They stopped to listen to children chanting behind an uneven cloth that hung at the opening of one building.

"It is Koran School," said Mohmud.

People hurried by, most wearing traditional robes.

"*Haiks, jalabah, baboush,*" Mohmud instructed.

Many women wore veils, and most were covered from head to foot (except the tourists, of course). When she considered them, it made Alice self-conscious to have her legs sticking out. Previously in her travels, she'd felt detached. It was the feeling that she was most comfortable with. But instead of her mind wandering to dead friends and family, in this place it wandered nowhere – everywhere. Things were no longer what they once had been, but a universe of swirling colors, the scent of cinnamon and jasmine, the tinkle of camel bells. In the background there were Egyptian singers whose pinched voices came out of ... were they transistor radios? In Europe, remote feelings in breathtaking surroundings were a dilemma. Here, alienation seemed to enfold her and mark her place in the ethereal setting. It seemed fitting, this combination of fervent, fascinating, and intangible.

Mohmud kept up a running dialogue which she tuned in and out of. He kept beggars and hawkers away, and did not intrude upon her thoughts. He pointed out the mosque's fine minaret and kept her from being run over by school boys with their books wrapped in prayer rugs. He commented on the anonymous checks which had rained down during the stay of Barbara Hutton to alleviate the suffering of the poor.

The mention of Barbara Hutton attracted her attention. The people of Tangier spoke of her often, as if she were still alive. She'd always thought of Barbara Hutton as a woman of obsessions and delusions, but the Moroccans thought of her as a distinguished celebrity, a generous lady, and a visionary with the means and fortitude to transform reality. Certainly, the components for such a transformation were here. Past, present and future intermingled and left only a primeval unity of feeling. The rules of logic did not seem to apply.

At the marketplace he pointed out cosmetic powders and incense, dates and rice, precious stones and household goods; caravan goods that became a sensory tumult in Alice's head. the ghosts that filled her life and caused great agitation seemed to float quietly around her, silenced by the exotic clatter and the scent of freshly baked *khobz*.

"What is that?" she asked of a sound that caught her interest late in the afternoon.

"It's the muezzin's summons to prayer," Mohmud answered.

"Do you wish to stop and pray?"

"It's not necessary. I am not so devout."

She almost told him how she was searching for her own truth and seemed to drift further and further from reality, but thought better of it and only nodded understanding.

The abrupt transition to the reality of communication, made Alice realize that it was already mid-afternoon. They ducked into a cafe for couscous and mint tea. Old men smoked hashish in the corner.

Mohmud chattered on about school and his sisters–Alice barely noticed – then excused himself to greet friends at another table, all the time keeping an eye on her, shooing away the riffraff.

Alice's thoughts in the cafe were not thoughts at all but feelings; she drifted from one memory to another. It was strange to be with someone and not be with him, to be here and not here. Mohmud didn't seem to notice or care, or perhaps he understood her need for solitude and respected it; it didn't seem to offend him as it did Americans and Europeans. Perhaps everyone was marginal in this strange milieu. Alice wondered if she could drift along this way for the rest of her life, without connections to anyone. She'd nursed too many sick people, eaten in too many hospital cafeterias, sat in the front row of too many funerals. she no longer hoped for the best or breathed easy after a crisis; for after one crisis, one never had to wait long for the next.

"Do you wish to see the Kasbah now?"

"No, not today. I'm too tired. I must go back to the hotel and rest."

"Tomorrow, then? I will wait for Madam."

"Yes, tomorrow."

They walked back silently. For a moment Alice thought she should be frightened, alone with a strange Arab boy, lost in the maze of the Medina, the sun due to go down any time now. But she wasn't. And she was amazed that Mohmud found his way back to the arches and the place where the Bedouins had been. What an odd thought–Bedouins not there ... Had they become a part of her catalog of missing faces?

"What shall I pay you?" She dreaded bargaining and the Arabs seemed so fond of it.

"Pay me tomorrow."

She knew she should settle now, but didn't have the energy to argue and so, saying good-bye, went up to her room and had a long bath with soap that smelled of some magical desert flower.

Dinner was pigeon and *harira*. She drank a traditional French wine and finished with another succulent pastry. An Englishman at the next table tried to speak to her; his dinner smelled of peppers and fennel, lemon and saffron. He smelled of tobacco. She only shook her head and drifted back to her room. Her eyes closed with a vision of infinity that was a whorl of dancing arabesques in gold wash upon a sun-washed wall. It was the first good night's sleep she'd had in ages.

She took breakfast on the terrace under a serene blue sky. Oh, Marty, if only you had lived to see this! And my dear friend Joya, wrapped around a tree in your new Audi. What a waste of talent and happiness. Would you, Marty, have spent all those long hours in your dry cleaning store, building up business if you had known about the cancer incubating in your cells? Would you, had you known there was such a sky in another part of the world? She put on her sunglasses to hide oncoming tears.

An emaciated elderly European woman was speaking to the cook just below. She was wearing a vintage Chanel suit and a bit too much makeup. Alice had been unconsciously staring at her; the woman made a sympathetic gesture. Alice thought she looked familiar but fearing another ghostly illusion, buried herself in her newspaper.

The *Herald Tribune* described Shiite assassinations but could not really hold her attention. Tomorrow she must return home. To what? A small house that would be too big for her to rattle around in alone? A street full of people who felt sorry for her? Wasn't it bad enough that she felt sorry for herself? Civilization and telephones. God, how she hated telephones, a piece of equipment which, in her experience, was used mainly to spread the news of Death. Horrible that people actually carried them where ever they went these days.

Morose thoughts. They infiltrated because she was lingering over breakfast. She must go. No matter that Mohmud would never expect her to be out this early. She would find the Kasbah on her own.

But Mohmud was waiting outside the hotel, as if he'd never left. Waiting. "Like Death," she thought. The other guides hadn't arrived yet and he was reading. He stuffed the small book into his back pocket when he saw her.

"Where to, Madam?"

"The Kasbah, Mohmud. Let's see this Kasbah of yours."

Down through the network of the Medina they plunged, both lost in their own thoughts.

"Who are those men with rifles?" alice asked.

"Mercenaries. Just walk quickly. They are not crazy; Tangier is dependent upon its tourists."

She wondered if this were true; but could anyone who smelled of sucre and pistachio be dangerous?

They began climbing out of the shadows of the Medina and into the sunlit nimbus of the great palace where the modern world did not intrude. They stood on the threshold of a world of harems and dancing girls.

"Do you see the dervish over there?" Mohmud pointed.

"Dervish?"

"The strange man sitting by that door."

"Yes."

"That's the apartment of Barbara Hutton."

"Oh, yes, the heiress." Occasionally the Moroccans mentioned the names of other celebrities who'd resided here – Jimi Hendrix, Brian Jones – but never with the reverence granted the name of Barbara Hutton.

"Before that, it was the palace of Sidi Hosini. Barbara Hutton outbid Generalissimo Franco for it. My grandfather remembers her well. All of Tangier remembers her parties." He studied her face for a moment. "It is customary to bring your friends to a party in Morocco."

Could he see her ghosts as well as his own? There was something about this boy.

As they stared at the protective stone walls of the tall, whitewashed structure, the dervish stood and waved at them.

"*Taqabbil Allah*," he called.

"May God accept your prayer," Mohmud translated.

Did she have a prayer? Alice couldn't take her eyes off the strange man and yet, could not see him clearly. It was as if he were a heat mirage from the desert. How safe it must be behind those walls. She could well understand Barbara Hutton's need for a refuge from curiosity and judgments, from pity. She'd read, in a book that she found in an alcove of the hotel, that Barbara Hutton had taken great pains to transform reality into a continuous fantasy. Perhaps this was why the Moroccans revered her. Perhaps it was why she, Alice, felt comfortable in this enchanted milieu. This was the only place she'd found where she could live undisturbed in her cocoon of thoughts.

"Come inside." Mohmud guided her into the Kasbah. "Soon he will come begging." Mohmud's hand brushed her elbow, warm and alive, the first human contact that wasn't an indication of pity in – oh, how long? Perhaps he had lost someone too.

Inside, a few tourists huddled in corners with their guides. Mohmud murmured tales of the history of the palace, but Alice didn't hear; it was the voice of the genie instructing the infidel. Often, he mentioned Barbara Hutton as if she were the patron saint of the city – if Moslems had such a thing. Alice trailed her hand along cool tiles and studied the graceful writing, a never-ending dance of prayers and praise to Allah. She noticed very little else; it was as if she were searching for something, some cipher that would connect her to the living.

It was not to be.

"Many tourists find Tangier oppressive. It is a matter of temperament. Others, like Barbara Hutton, seem to have it in their blood," he was saying. For a moment she thought of the poisonous things that were in Marty's blood but was lulled back by a vision of fig trees in a courtyard below. What a luxury to have your painful memories tempered by this mythical environment.

Finally, they stepped out onto a mosaic balcony overlooking the sea. Again the perfect blue of Allah's heaven astounded her and she must have stood watching the sea crash onto rocks for a long while. Perhaps this was the place she'd looked for, perhaps it was in her blood. Mohmud was silent. She smiled at him, thankful for his patience.

Then the two mercenaries appeared on the terrace; they murmured prayers and turned to her.

"Unworthy foreigner. Infidel pig – you defile our homeland! *Allah akbar!*" They raised their rifles but Alice felt no fear about joining her friends and family. It all seemed so natural, inherent in the hypnotic situation. She watched their nicotine-stained fingers tighten on the trigger. Certainly not religious fanatics, she thought. She knew that if she closed her eyes, she would see Joya's face as the car slid uncontrollably toward that tree; it was the only thing that scared her.

"No!" Mohmud leaped toward her just as the men opened fire.

In a moment they were gone, the sounds of a chase following them through the palace. People, police, screaming, hysteria. Mohmud was the calm in the center of chaos. He was lying in a pool of seeping blood, eyes open, but no longer seeing this world. Alice knelt above him, the sound of the sea momentarily drowned out by the ghostly echo of gunshots, footsteps, and screams. It had happened so fast; now you see him, now you don't. The familiar smell of Death was in the air.

"Another one," she sighed. The world around her swirled in pastel colors and wails. "You didn't have to do that," she told him. What would she tell his brother? She could remember a time when the death of a bird would have affected her. Now grief was her prevailing emotion; one more seemed to make little difference. A voice from deep inside her spoke: the spirit of the dead is the same as that of the living; only the appearance has changed.

Why so calm this time? Was it shock? Was it the general inertia of Tangier that had penetrated her soul? Or something even more devious?

She could easily have done an entire funeral service, she was that familiar with death. Perhaps she should throw him off the balcony into the care of the sea, but no, instead she put her hand to her temple and felt the warm ooze of blood. She'd been hit. Little droplets splashed into the larger pool that came from Mohmud.

Slowly she stood. "Come with me," she whispered to the spirit of the dead boy. It is customary to bring friends ... "

Her shoes tap-tap-tapped through the tiled corridors. Outside the palace, clouds swirled in front of the sun, diminishing its angry glare. The sky had changed to a more sober color, the gray of obelisks and tombstones.

She stumbled through the shadowed streets of the Medina. Mohmud, Marty, Uncle Hal, Joya, mother, father. Nothing to go home to. Businesses dead, whole towns gone with the coal companies. Steel mills collapsing, rivers loitering to a trickle. People looked beyond her but she was not embarrassed today, she'd worn pants and a long-sleeved shirt, even a scarf tied about her hair. She was well covered. Where was the hotel? Must get out of the gloom.

Finally, a patch of sunlight. The rue Ben-Raisul: she'd never paid attention to street names before — what made her think she recognized this one? Hawks circled above her. Was she back at the Kasbah, or was this the entrance to the hotel? Her eyes were starting to play tricks on her, perhaps it was stress or hallucinations caused by the variegation of light and shadow. Perhaps it was the spell of Tangier that confused real with unreal. She felt faint. Was that the dervish in front of the door to Barbara Hutton's apartments, or the hotel porter? He was motioning to her. She was out of breath.

"Toujours?" she managed to whisper. "Is this Toujours?"

"*As-salaam alaykum.*" The man smiled and bowed as he opened the door.

Inside was cool. Not the hotel but endless corridors with arabesques and mosaic patterns multiplied forever. Oriental carpets, gold candelabras, cushions, flowers, splashing fountains. the sent of rosewater and pastilles, aloes and ambergris. She put her hand to her head. The wound had stopped bleeding.

A handsome young man approached. He was carrying a very thin woman with thick dark eyebrows. She was smoking a cigarette and wearing an astrologer's robe and an emerald and diamond tiara.

"Meet the Queen of the Medina," the young man said, and he placed her upon a large throne-like chair.

"It's the librarian," the woman said. "We're so pleased you've come. Many of your friends are here already. There are so many to catalog. But you must rest first." She clapped her hands. "Mohmud will show you to your room where you may wash and perform your devotions."

"Mohmud?" Alice's eyes would not focus.

"Oh, yes," said the woman. "They're all called Mohmud or Hassan here. Take this ointment for your injury."

She pressed a small brass bowl in Alice's hands. In it was fiery water.

"Thank you."

"Life is whole here. Undivided and undiminished, continuous. There is no hierarchy, no barriers between different spheres."

"I understand."

"Good. Now rest. The fleet's in tonight and we've prepared an entertainment."

She was so frail and delicate, but the light in her eyes made Alice confident that this woman was capable of rearranging the elements of reality, of combining all of nature into one great society of life; past, present and future, all one.

A strong hand led Alice through corridors, up and down staircases. The liquid in her bowl turned luminous in the dark. She was so tired. Each room had a clock and many had smiling people lounging with books or drinks in their hands.

"Was that Barb ... " She was really too exhausted to speak.

"Muhammad, himself, was an orphan," said the voice behind the hand that led her. It was as gentle as the breeze from the terrace.

Alice felt a great relief. She had grown so used to being alone with her thoughts; now, strangely, she was thankful for company. She was thankful to be within someone else's fantasy. Her eyes strayed to the chambers as she passed was that Marty on the terrace with a bowl of walnuts? Was it Joya grinding limouns in the kitchen?

The Importance of Cheese

The Bathroom Ghost sighs when I take my clothes off, moans when I leave the room too smelly, disturbs the water in the sink and splashes. The Bathroom Ghost leaves odd puddles for me to slip on, uses the towels, dances in the steam.

I don't need the aggravation or the scrutiny. I'd like to be left alone so I can believe I'm aging well. But it snickers when I pose before the mirror, makes "tisk tisk" sounds when I put on makeup. (Surely it's a "He," a female ghost would have more sympathy.)

It will have to be exorcized.

Explaining this situation to a priest is out of the question, not that I know any as I am long lapsed. So I settle for Mrs. Sanchez down the hall. She agrees to check it out, goes into the bathroom and closes the door. It's quiet for a while, then an unearthly laughter and she careens out.

"He is a bastard," she says. "But no match for me."

She sends me to the Botanica for candles, herbs and other supplies that I don't ask the English translation for, and we meet back at my apartment an hour later. I'm relieved that there are no live chickens involved.

"Do you have any wine?" she asks.

I open a bottle of cheap Cab and she fills a water glass for herself.

"Aren't you having any?"

I pour a more modest amount for myself.

Mrs. S proceeds to line the candles up inside and outside of the bathroom. She pounds and mixes herbs. We munch pieces of sausage she's brought, discuss the Eberhards on the fourth floor, the Wingrove boy on two.

I open more wine.

She lights candles and throws pinches of herbs into the flame. It smells like when my dad burned trash in the backyard, only worse.

There's a lot of smoke.

I open a window and stick my head out. When I feel restored and turn around, Mrs. Sanchez has passed out on my couch.

"Leave the window open," she says suddenly, with an odd accent that sounds more Central European than her usual Newyorrican.

I wonder if she's OK. "Mrs. Sanchez?"

"No."

I feel a chill that has nothing to do with the seventy-five degree breeze coming in the window. "Who?" I ask.

The answer is in a language I don't understand. It comes from Mrs. Sanchez's lips but she appears to be asleep. Her eyes are closed and between sentences, she snores.

"I don't understand," I say. "What are you trying to tell me?"

"Velvet doesn't last."

"Excuse me?"

"Your idols will disappoint you." Then she snores so loud, she wakes herself up.

"What happened?" she asks in her Newyorican accent.

"What languages do you speak other than Spanish and English?" I ask.

"You think I'm the UN? No other language."

"How do you say oy vey' in Spanish.?"

"Oy vey," she says and I tell her she was speaking with a completely different accent in her sleep.

"It must be the ghost. Was there a message? Surely it's come to give you a message."

We drink more wine and I tell her what it said. "Do you suppose that's the message?" I ask. "What does it mean?".

"I'll sleep on it. You can use my bathroom tonight."

I follow meekly but Mrs. Sanchez's bathroom is a horror, open make-up dripping into the sink and down the wall, smeared on the towels. Smudged mirror, shelves crammed with hair and skin products. You can't imagine how much effort goes into a "look" that seems, well, haphazard at best. I hadn't given much thought to her bright red curls and stage make-up before, hadn't considered how much time and effort it took.

"It's fine," I say. "I'm used to my bathroom. Thank you anyway, Mrs. Snachez."

I go home and clean up as much of the mess as I can by hand and take out the vacuum, but I have to use the bathroom first.

"Look here," I say to the old tile. "I'd like you to keep your comments to yourself. This is what sixty looks like. This is what sixty looks like on me. You'll have to get used to it. Or go elsewhere."

Do I hear a sob?

"Velvet doesn't last and neither do people." I tell it. "A lot of people have disappointed me and my idols are the least of them. Discovering that Mel Gibson is a schmuck or that Tiger is a two-timer, or twelve-timer or whatever ... isn't nearly as bad as loosing my Henry, or mother, or my best friend moving to Alaska. People come and go, fabrics rot, fortunes are lost, idols fall. That's life."

Now I'm sobbing.

"We fuck up."

The ghost was silent.

When I first came to this city, I had a job in an auction house. Two weird characters came in without an appointment and I, a mere assistant, was sent to deal with them. They showed me photos of a jaw-dropping collection of jewelry. When I explained the auction process to them they said they wanted to sell it outright and when I said we didn't do that or give out the names of our customers, they left.

Later, we discovered they'd stolen the jewelry and I was called to the courthouse to give a deposition. All I could remember about them was their suits. They looked like characters out of a Dickens novel, cartoonishly thin, one in an orange plaid suit, one in a tight gangster penstripe. There was nothing I could tell the DA that would be helpful.

I'd never been to a big city courthouse before and my boss's lawyer went with me. After the deposition, he took me to a cheese store in the area. Having grown up in the country, I never imagined there was any other kinds of cheese than American and American with pimento embedded in it. I was amazed by the variety of cheeses. They let us taste several kinds. I thought I was in Oz. (I was.) Diamonds meant nothing to me, I saw them every day at my job – crowds, architecture, fashion, unattainable by someone like me. I was beguiled by the the extensive variety of cheeses available: creamy bries, tangy Cheshire, strong marbled blues. (You'd think the obsession would reduce the number of my bathroom visits, but no ...) These delicacies were accessible to ordinary people, even offered free to taste.

"There's a world out there to haunt," I tell the ghost. "Why keep yourself huddled in a bathroom? Your spirit is free. Get out there and look around. Go sniff a good restaurant. Take in a Broadway play. Meander in the park. Get some air, for heaven's sake. Let your soul float to the dome of the universe," (something Mrs. Nirmaan in 4B told me when Henry died).

At this, I fling open the front door to find Mrs. Sanchez poised to knock. She emits a loud gulp and look of surprise like she swallowed a bug. Then she goes down with a thud, landing on her ample derrière.

There's no chance I can lift her so I run for some water and a magazine to fan her with. When I get back she's sitting up in the doorway, looking around my apartment like she's never seen it before.

"Vat ave you done wit to this place?"

"You're scaring me, Mrs. Sanchez."

"Vat you call me?"

I help her up and over to my couch, give her the water. She looks suspiciously at my *O Magazine*. "You vere going to read me something?" she says. "Or ver you goink to svat me like a fly maybe?"

I put the magazine down.

"Is better," she says.

"Do you have a message for me?" I ask.

"A message, yes. Let me think. You have food? Maybe some vodka? Scotch?"

"I have beer, and some wine. You like wine. And cheese." I jump up and run to the kitchen. Anything to get away from her.

"Cheese," I hear her mumble. "Now I'm a rat."

When I come back, she's draped across the couch in an eerily familiar pose.

"You're not Mrs. Sanchez," I say.

She takes a huge gulp of wine and sighs. She drinks like Mrs. Sanchez. "You may call me Garbo."

"Garbo!" Now I wish I'd poured wine for myself. "That's who you are?"

"Of course not, darling, that's the name they gave me."

"The studio?"

"You think I didn't have parents like everyone. Maybe I'm Garbo Eileen Horowitz." She nibbled the cheese. "Vhat is this? Oooh, I like."

"Manchego." Mrs. Sanchez might have known that.

"You have maybe a cracker to go with it. Aye!" As she swallowed her face changed from boredom to surprise; she sat up.

"*Dios, mi*. What happened?"

"Mrs. Sanchez? You're back?"

"Back! Where have I been? I was coming to you ... the door opened ... then ... I'm here on the couch ... with cheese. And ... " She looked at the glass of wine. "Oh, yes." She brought it to her lips, shook her head and put it down. "Ay! I shouldn't drink. I shouldn't play with the magic." Then she does drink.

"You said you were someone named Horowitz, but I think you were Greta Garbo. You had the same gestures, the same accent, sort of Central European."

"Garbo, Central European? No, the woman was Swedish."

"I know but she didn't sound Swedish, or maybe that what Swedes sound like, not like that muppet chef. She can't seem to remember her message. She's trying to fool us."

"Fool us? Muppet chef? Have some wine, dear. You're babbling. You know, I believe Greta Garbo did live down the street."

I take a tiny sip of wine. "Yes! I think it is her. How do you think she got to my bathroom?"

"*Dios sabe*. How do any of us get where we are? Maybe it's the only place she could be alone. Oh! I think it's happening again ...

"There. That's better. I never said I vant to be alone. I said I vant to be left alone."

"Well, so do I. Especially in the bathroom. You must understand that."

"I lov this cheese."

"Yes, well, I don't think I want you in my refrigerator either," I say. "Why don't you go haunt the Cheese Shop down the street."

"You vant me to go to a shop of cheese. Maybe I can't stand the smell."

"So you'd rather stay in my bathroom?"

"You haf a point, darling. Is it crowded, this cheese shop?"

"Sometimes, yes, but it's the best way to be left alone, in a crowd."

"Is like crying in the shower? Nobody knows ... "

"My husband died. My best friend moved to Alaska. I haven't cried in a long time."

"He vas an irritating man."

"Please! We don't speak ill of the dead. OK, yes, he could be irritating."

"He vas grouchy. He talk nasty."

"He didn't mean anything by it; it was just his way ... "

"Better is what you deserve. Vat about the computer boy who comes here?"

"Sam is twenty-eight years old. I have children older than him."

"I vould do it."

"I am not you. And I do not want another man."

"I don't say marry the boy. Americans! Vat am I doing here?"

"I don't know! What are you doing here? You do know you're not alive?"

"Phhha, and what are you? Oh! Oh, no! Where am I?"

"Mrs. Sanchez? Is that you."

"I think, yes. It's me. Dios! What's happening?"

"You keep changing into this person who may or may not be Garbo and doesn't seem to have any real message. Here have some cheese."

Mrs. Sanchez nibbles thoughtfully at the cheese. Every time she feels the change coming on she takes another nibble. The cheese seems to help. She drinks a little wine and we perform another ritual to exorcise the ghost from her body. There are herbs to be mixed, candles to be lit and chants, endless chants. I am completely exhausted and plop down on to the couch at exactly the wrong time. A candle falls and I strike the carpet with a pillow to extinguish the sparks. Smoke billows and Mrs. Sanchez is horrified even though there's no fire. I'm too exhausted to speak so I just wave my hands in frustration.

"*Oy, dios,*" she says.

"I'm going to take a nice long shower."

"Mas adelante."

Suddenly I feel strange, not myself. "Watch out for those kids with iPods," I say. "They can't hear themselves fart."

Mrs. Sanchez turns back.

"Never trust anyone with bangs," I say.

She freezes in the doorway.

"Keep moving. Don't block the intersection."

Mrs. Sanchez comes back in.

"Welcome back. You're in a safe zone. You may rest."

She hands me a piece of cheese but before I put it in my mouth I hear myself, in that psudo-Swedish accent, say: "How do you like my imitation of American, eh? Silly people. Never speak to anyone wearing a brown coat."

Candles are lit, herbs pounded, chants ... The room spins and then Mrs. Sanchez is patting my back. I burp and feel like myself again.

"What do you want?" I scream.

Now the voice comes from my TV. "Jimmy Stewart vas a weasel."

Mrs. Sanchez and I settle on the couch. There's nothing more we can do.

"Marlene got all the best gowns." This kind of talk goes on for a good twenty minutes, then there's a litany of authors who are "a waste of time and tree."

"Well, I certainly don't have to listen to any more of this," I say.

"Nor I," Mrs. Sanchez.

The smoke alarms go off. The TV blasts — some loud preacher wearing a bad toupee. Lights flash. The blender whirls; the toaster pops, water runs; objects fall. Mrs. Sanchez and I run around catching things, turning things off. When it's quiet again, we plop onto the couch. Mrs. Sanchez takes her shoes off and rubs her feet.

"What is all this?" I ask

"Magic," the voice says.

"Magic? You call this magic? Magic is having your wishes granted. Magic is fairy godmothers dressing you up to meet a prince. It's floating ladies, pulling cards out of the air, doves ... and guess what else? There's no such thing."

"Wrong," the voice says. "Here's my message: there is magic in the world. It's just not always convenient."

Then "whosh!" There's an awful stillness.

I look around at the mess in my apartment. "Where are the elves to clean up?"

That evening, after I've taken out the garbage and vacuumed, my granddaughter calls. "Look out your window, Nan," she says. "Can you see the moon?" Sure enough there's a huge full moon with what appears to be a vague smiling face on it.

"What's he doing?" she asks me.

"I think he's having some cheese."

"Can we have cheese with him, Nan?"

"Of course we can. Have your father bring you over."

Abracadabra. Now this is convenient.

Unto Others

Our neighbor, Mills, hated us. When he got real drunk he'd go out on his porch, shoot his gun into the air, and scream, "Git outta here, you Commies." Meaning us. We knew that if he ever decided to aim his gun at our trailer, the bullet would go right through and heaven help us if we happened to be in the way. We kept the couch on that side of the room so we could hide behind it when he got into his shooting mood but sometimes we were in bed or doing something in the kitchen when he started up.

We rented the trailer from Mz. Murphy who lived further up the mountain. Mz. Murphy hated everybody – in her words, "blackies, Chinee, towel-heads, all them hippies, and heathens that are out to kill babies before their borned and blow up good Americans." Despite all this hatred, Mz. Murphy considered herself a "Good Christian Lady." Being a good Christian was not an option for Mills who was usually too hung over on Sunday mornings to make an appearance in church or elsewhere.

There was a bad smell that came out of the woods behind us, like dead animals but we could never find them. We always had a rash and you couldn't drink the water, but the rent was cheap.

My roommate Maureen was living there because she got a job at the foundry in town for good money and she needed money to get out of Hunker County. I moved in with her when Carl got called to duty in Africa, one of those countries where the name changes with every new regime and there's been war for so long that nobody knows how it got started. The UN asked for troops to take water and milk to starving kids without families – and sometimes without arms and legs and eyes.

I was working at the Dog House even though the smell of hot dogs turned my stomach.

We didn't get a lot of TV reception around the county and the cable didn't reach where we lived. Most folks, like Mills and Mz. Murphry had dishes, but me and Mar didn't on account of we were tryin' to save up some money. When we wanted to see something, we had to go down to Jake's Bar which showed sports mostly but we could get the Real Housewives and Survivor LX on week nights when there was no big game.

That's where we were the night the Indian astronauts (those are the fellas from the country of India and not the ones that run the casinos) landed on HD4 … something, which they call Hanuman.

I was always one to tease about going to Mars, being a friend of Maureen and all. Like, "Oh, yea, I'm staying at Mar's a while, till Carl gets back." Or, "I gotta get back to Mar's and help her with the broke cinder step." You could only do that if you had a friend you called Mar. I didn't know nobody called Hanuman, so I couldn't kid about going there. Hanuman is a kind of monkey god that jumped from India to Sri Lanka, which was the name of another country that changed a few times in the last fifty years. The monkey did this jump to save a girl (wouldn't you know) but it wasn't even his girl, so go figure that one. The Indians figured it was a big jump from earth to HD4 … whatever, and that it looked like a place where monkeys might live, jungley and wet.

Mz. Murphy was all heped up about "them black heathens going to space. Let 'em all go and stay there. Sweet Jesus!" A lot of the folks at Jake's seemed to feel the same. You could taste the tension in the room but Mar and me wanted to see them touch down on this faraway planet, like the Americans did on the moon. We wanted to see them take one step for the Third World, which us American Rednecks were a part of, whether all of us knew it or not. And we didn't have army guys bringing milk for our babies nor clean water, which we don't have on account of the chemicals seeped in the wells from mining –

You should see the freak things that grow up outta the ground around these parts. And we sure as Hell don't have no space program to get us outta here.

Carl told me one of his army buddies, a college boy, told him the Indians weren't a part of the black race, despite the dark color of their skin, that they were "Caucasian" like us. This was a little disappointing since I was hoping for the other races to take over as old white men like my daddy and Mills had run this world into the ground and it was time someone else took a crack at saving it – OK, so maybe it wasn't ONLY old white men ruined things; there's greed in every race. So let's get rid of the greedy who get to power because of a lot of lies and underhanded shenanigans meant to keep poor folks down and make big money off of them.

Me and my friends kept our heads down and were determined to bide time till we could get to a place more open minded – it ain't easy to find your way into the world from these hills when you come up in them. In my granddaddy's day it was a fine place to come up, a place where every person thought for themselves and everyone else let them do it free. You'd argue with a person one minute and help them build a barn the next. Neighbors looked after neighbors no matter what their differences were. (This is mostly true except for a few feuds in the backcountry.) But something happened. Maybe it was the foolish TV shows you get on a dish, or the crap they feed you at these new strip malls, or the mines closing, or just a sickness come up out of the ground from them old shafts. Folks around here was always fearless but suddenly they got scared and they started to hate. It's a sad thing 'cause these mountains was once a beautiful sight before they got spoilt by folks like Mills and Mz. Murphy, the Hinkies and the coal companies. There seems to be hateful folks everywhere and maybe we're better off stickin' with them we know rather than them we don't. Still, I was hopin' to get out for a spell and see what the world was like. I admired how them Indians struck out for space as they was crammed into some crowded places that was as polluted and sploit as our mountains (but in different ways).

Me and Mar was in Jake's for a long time because of delays in the landing. We did a lot of drinking. Everyone else did too but luckily, the rowdy ones left early to race cars with the Hinkies. They didn't believe what they seen on the TV was real – like all the channels would get together and play a joke on us when there was so much else happening in the world, and the companies that paid for commercials and programs that weren't showing would go along with it.

Like all foreigners, the Indians spoke American and only mumbled a little now and again in their own language. How is it, Mz. Murphy, that all these "backward races" can speak a bunch a languages and you and me can't even speak good American? Carl said that it was old white men took all the resources out of that African country to get rich and left the Africans to fight over the little they had left. It's kinda like here, ain't it? We come to find out that although the Indians were in charge, there was a passel of little countries contributed time, brain-power and some money: Cuba, Cambodia, some a them African countries whose names kept changing and a few Pacific island countries with names you never heard of or thought were fairytale places. It was like watching the little guys win, kinda like the Mets, or that first black president, or a Hunker county girl landing on Mars. I don't see why that should scare anybody, but it did.

Now the fellas on this trip were very serious and so were the ones in the base in India, but when they landed, they didn't make speeches like the American moon guys. They danced. Yes, sir, they danced in that Hanuman jungle and they frolicked in the control room in India. They moshed in the little countries in Africa and on the fairytale islands. They boogied in Cambodia and got down in Cuba (where they lit a lot a cigars too).

Our president, who wasn't a bad guy but just had way too many troubles to deal with, congratulated them with a grim face, as did all the leaders of the big countries. It seemed the air was breathable up there and there was plenty of growing things to study. Them Indians had found another world, like Columbus. "Hot damn," is what we said. We wondered what else they'd find …

I thought I saw some movement behind them on the TV, but the picture wasn't all that clear. I guess I wasn't the only one 'cause when the dancing and congratulating stopped there was a finger-chewing quiet. Everyone up there started looking around and there was a lot of mumbo-jumbo words going back and forth and then the transmission ended. "Back to your regular programming," just like that.

We didn't know what was happening for a long time.

It finally come out that they'd found some kind of animal there.

They called them "animals" because they didn't look like us. They were small and hairless, with some webbing in their hands and feet. They had a large head that might have been considered snake-like since the nose didn't stick out like ours and they had big soft eyes that turned down at the corner. We come to find out a lot more about them as time wore on. They communicated with one another and carved towns out of stone and enormous hollowed trees. They wore clothing made of something soft and flowy like our silk, but sturdier and the kind of colors that don't look like color but show up in certain kind of lights. They all wore loose shirts and a kind of pantaloon so you could only tell the boys from the girls by their ears. They had officials and families. Mar and I couldn't understand how folks could think of them as animals but there wasn't too many folks wanted to go there and stick it out to find out about them.

We watched a lot a news in the next few months but none of it stuck because I got word that Carl had contracted one a them weird African diseases and was flown into some special army hospital in California. I wasn't allowed to see him for seven months as this disease was so contagious they kept him in a sealed bubble-thing and a kinda sleep they controlled with machines. They moved him back to the big hospital in Morgantown for another three months of therapy and I was close enough to see him every now and again. He was in mighty poor shape, his parts didn't work so well and some of them were gone (spleen, a piece a thyroid, some toes, a finger). His head was muddled and sense came and went. They said he wouldn't get much better. Since we was good friends and thought one time to get married, and since his people had mostly all died and he didn't have anyone else, I took him home with me. Mar's job at the foundry was cut down but with Carl's disability check we made out ok.

Mills was a little kinder since he seen we took in a sick veteran and we talked enough about how contagious Carl's disease was that he stayed clear of us. Mz. Murphy give us a wide birth too.

What also helped us was that Miss Lucy Oglethoren lived down the hill. She gave us vegetables from her garden and homemade jams. She gave us cookies she made for the neighborhood kids and casseroles like she made for all the sick and bereaved in the county. Time and troubles wore on all of us. Miss Lucy was a fine neighbor till her parts started to wear out. She was lively for a gal in her eighties but pretty soon we was helping her with chores and delivering her home-made food to the needy. So here was a woman never went to church and did a lot a good and loved everybody, and there was Mz. Murphy always going to the Resurrection Bible Hall and never done a lick a good work I could see, and hated everybody. (I can't say everyone in the RBH was the same as Mz. Murphy. Some was fine folks.)

Now the coal companies around our mountain had a big mess to clean up and they'd been dragging their feet for neigh on to six-ty years when they started bringing in the Citu, which is what the creatures from that foreign planet called themselves. Folks like Mills called them "monkeys." I was surprised he knew that much about the Hanuman story. Pretty soon a lot of folks was calling them monkeys.

The companies housed them up in some old concrete army train-ing barracks mostly, but some ended up in abandoned coke ovens on Jack's Run. It was a pity looking into those creature's sad eyes. They was quiet and kept to themselves; most only learned a few words in our language. Nobody except for some scientists learned much of their language and these fellas were called crackpots since they insisted the Citu were intelligent beings.

The Hinkies routinely got drunk, drove around and threw beer cans at them. Mz. Murphy wrote a letter to the Morgantown paper saying they should be locked up at night like all animals.

"Do you tie your dogs up?" Miss Lucy asked her one day on the street.

"I sure do."

"It figures. Look who I'm talking to …" We pulled her into a store before she could say any more. Miss Lucy was old and feisty but Mz. Murphy was capable of setting the dogs on her, and if that happened Miss Lucy didn't have a chance.

They sent the Citu into the abandoned mines to suck up the gasses with some machine they'd invented. They put them to shor-ing up places miners had marked as too dangerous fifty/seventy years ago. Lord knows what they gave them to eat. They didn't pay them any money, said they weren't capable of handling it. Occasionally, one or more of them would run off and a posse would go after them. The Hinkies and Mills, would always go with the company men. Sometimes they brought the Citu back bloody; sometimes they brought them back dead.

This was not unusual treatment for the Citu anywhere and some-times they were treated worse. The world had a new pack animal, but "it looks like slavery to me," Carl said. He'd learned a lot in the army. He couldn't always bring this learnin' up out of his addled brain but when he did, it was worth listening to.

Four years went by from that first landing. The Citu had been among us for nearly a year when Mar lost her job. We were about to be in dire straits but Miss Lucy stepped in to save us.

"I want you all to move in with me," she said. "You're there half the time anyway and the rest of the time I'm rattling around in that big old house."

Miss Lucy got her house and money from a long line of stingy folk who hoarded every penny they made. Miss Lucy was the last of her people and had vowed to blow it all in her youth. But after years of travel, she got tired, came back to the hollow, taught school for a while, and was hard put to spend it as fast as she found it stuffed in ev-ery corner of her house and coming in monthly from old investments.

I didn't think the trailer would last another winter anyway.

"There's just one secret you must keep. I know I can trust you."

"Sure, Miss Lucy."

"Go get your things then."

We had a little clothing and some knick-knacks but most of our things consisted of Carl's paraphernalia, his chair, oxygen, testers, drugs …We packed it all up in a borrowed pick-up and got to Miss Lucy's for a late supper.

"Just put everything in the front hall and come to table," she said. "We'll put it by later. You can wash up in the hall powder room first."

The drapes were drawn but the dining room was glowing with candles like a fancy restaurant. The table was set for seven. Three Citu stood up politely as we came in.

"Carl, Maureen, Cerese, I want you to meet Amu, Bao, and Fee."

We all nodded and sat down.

"You must promise not to let anyone know about them," Miss Lucy said.

We had no problem with it.

"We ran away from the mines," the one called Bao said.

"Our people are getting sick, dying," Amu.

"We're afraid for the unborn," Fee.

"What's wrong with you people?" Bao's eyes lost their softness for a moment.

"You can talk!" Mar said.

"Better'n us." I added.

"Of course, dear," Miss Lucy said. "I've been helping them with their English. They're perfectly intelligent. We must free them and change people's attitudes. I'm part of an underground movement."

"Railroad," Carl mumbled.

"Why, yes, an underground railroad. It's like a bad *deja vu*, isn't it?"

"Very bad," Carl said. "What can we do?"

Miss Lucy and the Citu outlined the situation. There were pockets of freedom fighters around the US, but West Virginia was the center. I was relieved to find out that people like Mills hadn't overtaken the spirit of the mountains. The Indians, who'd known the Citu longer than anyone, were beginning to relent on their status as animals despite a history of "castes." (Carl told us about these classes that you were born in and stuck for the rest of your life! I guess nobody's perfect.) There were small movements to help them in other countries too. Cuba was the only country that had fully accepted them as human; as long as they went along with the program they were treated like everyone else. The moon colony had no qualms about slavery.

My people had fought the big coal companies before, fought and won, then grew disgusted with their own officials who got greedy after a time. My granddaddy and his before was encouraged to get out a the mines, which had pretty much disappeared by their time anyway. Then there was a time when politicians dreamed up this idea of "clean coal." Now, wasn't that a crock … it gave the companies license to come in and blow up mountains, pollute water, destroy whole communities of good folks, and then up and leave. Folks that didn't die off from the gasses and the water, tried to get out but there was no one to give us jobs except the army and you could get into some crazy trouble there – just look at Carl. Them that stayed mostly got bitter like Mills and Mz. Murphy.

The way I figured, just because me and mine had it rough was no reason to wish it on any other creature, human or not. They weren't going to pull me down, and Mar, Miss Lucy and Carl felt the same way. It was gonna be a fight; we could tell by the sound of Mills gun going off above us night after night.

As the months wore on we got a few Citu out, and a few more. It seemed that just when it would get crowded in Miss Lucy's house, a wind would blow strong enough to send folks running and we could get Citu out of town without anybody seeing. Bao stayed on to translate and help out. He did a "laying on of hands" to Carl and put some circulation back into his feet. Carl's hands started to work better and his head started to clear up some. The best Bao could explain, it was a transfer of the energy from his body to Carl's, but we didn't have the words in American.

I took on a better waitress job at the Lost River Inn. That river was lost all right; nothing come out of it but black silt and oily goo. The inn washed their dishes in it, so I didn't eat anything there. It was a good thing because cook and Al Ranger, the owner, were sick all the time. The rest of the folks that worked there were sick a lot so I got a passel of overtime.

I was feeling pretty good about things. Then one night Mz. Murphy come in off the street when she seen me in the window.

She shook her bony finger in my face. "I know what you're up to," she said. "I know whoall's in on it too."

"Mz. Murphy, you've got yourself all worked up. Why don't you sit down and have some of our fine lemonade, made from pure store-bought water."

"I make my own lemonade, thank you. I don't have to pay fancy prices for lemon sugar-water. You mind my word; you're little game is about to end."

It was like she put a curse out into the air. It got dark as night in the middle of the afternoon and a storm come up so fast they closed the restaurant early. The five of us sat around Miss Lucy's table and worried over Mz. Murphy's warning while the wind settled some and the rain threatened to bring the rest of the mountain down on us.

"I have word of a ship leaving from Cuba," Bao said.

The Citu had decided to return to their planet. Not many of them thought earth was worth fighting to stay on.

"Will you leave us then, dear?" Miss Lucy asked.

"I can't leave until my people are safe. But you four have done your part. I see no future here for you. Carl could be helped with our herbs and treatments. Our world is clean and your lives would be easier."

"I couldn't leave," Miss Lucy said. "I'm an old woman and this is my home, but you young people should go."

"I'm down," Mar said. "Where do I sign up?"

I looked at Carl. "You should go; if they can help you … "

"I will, if you go."

"Come on," Mar said "What's to hold you? You ain't got no people here anymore. You can be a waitress anywhere."

"Oh, I'm sure there are many more things you could do," Bao said. "We have an open education system – if you're interested."

I thought about studying stars, about studying herbs, about nights without Mill's gunfire (I know Carl was thinking about this too).

How we got out was, Bao had this little spinning thing, like a top, that he put under the big willow in Miss Lucy's backyard. It stirred up a wind and that wind got bigger and bigger and turned into a storm that sent everyone running and Carl, Mar and me lit out in Miss Lucy's old Volkswagon car to a house in Morgantown. I asked Bao how this worked and he said it was like the butterfly wing and the hurricane, whatever that means. They flew us in airplanes to Pittsburg; Cancun, Mexico; Havana, Cuba and the Gitmo Space Center.

Even before we got here there were so many new things … my first plane ride, Mexican food, Cuban music, the quiet of space, the gentleness of the Citu. Carl says history repeats itself, but I hope that don't happen up here and why would they repeat a history that's clearly not theirs? The Citu are good neighbors and Hanuman's a place without fear and hate, a place where simple things (like Bao's spinning toy) do the job of big dirty machines. The Citu now have a strict policy about who they let in, so I think it'll stay this way.

Carl's walking short distances; Mar's studying to be a kind of midwife, though the Citu don't have babies like we do but that's another story I might write about someday. Everyone's willing to teach what they know to anyone who wants to learn. I'm learning a lot. So far I study about anything that takes my fancy, and there's a lot that does. I don't know where it'll take me but the Citu say it'll take me somewhere and not to worry. We all work but it don't take much to live here. I'm thinking our own world musta been a lot like this once. The trees and the plants look different but the water runs clear and cool down from a mountain that reminds me of home.

Wait, it is home. And it wasn't such a big jump after all.

Breakthrough

(A passage for ventilation that is cut through the pillars between rooms in a coal mine.)

In past lives I was a a princess in Sheba, a Chinese dowager, a Viking soothsayer, a Roma gypsy, a Zulu dancer. I have memories from all my past lives: the magician/king Solomon who seduced our queen, the pain of bound feet, Norse winters, the red velvet skirt my mother made for me to dance in, and the rumblings of a hungry tiger nearby. I remember the world as it was in many eras.

In this life I live in a tiny house in a hollow above Mahulda, West Virginia. I haven't left my house since papa died, twenty-two years ago. RayJay, Mr. Handler's boy from the general store, delivers necessities and my neighbor Mz. Altusson checks in on me and brings me herbs and vegetables from her garden, chicory and wild ginger from the woods, apples from her tree. I sew and I have the TV to keep me company. Time passes. Papa said a body only needs three things to keep a house up: duct tape (if it moves to much), WD40 (if it's stuck), and a good screwdriver (one with a variety of heads). Still, it's a race to see what'll wear out first, the house or my body.

Twice in that time I thought I was dying and Mz. Altusson found me (she has The Gift), and called Doc Mathias who brought me back with his medicine. Mostly I tend to myself with teas and poultice and such, but Mz. Altusson looks in on me like she does everyone around here. She's old but she's spry.

I get the National Geographic which is how I first remembered my past lives, recognizing pictures of places, people and objects. Funny thing is, papa always got the Geographic and never let me read it because it was "full of Heathens and not fit for the eyes of a decent young lady." I didn't start reading it till after he passed. It wasn't until then that I realized what all those strange memories were. I've been reading it ever since.

Mz. Altusson also brings me ironing from the Benson's, who own the mine, and she takes it back when I finish. This is how I make a little money beside what I get from Social Security. Mrs. Benson doesn't like how they finish laundry in Mahulda. She likes her fancy bed sheets ironed every week and her five kids clean and pressed. I do a little mending for her too. I've never seen Mrs. Benson nor any of her kin but I know clothes and bedsheets that are too posh to be from any of the stores in these parts, so I'd recognize the folks that wear them, right off, if I was to run into them – which is unlikely as I don't plan to go out any time soon.

Mrs. Benson wrote me a note last Christmas thanking me for my services and for allowing her and her children to live like "human beings" in this "god-forsaken hillbilly wasteland." I hear stories about her saying things like this to others, which is why she's not well-liked around here. I feel sorry for a woman who can't appreciate the hills and woodlands and the good folks who live here – but then I guess there's some who'd say I'm not much better.

Lately the house shakes from the blasting on the mountain. Mz. Altusson doesn't like it. She says they're blastin' out the ghosts of miners lost in the tunnels and I reckon she knows what she's talking about because she's got The Gift. She says we better all watch what we're doing or learn to swim, but I'm not sure what she means by this. I've seen some strange things on the mountain lately, lights and such, trees just fallin' over for no reason, creeks that rise up fierce, and drop down to a trickle. There's a sink hole in my front yard and sometimes a stench comes up out of the ground. The marigolds on the kitchen sill die and the grass is brown and weedy. I worry about the beech trees and the old sugar maple at the foot of the yard. Of course, I haven't gone out to tend them in an age.

Mz. Altusson says we have to get out of here one of these days soon before all those ghosts get really mad at the ruckus being caused by the mining companies, trucks and road crews; and before the whole mountain comes down on us. She thinks her house is sinking into one of the old shafts. She wants me to come see it but I tell her I'll take her word for it. I haven't told her I'm not leaving but she surely knows it anyway.

On the day the mining alarm sounded, I was waiting for Mz. Altusson to come for Mrs. Benson's clothes. It wasn't till the next day she came for them and then she was in a snit because Mrs. Benson didn't have the decency to stop bothering her about them, or come herself when Mz. Altusson's brother-in-law, Al Conner, was lost in the mine.

"Twelve lost all together," she told me.

"Did they give up searching already?"

"No, can't give up yet, but they gone."

"Well, you have The Gift and should know."

"Don't need no Gift with them ghosts moanin' all night."

"I heard them."

"They gonna blow up the mountain now for sure. Tunnels ain't safe. Time to git."

"Got no place to git' to."

Mz. Altusson just shook her head, for she had no place to go either. She had no kin except her little sister and Al Conner. Her sister had but one leg and needed more care than Mz. A. could give her. Al may not have been the most sociable fella in Mahulda but he was a good husband to Mz. Altusson's little sister. Al's kin down in Beckley were decent folk and would care for Mz. A's sister but there was no room or money to take in Mz. A.

I wondered if my ironing days were over and if I could live on Social Security money, and was the mountain going to take me with it when it went. I was worried about Mz. Altusson and her sister and the other wives and children. And the ghosts – maybe it was time for them to move on.

In a few weeks the rescue phase was ended and the funerals began. I could hear folks singing in the cemetery on the hill. I could feel the pall that came over the valley and I closed my curtains and opened the door to the storm cellar in the back hallway, to see if there was any damage.

I don't use the storm cellar much since I put papa's guns and boots down there. It's a shame to waste good boots but you don't give away a dead man's boots. I always meant to put them in the garbage one at a time so nobody could take them to wear, but just forgot.

Three ghosts huddled in the corner. Al Conner was one, the others were too young for me to recognize.

"Where's the rest?" I asked them.

"Gone to glory."

"You boys are going to have to go too. You can take some time here if you've a mind, but then go on into the light, prepare for the next life like everyone else. I'm sorry but that's the way it is."

They just looked at me with their big empty ghost eyes.

"Listen," I said. "It's not so bad moving' on, better'n this cellar. The next life is a do-over. You get new clothes, a new name (something I was looking forward to), your feet don't hurt, you get fresh opportunities. Even if you've been very bad, chances are you've learned your lesson and you won't mess up as much next time around."

"That's blasphemous talk," Al said.

"You believe what suits you, Al Conner, and I'll believe what suits me. We'll know who's right real soon."

Al rubbed at his eyes that couldn't see the world any more. "I know you," he said. "You're Meme Cumshaw, from up the hollow. You was always a little peculiar."

One of the young ones spoke up, "He's sorry, ma'am."

"That's allright, son," I said. "I know Al and he was always quarrel-some. But he's harmless."

"Now see here!" Al stood up.

"That's what I mean."

The boys laughed. I guess that's what it was, but ghostly chortling is a mighty sorry sound. It made Al's knees buckle and he sat back down.

"Just how did you end up here?" I asked.

"I reckon we came to warn you," boy #1 said. "Your house is undermined."

"I know that, son. There's tunnels under every part of this mountain and in the town."

"And they're gonna blow the mountain," boy #2 said.

"So I guess you gotta git outta here too," Al said.

"Well, sir," I said. "I've lived in this house all my life and haven't been out of it in twenty-two years and the only way I'm going, is the same way you fellas are going. And that's into the light."

"What'd I tell you, boys," Al said. "Peculiar."

"Excuse me, ma'am," boy #2 said. "I wished it were true that we git another life but I sure would miss my mama, and my dog too."

"Son," I said. "Some souls are so tangled up that they end up together in other lives, some out of love and some out of lessons to be learned."

"You mean I could end up with ole Miss Kramer what teaches the forth grade?"

"You might."

"I don't think I'd like that."

"You don't know. She might have learned some lessons herself and be a better person down the line. It's never what you think it will be."

"Blast-phemer!" Al said.

No sooner did he speak than there was a rumble and the old house shook, dust kicked up and we heard hollering outside.

"You just stew down here a while and I'll go see what the ruckus is." I told them.

Sure enough it was Mz. Altusson and the Doc, come to talk me into leaving. She must have seen it coming and called on Doc to back her up.

"The mountain is speakin' to me," she said.

"Seems to me it should be speaking to Sam Benson about his mining practices," I said.

"If he don't hear it now, he's never gonna hear it."

"I'm afraid he doesn't want to hear it," the Doc said. "We been trying to get his wife to intervene but she's worse than him."

Mz. Altusson stood there studying me. I looked her in the eye and said, "You two better get along. You've got no call staying here. You've done your duty but I'm not going anywhere. I'm an old woman and I have no place to go to and no kin to take me in."

Doc put his hand on the porch beam, "Nobody wants to leave but it's not safe. We're all being evacuated. We know you've had some painful times in your life." (He was talking about my mercifully short and grisly marriage to Tom 'Jink' Fenster). "And your papa was the only one treated you kindly and since he passed – well, we know why you want to keep to yourself. But there's folks out here want to help you and won't hurt you. The Red Cross's set up a shelter down at the high school gym in Hunker. You can stay there till they decide if it's safe, and if it's not they'll set you up in a nice place."

"I'll take my chances here."

"You can't ... " he started.

"Go along, Doc," Mz. Altusson said to him. Then she turned to me, "I'm commin' in Meme Cumshaw. We're gonna have us a talk."

I said, "I'll put the kettle on," and the Doc turned to leave.

We were barely in the door when she said, "You are cavorting with dead folk."

"I wouldn't call it cavorting."

"Keeping company, then. You've got some a them dead miners here. Where are they?" Mz. Altusson started walking around, looking into corners and behind furniture. She noticed the open cellar door, got on her knees and stuck her head down the stairs. "Al Conner, Harley Shute, James Lee Booker, I swan."

Then she pulled herself up with a groan and told me to "go put that kettle on."

After a little tea and some of my pecan scones she said, "If we could just git these boys over to the Benson house and scare the beje-sus out of them ... then I could talk to the mountain ... "

One of the young ghosts, James Lee, swished up next to her and whispered in her ear.

"Well, isn't that Old Nick's dessert. I recon I'll be calling out those shadows ... "

"See here," I said. "I will not have you hexing in my house." I guess it was my tone of voice that scared James Lee back to the cellar but it didn't scare Mz. Altusson.

"I beg your pardon," she said. "I do not hex. Such pitiful deeds are beneath me. Wasn't it you tole me about harm retribution?"

"Do you mean karmic retribution?"

"You and your Geographic stories ... It don't take no Dolly Lama to know puttin' harm in this world is a bad idea. Bad deeds have a recoil like my daddy's railroad gun and ten to one, it's gonna come back to haunt ya. Even a not-so-good Christian woman like myself knows that the hand a God is gonna come down on evil. I seen it happen again and again. I'd say that abusing this mountain or encouraging your husband to harm man and nature so as you can spend money like water, is a bad idea. And if your house happens to be undermined, like the Bensons, that mountain's gonna swallow you up and the hand of god or your karmic whatits is gonna cut you down one of these days."

"Yes, but god or the universe or whatever the power is that's in charge of the Bank of Retribution, has time on it's side and a particular account may not come due for years or decades or another life. You know that's true. How does it help us here and now?"

"Didn't I tell you I would talk to the mountain?"

"Talk to the mountain? Now, Mz. Altusson, that's the sort of thing going to set folks to saying you're crazy, like they do me."

"For god's sake call me Evie. I'm only five years older than you and we've known each other ... forever."

"Well, Mz. Altusson, I think you should have another cup of tea and try to calm yourself down."

Then the house started moving. Dishes rattled. Furniture slid. Tea spilled and Evie Altusson jumped up.

"It's happening," she said. "They're not gonna get this mountain if I have anything to do with it. But there's gonna be hell to pay before it's over. Come on!"

"I'm coming."

She was out the door in a shot. "Leave everything, Meme. Just come."

"I'm right behind you."

And out she went, down the front steps, into the yard.

I was happy she hadn't looked back before she got outside because I had to stop at the front door.

"Come on, Meme. You can do it."

I couldn't.

"Thanks for everything, Mz. A. I appreciate your concern. Take care of yourself."

She started back toward the porch. The house gave a terrible shake, lifted right off the ground, and then fell back down.

Mz. Altusson turned away. "You do what you want, Meme. I'm gonna have a serious talk with this mountain."

I went back into the house and laid down on my couch. I wrapped my feet in the afghan I'd crocheted the winter before, and put my forearm over my eyes to rest. I could feel the mountain rumble beneath me and hear the pages of the National Geographic that was sitting on the coffee table flutter.

Dreams hit her one after another: the loud protest of the camel beneath her as the caravan left a walled city, playing a board game with her mother in the shadow of the Yellow Crane Tower, a voice telling her "Kjartan will die," the screams of her ten-year-old sister being kidnapped to become a child bride, bare feet pounding on dusty earth while drums and whistles called to the ancestors, and then a deafening rumble and dust that obscured everything and choking ...

Falling. Falling ...

When she woke, she was a young girl on a pallet built into a wall in a concrete room with a desk-ledge and chair. Drawers and terminal screen were embedded in the opposite wall. She jumped down and found her way to a bathroom. To her muddled mind it was vaguely familiar but didn't really look like a bathroom. The toilet had no tank; there was a waterless shower and the sink was a bowl on a shelf. One wall was mirrored and she stared at the reflection of her childish self. Her skin was smooth and brownish, her hair had some curl. She jumped up and down, pounding her feet as hard as she could. There was no pain. She twirled. New memories came flooding in: catching crabs in the surf, a little sister (was it hers or someone else's?), an accident that left a blue scar on her knee, something doughy and sweet and filled with nuts, that was her favorite food.

It was a long time before she realized someone was watching her from the doorway. Mother. "You're awake. Look at me. I know that look. You've inhered. I can see the difference," she said. "I remember when it happened to me. I was about your age and I'd been hiding in a cupboard. I fell asleep and when I came out, I understood something about myself and the world that I'd never been aware of before. We're not born inhered and it doesn't appear gradually. One day we wake up to it and everything changes."

Inhered? Carmah didn't know what she was talking about.

"Well, come on," the Mother said. "We'll be late for the parade."

The house and everything in it was very straight and square. The only color beside grey and white was bright blue. It was all familiar but other, more colorful and cluttered spaces hovered at the back of her mind.

Mother opened the front door. Carmah froze. Before her was a yard with a gentle drop at the end. Below the drop was an ocean, languid waves and a rocky beach. To both sides, as far as she could see, were other concrete houses, every one was about the same size and they all had porches. Curved, latticed, domed, embellished, the houses were scattered down the beach in both directions as far as she could see. Behind the line of houses, rolling hills with scattered stands of beech trees and sugar maples. The ground was covered with jewel-weed and vetch. Chicory and wild ginger grew along a path.

"Come on," the mother said. "I don't know why you have such a hard time leaving the house but once you're out, you're fine. Nothing bad's going to happen; I've taken care of it. Come on, you can't see from inside."

Carmah stepped out onto the porch. She could feel the warm wind. It smelled of ocean and something else, a familiar woodsy smell that didn't seem to belong near the sea, though she couldn't remember why she thought this.

"I told you I'd talk to the mountain," the mother said.

Before she could answer, Carmah heard music. Now she could see a parade coming down the beach. The music got louder and louder and then the bands and floats passed right in front of their house. Halfway through, a man stepped out from the marching crowd and came up onto the porch.

"Hello, Mitchell," the mother said and pecked him on the cheek.

The man seemed familiar but Carmah didn't recognize the name. He lifted her up easily. "How's my girl?"

"Say hey to your Uncle Mitchell," the mother said.

The man winked. "Uncle Al to you," he said.

"Oh, you two ... " the mother said.

Carmah felt memories swirling back: the mountain, the alarm, the ghosts ...

"I made pecan scones, your favorite," the mother said and went into the house to get them.

Uncle Al looked Carmah over and laughed. "There's been a change since I saw you last. You're growing up. I guess I can tell you now that you were right about my feet," he said. "I can dance all night. Why didn't you tell me that we were connected?"

"You've changed," Carmah said.

"You're darn right I have, and it's not just new clothes."

"Where are we Uncle Al?"

"We're still here, still on our mountain. A lot has changed, but the mountain hasn't been completely swallowed up yet. I guess folks can get linked to places as well as to people."

"And animals, Uncle Al. Don't forget animals."

"You talkin' about that miserable dog a yours, Mrs. Benson? I don't know what you see in that mangy critter."

The mother came in with a plate of pecan scones followed by a three-legged, half-bald, sad-sack mutt. She said, "I do believe this child was put on the earth to help that dog."

On Orly's Border

Orly's modest cottage was located in a mountainous region on the border between the Land of the Living and the Land of the Dead. The cottage was small but cozy. Orly had carved the eave timbers and posts in the form of trees and flowers that were scarce in the stark landscape. Villagers from the glens below helped him with the roof thatching and thick cob walls. Though the land was rocky, Orly had cleared a small garden around which he built a sturdy wood and wire fence to keep the wolves out. He built another fence and shanty for his two goats and a few chickens.

Folks rarely traveled into the Land of the Dead by way of Orly's homestead as it was an arduous journey and out of the way. They preferred crossing over tranquil waters in the company of the kindhearted boatman who operated a ferry in a distant valley. Orly couldn't take time out from his chores to lead them over the boundary; he barely had time to point the way. And because he wasn't endowed with a sociable nature, Orly never knew what to say to them. He kept his head down and carried on with his work, avoiding conversations.

When he was a young man, Orly took a wife. She was agreeable and pretty enough to wake up to each morning, a young woman who loved the mountain as much as he, but was a bit scatterbrained – perhaps it was the altitude. One morning she took the goats for a walk and stumbled into the Land of the Dead. Had her attention been on the goats, this would never have happened because goats are sure-footed and attentive. Orly's wife had been singing to herself and looking up at the clouds, which is not a very prudent thing to do when walking on a rocky mountainside but wasn't unusual behavior for Orly's wife. Orly tried to call her back but she wasn't quick-witted enough to realize what she'd done. He thought of going after her but was afraid he wouldn't be able to find his way back, and who would take care of his goats – and his baby daughter. His wife had left the baby sleeping in a cradle outside the cottage, which wasn't a wise thing to do when a gate is open and there might be wolves about. But this was the only way she could hear the child if she cried. (Perhaps "scatterbrained" is too strong a word for someone who's just relentlessly cheerful.)

Orly's daughter, Lhosi, grew up believing that Orly was her grandfather, as she'd read a book about a girl who lived in the mountains and thought it was about her, and because Orly was old-fashioned and very weathered (from mountain winds and lost love). But when Lhosi was fifteen and no handsome goat-heard had befriended her, and no one had asked her to move to the city to be the companion of an ailing rich girl, she realized Orly was her father and that she was Lhosi not Heidi.

Lhosi inherited her mother's lightheartedness, which frightened Orly. He marked the border to the Land of the Dead with wire fence and colorful flags on posts, and reminded her each morning, and several times during the day, not to go beyond them.

Lhosi hadn't inherited her mother's comely looks, so Orly was surprised when a young hiker from the city, a boy who thought of himself as an adventurer, took a liking to Lhosi and asked her to marry him. Orly didn't trust city folk and it took him a long time to accept the young man, but eventually he did and encouraged them to visit often. When Lhosi and the hiker had children, it became difficult for them to journey through the mountainous terrain. Orly had to go to the city to see them and though he loved his daughter and her children and had warmed up to his son-in-law, he did not like the city. He didn't like the crowds and the traffic. He was suspicious of the aromas, and he hated the noise. Lhosi asked him to come live with them as he was getting old, but he refused to leave the mountain.

Lhosi understood she couldn't change him and sent packages with food and clothing and books so he wouldn't have to work so hard. For the first time in his life, Orly had time to sit and watch the clouds pass and the stars come out. He had time to read the books Lhosi sent him, though he had a tendency to fall asleep while doing so, forget what he'd been reading, and have to start over. And he had time to watch the travelers and even say a few words to them (having grandchildren had made him a lot more sociable).

Most of the people who journeyed to the mountain in order to cross over to the Land of the Dead were very old, or had been sick for a long time and used up all their savings, or had to leave whatever they had to children and spouses who were destitute. They had no money to pay the boatman. The boatman, who was a kindly soul, never asked for a fee, but it was customary to give him a coin and it embarrassed people not to be able to do this. So they braved the treacherous path up the mountainside and were so relieved to see the border that they didn't have much to say to Orly. Often they dragged themselves over the border without even taking time to sit and catch their breath or ask for a cup of water.

Occasionally, someone who was reluctant to cross would sit on Orly's porch with him and tell their story, for everyone has a story. Sometimes Orly would nod off during the telling but most of the stories were better than the ones in the books Lhosi sent – they were stories of love and betrayal, murder and escape, invention and deception. Some stories made Orly sad and some were downright silly. Orly liked to see people laugh when they were about to cross over to the Land of the Dead. Though he'd improved, Orly still wasn't very good at conversation but folks seemed to appreciate that he took time out to listen to them.

He told everyone to look for his wife and tell her he loved and missed her and that Lhosi was well and had three fine children of her own. He told them to tell her to come to the border so he could talk to her. If it hadn't been for Lhosi and her children, he would have gone to look for his wife himself, but it always seemed there was some reason to put it off, a school play, a ball game, a dance recital, or a holiday.

Then the Children of War began to arrive.

They were burned and limbless and blind but the kindhearted ferryman kept sending them back to be saved even though there was no place for the maimed in the Land of the Living, and they were sent from there to Orly's boarder. They camped on the mountain subsisting on squirrel meat, insects, and roots. They persisted with the hope that a miracle would occur and someone would come up with a way to give them back what they'd lost. But what they'd lost was much more than limbs and organs. What they'd lost made the winds blow cold and the spirits of the dead moan in compassion when darkness came. Their loss wasn't something you could hide beneath a rock and retrieve after a fight. It wasn't something you could buy at the market or pull out of the sea. It wasn't something you could grow in your fields or mix up in your kitchen. What they'd lost was buried deep beneath battlefields or had been vaporized into the smoldering pall of fear. If they were to get it back (and one or two had – which only succeeded in giving the others a flimsy hope), it would take a miracle of cosmic proportions.

What they'd lost was something Orly'd had little of since his wife died, and hadn't understood until he was surrounded by it's absence in others. He realized that it was the one thing Lhosi had in abundance, the thing that had seeped out of his wife slowly from living so near to the Land of the Dead. It was the thing that made her look up at the sky and sing the day she stumbled into the Land of the Dead – odd that such a thing wouldn't lead her in the opposite direction. Orly wondered how his wife and child had sustained the fragile attribute so close to the Land of the Dead.

He decided to ask Jaijai, the wisest man in the valley, about this. So Orly journeyed down to the tiny village at the foot of the mountain.

Jaijai told him, "The proximity of the Land of the Dead has different effects on people. It stimulates some; it numbs others. It drives some people crazy; while others pay little attention to it. There's no predicting what effect it'll have."

"Do you think I should move?" Orly asked him.

"Where would you move to?" Jaijai asked. "Perhaps you haven't noticed, none of us are too far away from the Land of the Dead."

Orly climbed back up the mountain. It was becoming even more crowded day by day. Orly wove through the tents and the sleep-sacks, avoiding the eyes of the maimed. They didn't ask anything of him as they understood he had nothing to offer, but their eyes made Orly's heart heavy and his head throb.

At home he sat on the porch eating salted butter beans and looking over at the Land of the Dead. Sometimes the only way he knew he was alive was by the taste of salt. When his wife was living there was pomquat cake, but he'd forgotten the taste of it.

At sunset he walked along the border checking his fence and line of flags. Beyond the low murmur of the Children of War, stillness from the Land of the Dead spread over the mountain like fog.

Then he heard a low whisper coming from the border, "How are you, Orly?"

Orly looked into the Land of the Dead and saw a ghostly figure, one that looked remarkably like his wife.

"It's me, Orly," she said. "I was sent ... I miss you."

"I miss you too," he answered. "Come back. Lhosi is grown; she has children. You should see ... "

"I can't; it's been too long."

"I'll come to you then."

"No! Don't do that. You'll be called soon enough. Stay with the children as long as you can. But sit for a while and tell me about them."

So Orly sat on the hard ground and told her about their grandchildren. He told her about the songs they sang and the toys he'd carved for them. He told her about their sticky hands and what their favorite foods were. The ghost wife laughed and cried, and then she said, "I must go."

"Will you come again?"

"I can only come when I'm sent. Oh, silly me, I forgot that I was sent for a reason." Dwelling in the Land of the Dead hadn't made her less capricious. "Something must be done about these people."

"You mean the Children of War?"

"Yes. They disturb the dead."

"They disturb the living too. That's why they're here."

"Well, you have to get rid of them. They have to make a decision. They can't stay on the mountain; they can't make a real life on this border."

"Where can they go? There's no place for them in the Land of the Living and it's not fair to force them to crossover before they're ready. The boatman sends them away and the living send them here." Orly didn't realize that he spoke for himself as well.

The ghost wife thought for a while.

"You must stop the wars," she said finally. "That way at least there won't be any more of these poor souls hovering about."

"Stop the wars? Me? How would I do that? There's been war as long as there's been people."

"Where did the maimed go before?"

"It was easier for families to tend to them; life was simple and there weren't so many. Most of them crossed over. Doctors and treatments weren't as good in the old days."

"It isn't as if they're made whole now."

"Still ... "

"I don't know, Orly. This is not a problem the Dead can solve, and it's not only our side that suffers – the animals on the mountain have been killed or displaced, the water and land defiled. Soon they'll have used up the mountain itself. Then what?"

Orly had no answer.

He watched his wife disappear and wondered what he could do. He'd gladly give his life to end war, but many people had given lives over the years and it hadn't done any good. He could assassinate the warmongering leaders, but that never worked before either. He could go from town to town and deliver an antiwar message, but such men ended up imprisoned or dead and some became the cause of terrible wars themselves.

How was he to bring the Children of War back to the Land of the Living and encourage the Living to take them in? The maimed weren't capable of establishing a town without some support and that wasn't obtainable in a time of crisis and war. If he was to lead them to a town where they outnumbered the Living, there'd be no choice ... but wasn't that the same as attacking? If the town people were to retaliate, which they surely would, it would create more war. Perhaps war is the only answer, he thought, a grand war to end all wars ... but that had also been tried.

Orly sat on his porch, at war with himself, trying to come up with a plan. Occasionally he'd see some of the maimed crossover and he'd hope the siege would end without his participation, but more Children of War would arrive and build their leantos and light their fires and tell their stories.

Some stories have happy endings and some have endings that are dreaded from the first "once upon a time ... " Some endings are a relief, and some are torture. Some are agonized over. There are stories you wish would never end and regret it when they do as they leave you forever yearning for more. There are stories you wish would have ended long before they did. Occasionally a story ends before it begins and we never hear it. And some stories are circles, beginnings and endings so entwined that you can find neither. They always were and always will be; they go on and on. Regrettably, this is one of those. For how can we say that the story ends when Orly (or anyone else) crosses over? There's still war; there are still Children of War, maimed and waiting. This story goes on no matter who passes over Orly's fence to the other side, sadly, after Orly's story ends, after Lhosi's story ends, after her children ... It began before we were born and it's set to go on after our story is finished. It's a story that deserves a peaceful resolution, a story that should end. But, try as I may, I can not end it.

Or can I? Time and Lhosi go on, for mothers are dauntless and those who keep their children from war possess a strength that's undiminished by frivolous conflict. They teach their children tolerance and kindness. They teach their children the power of nonviolence.

Perhaps one of Orly's descendants rebuilds the cozy cottage and repairs the wire fence that separates the Land of the Living and the Land of the Dead. Perhaps he/she adds lanterns and colorful murals to the fence, repairs the road and opens an inn that serves fine food. Perhaps there's music and dancing, and games for children. Perhaps the rocks are cleared, terraces built for crops and the maimed find hope.

Perhaps one day, amid all this gaiety and abundance, war is forgotten.

Episcatory

Occasionally, I raise my head out of the water to scan the land and see what I might be missing. I do this in the evening so as not to be blinded by sunglare. I can't imagine why anyone would want to live in such a tangle of vegetation and humanity, noise and pollutants. I can't imagine why anyone wouldn't appreciate the caress of water about them or the certainty of current to carry them to a destination orchestrated by the power that created all. I barely remember the *sturm und drang* of life lived in rich air, only that my gentle and compassionate nature was neither advantageous nor desirable there. Thankfully, my physical body took measures to save me from inhospitable environs.

There is much I've forgotten about being human. It was so long ago that I stood on feet and attempted to walk on coarse earth. Was there a time before I could swim? If so, I can't remember. I realize now that air was my nemesis, that by taking it in wantonly I put myself at great risk, for I am allergic to earthy things. Each breath I took brought with it a taste of melancholy, the ache of annoyance, and stench of despair. Effects of the oxygenated environment varied from wearying distress to painful torment. I suffered from acrophobia and was prone to fainting spells.

I knew, even as a child, that my awkwardness on land was eradicated by water. I was strong and graceful in water, clumsy and unbalanced on land. How can one hope to balance without a supporting element to buoy one of them up? Air is so flaccid, the pull of gravity sadistically brutal. There is comfort and ease in the soft embrace of liquid, the engram of nurturance.

My transformation began with intermittent sleep disturbances. I remember lying in bed as a child, holding my breath so as not to suffocate in cloying air, while pores struggled to take sustenance in a more suitable measure – the purity of oxygen without the contaminants of your atmosphere. At first it was only a dream that I could breathe under water. Then one day I dove into the cool arms of the river, and sank to the bottom in peacefulness. The silent, slow, even rush of life there was a welcome antidote to the chaos of earthly endeavor above. I shimmied out of constricting clothing and worked my limbs with the current. Within days webs began to form between toes and fingers. My former breathing apparatus, already obstructed by pollens, sealed itself off and withered.

Do not assume that I am a singly mutated monstrosity, incapable of reproduction and doomed to extinction. There are others like me, our genetic factors re-assorted into revolutionary (dare I say, groundbreaking?) combinations. There are new generations bred in a union of liquid sensuality unimaginable to lesser creatures bound to land. I will not demean our devotion with descriptions or labels of biological urge, for it entails a compulsion for purity beyond the comprehension of philandering terrestrials. It is unpretentiously beautiful, symphonic in light of your loamy crudeness.

We do not concern ourselves with the gratuitous trivia of civilization down here. There is no need of economic scheming or exploitive organization in a perfect ecosystem. What do shelled creature or fish care for politics? No more than algae and bacteria. It is rare that any life-form here disturbs peaceful silence with discordant noise, unthinkable that one should disrupt the balance between silent fellowship and solitude. Whereas land creatures consider grace of movement an art form, here it's the norm. We do not corrupt our environment with arrogant creations; we do not presume that intellect will reveal Truth. We do not "hold beliefs;" we do not behave in ways that might undermine the dignity of others. We never "thirst."

I've heard whispers from above that our conditions are primitive, barbaric. It's true that the larger, more aggressive among us regularly consume the smaller. But is this not true above? Yet, when we do it, it's not out of malice or greed, nor is such action bemoaned by others; it is the accepted way of nature. We are the Ur-creatures of your fallacious construct. Do you not wistfully speak of "simplifying," "returning to basics?" We've taken those aspirations to their farthest, disengaged from social and species pretext, receded from your convulsive evolution and reverted to conditions fundamental to the genesis of life. We are sustained by a basic element and live accordingly.

Such a life would be paradise were it not for your interference: the noisy splashing, filthy residue, intrusive edifice. Fortunately there remain some waters uncorrupted by your influence – waters distant and deep. We rely on the hand of the creator and the current to lead us there until that time when your own conduct purges the land of your tenuous purchase.

Timepiece

After the dogs chewed the hands off the clock, we had only the chimes to remind us of time. If we were engrossed in our work and missed the sound of them, we lost the hour. This occurred often, as you might imagine. Winding the clock became the most crucial task of our day. We were afraid that sooner or later someone would forget, then time would stop and the rest of the world would go on without us. But this was in a time before Timelessness.

It wasn't that our standards were as consistent as that of the outside world. After we moved to this place, the old clock took on a mind of its own. Like indulgent parents, we overlooked its early misconduct. The chimes were not as reliable as they had been – they began to strike odd combinations at quirky intervals, and sound out in peculiar tones.

Perhaps we should have considered the possibility of defection in a more serious light.

Perhaps we should have thought about the inevitable lapse of synchronism, however tentative it might have seemed then. Perhaps we should have made contingency plans, studied shadows or celestial bodies.

We chose to allow its quirks.

We might have recognized the old clock's inclination to "strike out for attention" as opposed to the smooth performance of contracted function – that being the regular and consistent process of marking increments of time. Beyond the pretext of furniture, it stood proud and tall, covetous of its role as Keeper of Time, reveling in the attention of careful polishing and regular winding by acolytes. For love of furniture goes beyond person-to-object or object-to-object, or even object-to-itself, itself-to-itself; inspiring ever more perverse pairings of which we dare not speak.

Chronometric decline ensued sometime after the move, causing distortions in the pervading continuum: the doors that opened to the clock's face and works commenced to hang ajar in a state of warp; chiming became garbled and erratic. Ministrations of chronometric practitioners were to no avail. "Best to grant evolution with dignity," they advised.

"But what of us?" we asked him.

Committed as he was, to the wellbeing of such crucial devices, he could only shake his head at such a question. We were chagrined at our pettiness, shamed to silence.

It was not long after this that the dogs took matters into their own "hands," as it were. Ordinarily, we trust them to follow their own nature which compels them to protect us from abstractions and affectations. The act of consumption against the agent of continuity was their greatest and most defiant exploit, so far reaching in its effect that we're humbled by their audacity. We were stunned by their duplicity as our tenuous confidence had rested solely on the dependability of their instincts. We had believed they were the only creatures that could be trusted to be vigilant and responsible. We might not have credited them with this surreptitious act had it not been for their lethargy and metallic-smelling hiccups after its discovery. We awoke that morning to find them lying smugly at the foot of the afflicted timepiece, daring us with hard eyes to challenge their priority.

Thinking back, there had been signs of impending canine betrayal. They'd taken their position weeks before the event. Daily, they lazed at the foot of the clock with looks of boredom and innocence, quietly observing our movements. We attributed this indolence to age and the palpitant quality of ticking, which seemed to function as soothing anodyne. We dismissed intermittent growling, raised eyebrows, and furtive glances. We ignored eyes obsessively following movements of the pendulum.

Reluctance at outdoor excursions was regarded as laziness, aversion to cool weather.

The ill-fated morning arrived in fog-draped chill, resistance to endeavor, and the shock of bare feet on cold floor. The dogs, strangely indifferent to our delayed emergence, languished quietly until discharged to their morning run. Housemates went about appointed tasks reluctantly, idling in snug wraps at the windows. We sipped warm liquids awaiting purpose. We watched the river Absolong flow beneath the cliff on which the old house rested. It wasn't long before the deed was discovered. A call went up, and choking gasps interrupted the quiet morning.

The dogs lapped at water bowls and lounged shamelessly, but there was no mistaking their brazen impropriety; each human sigh and timid admonishment was met by low menacing growls. The pack would not be separated. After that we had no recourse to the collapsing undertones despite attempts at jerry-rigging and maintenance supported by regular and ardent windings.

The dogs were indifferent.

Housemates fell into a state of witless communal agitation that degenerated into bouts of coarse blame aimed at one another. They became careless about the winding schedule, futile that it was. As duration and tempo disintegrated, the old house contorted; assessable space contracted, groaned in garbled protest and facilitated invisible leaks. The competent, among which I've never been included, regressed and the impulse for polish and winding flagged.

Once abandoned, its primacy surrendered, the old clock betrayed its illusion. As with the flow of the Absolong below us, the moment stretched out ceaselessly. We watched at the windows as the world moved away, expanding beyond our reach. The doors and windows, caught in the distorted framework of the house, held fast. There was no escape. We began a nervous pantomime to counteract the wayworn stillness.

Now only vision remains, and of that there is no limit. It will feed and clothe us and lull us into complacency until rogues climb the steep path along the cliff and break in with their tents and wagons and wives to reconcile world and dog, memory and imagination.

A Gray Matter

Millard Augustine came home every evening promptly at six-fifteen, unlatched his skull port, removed his brain and placed it in the Bolivian Rosewood box lined with Thai silk that had been given to him by his grandfather on his thirteenth birthday. His wife swabbed out his cranium with sterile cotton gauze and Neutragentle™. Then she put supper on the table. Millard's brain would remain in the rosewood box until he was ready to leave for work the next morning. He rarely took it out on weekends or holidays. He was proud that in his fifty-seventh year, his brain remained pristine, rich in little folds, lively of color, vibrant with energy.

One would think that not much could be accomplished without the brain being stowed in its familiar cradle, but this is not so. Millard Augustine carried on conversations, drove his car, operated his computer (various social networks, shopping functions and gaming sites), enjoyed a variety of entertainments which included reading newspapers and light novels, and occasionally had sex with his wife.

In fact, Millard Augustine was much more pleasant without his brain. He didn't worry or obsess on tasks. He didn't struggle to "understand" what he saw or heard. He didn't read unpleasant meaning into what was said to him or what was going on about him. He didn't try to figure things out and he didn't hurry.

He puttered. He dawdled. He relinquished his hold.

He didn't resemble the high-powered, driven, manipulative factory manager he was during work hours, the man his wife avoided speaking to during the day except in case of dire emergency. He wasn't the scheming, ruthless entrepreneur that unnerved his employees and associates.

He was barely noticeable and more than a little boring.

His wife didn't mind. She was happy to tend to their little house and not have to explain herself. When she wanted more lively conversation, she called friends on the phone. When she wanted excitement, she went to the movies. When she wanted passion, she read novels. She complained sometimes because that's what wives were expected to do, but deep down she was content. She had twenty-eight pairs of shoes, perhaps a modest amount to some but a dream come true for her, despite the fact that they all came from Sears, Target or Payless. She had her own Sand Metallic Hyundai Accent to drive around town and she had a standing appointment at Amberly's Stitchery and Salon every six weeks. What more was there?

One Wednesday night the Friskin's, next door, had a fire. It ruined some furniture and wallpaper and melted some of the children's plastic toys, but no one was hurt. It took the firemen two hours to put it out and pack up their equipment. Millard Augustine's wife invited the Friskin's into their house for tea and banana cake. The commotion kept Millard up until three in the morning and caused him to sleep in. His wife, who had her appointment at Amberly's that morning, hurried him out and he forgot his brain. Mrs. Augustine, busy with her hair and some dress alterations she needed done, didn't notice.

As was their habit after the Mrs. had her hair done, the Augustines had dinner at Rita's, their local Italian restaurant. They got home late as they had to discuss the fire with Miss Lucy and several of the other diners. Millard forgot his brain the next day, and then it was the weekend. While Millard played golf on Saturday morning, the Mrs. invited the Friskin children in to watch TV while the Friskin parents cleaned their den, where the fire had occurred. Millard's wife was quite shocked at how spirited the Friskin children were after such a disruption. Unnerved by such activity, she put the rosewood box on top of the credenza where it would be out of the children's reach.

So the weekend went: an evening at the Elks, church, dinner with his mother-in-law and, of course, the bustle next door as the Friskins cleaned and repaired their house.

And Millard's brain? Out of sight, out of mind.

Amazingly, Millard's business began to improve. His employees got used to not being yelled at and productivity increased. Word spread through the industry and new contacts emerged, old customers increased orders. Millard bought the lot next to his factory and began building. He hired more people.

If this should sound strange, you must remember that the brain isn't the only organ capable of controlling a body. Nerves fire, muscles have memories, other organs continue humming as a result of momentum. Surely you've known people who carry out daily activities without using a brain. You must have done it yourself. Millard Augustine had performed the same activities for thirty years, he did not need to think in order to do them.

The rosewood box sat on the shelf for six years, until Mrs. Augustine choked to death on a locker key (which she put in her mouth in order to tie her shoes), after forty-nine minutes in the steam room and two dirty martinis at the country club.

Millard Augustine was surrounded by friends, business associates and acquaintances offering their help and advice, but he couldn't decide what to do.

His sister Maybelle came from Akron to take charge but she couldn't get him to make a decision. She couldn't get him to leave the house. He went from bed to couch and back in a fog of confusion.

"I can't stay here forever," she told him. "I have a family back in Ohio."

"Of course."

"Do you want to come back with me?" She asked him halfheartedly.

Millard Augustine couldn't imagine what Ohio would be like or what he would do in a big city like Akron. He couldn't imagine at all. And though he liked Maybelle well enough, he didn't want to uproot himself on her suggestion, which even he could feel was unenthusiastic.

"I'll stay here," he said.

"I suppose if you sell your business you could live out your days here easily enough."

Maybelle stayed to help him make arrangements, as she could see he was in no state to conduct a business deal. Before she left she hired a housekeeper for him and was supervising in the living room when she spied the rosewood box.

"I remember this box," Maybelle said and brought it down from the credenza. "Grandpa gave it to you, didn't he? Is there anything in it?" Maybelle lifted the lid and a vaguely bitter odor emerged. "What is this?"

Millard looked but he didn't recognize the shriveled thing inside.

"It looks like an old piece of fruit," Maybelle said. "A mellon, maybe? Is it something you brought back from a trip? A keepsake?"

"Never went anywhere but the lake and your house," Millard said.

"Well, do you want to keep it, or shall I toss it?"

Millard took another look at the thing in the box and tried to remember ...

"Keep the box," he said.

Douglas Dhubhagain

Douglas Dhubhagain was born with a hole in his heart. It wasn't the kind of hole you could see on an x-ray or CAT scan (though doctors tried), but a breach in the metaphysical organ that pumped buoyancy into his spirit. Douglas and the people around him could feel the void even if they didn't always know where it came from.

Many people tried to fill the hole. His parents were told to fill it with love, which usually works to mend such rifts, except when it's conditional. They sought to cram it with duty and honor, custom, piety, resolution. They allowed some unscrupulous practitioners to pack it with fear and envy but everything oozed out and stained the fancy carpets. Other "experts" tried cotton balls, steel wool, table scraps, kitty litter … These fell right out. His grandmother tried to fill it with chocolate but that melted down his shirt. One of his teachers tried algebra and it nearly killed him. His baby sister stuffed a marshmallow in the hole with her finger. The marshmallow stayed there for nearly three hours before it disintegrated into sweet motes that floated out behind him as he walked.

People who looked into the hole in Douglas' heart had varied reactions. Some felt hopeless, some were elated, others fainted or threw up. Two people tried to reach in, but Douglas' mother pounded them with her shoe until they ran away.

Douglas grew sadder and sadder. His grandmother fed him fruit to cheer him up, strawberries and cherries, figs and pomegranates. The other children either made fun of him or were frightened away so Douglas Dhubhagain kept to himself at school, played with his Hot Wheels in the back yard afterward, and waited to grow up.

Mostly what he lacked because of the hole was hopefulness.

Douglas Dhubhagain attained adulthood despite this disability. He got a job entering data at a company that did Acquisitional Rewording. He moved from apartment to cubical and back, stopping at the corner store for supplies once a week. He was little more than a shadow in his town and if he was happy about anything, it was that his parents had his little sister to dote on and bestow all their expectations on so they weren't overly concerned with his condition, especially since he'd done pretty well for a person with a hole in his heart.

There are people with similar flaws who quietly go about their lives until they expire, but this was not the case with Douglas. On Douglas' twentieth birthday, his little sister brought him a cake she'd made out of marshmallows. Marshmallows were her favorite food and even though they hadn't worked to fill Douglas' hole, she believed they had magical qualities that could affect maladies in a positive way. She believed this because of the way marshmallows fill the mouth with an airy sweetness like no other food, and then deteriorate into sugary granular saliva.

But it wasn't the marshmallow cake that affected Douglas that day; it was the birthday gift. What she gave him was a small red flashlight, about the size of your thumb. "In case the lights go out," she said. "You'll be able to find your way."

Douglas thanked her and ate as much as he could of the marshmallow cake, which wasn't much since he didn't particularly like marshmallows and doubted their mystical powers – but he couldn't tell his sister this because he didn't want to hurt her feelings.

After she left, Douglas studied the little flashlight. He turned it on and off; he put it in his shirt pocket, took it out and put it in his pants pocket, practiced drawing it out smoothly like he'd seen guys do in old cowboy movies. Then he went into the bathroom, stood in front of the mirror and shined the light into the hole in his heart. For the first time he could see what was in the hole – and what wasn't.

There wasn't anything you might expect, no veins with blood pumping through, no muscle tissue or torn organ parts. There was no recognizable landscape, no beautiful meadows or snow capped mountains, no dark forests or sunny beaches. There were no zoo animals or bothersome insects, no mythological beasties. The hole contained no postmodern compositions or sculptural entities.

Douglas Dhubhagain stood in front of his bathroom mirror and looked and looked. How can you describe what he saw? Emptiness is not what you might think. Emptiness isn't really "lack of," but more "space between," the "nothing" that gives essence to "something," as they say. But it's even more substantial than that. It can't be described without getting philosophical, and philosophical is not at all what it is. It's about as philosophical as your toothbrush or the cardboard box your cereal comes in. Can you picture the world all filled up with "somethings?" No space between ... well, maybe you can and maybe someday it'll be like that (it's going in that direction) ... but right now there's still room for a hand or at least a finger. When you pull it back, where has it been?

Exactly.

Douglas thought about his little sister's obsession with marshmallows. He realized that there were other things she might have obsessed on in order to cope with the universe, many other things, but marshmallows fit her personality and her immediate world. They were light and spongy, sugary and playful. It was the reason she wanted to be called Marsha and why he would be called, from then on, Doug.

In his cubical the next day, Doug aimed his desk light at the hole in order to feel light and warmth. He looked at his computer screen and saw the hole reflected behind the rewording data. For the first time in his life he smiled. He even giggled a bit. Although he was looking at the same sort of data that corporate reworders had always acquired, it seemed quite different superimposed on his hole. Coworkers looked up from their screens and over cubical walls.

That evening, on his way home, Douglas stopped at the corner store for extra flashlight batteries and bought marshmallow in a jar for his sister. He'd never noticed that it was possible to buy marshmallow in a jar before, and thought she'd be pleased. He wondered if there was something (or naught ...) that he could market in a jar, a kind of cottage industry. But, of course, he realized as he looked around, jars weren't always necessary. Then again, someone had convinced the world that Aquisitional Rewording was necessary. Someone had decided that emptiness could be promoted as an affliction. There were zilches and nils purchased everyday, an extensive and costly industry in voids and vacuums. There were people who made Herculean efforts that ended up "all for nothing." Successful lovers whispered "sweet nothings," and there was a store on his own block called "Gap." What about the ancient and recently expanding belief that Nothingness was a state of grace?

Why then, he wondered, was everyone so troubled about the hole in his heart? Douglas had the feeling that there were other breaches concealed or better disguised than his own. Why should he be scorned, scrutinized and questioned? Perhaps his hole was a place of solice.

The name of the marshmallow in a jar was "Fluff," which, if you think about it, suggests that it's only a trifle above "nothing." There are a lot of other things that could be called "Fluff," though they don't leave as good a taste in your mouth.

When he took the Fluff to Marsha that night she was ecstatic, even though she'd had it before. She asked him, "Do you think the hole was always there?"

"I suppose so. I know that mum and dad were always concerned."

Marsha thought this over. "Their only concern regarding me was what I might achieve," she said.

"Well, of course. You have no flaws."

"Don't I? It would seem to me that everyone has flaws."

"What then?"

"I suppose I'm too fond of marshmallows for one thing."

"Is that a flaw?"

"Well, they're not very healthy and they're too easy. You don't even have to chew them."

"Still, it's not a hole." Doug decided he might as well tell her … who else could he tell? "I did something – I used the flashlight to look into my hole."

"And … "

"And nothing, there's nothing. I can't see what all the fuss is about."

"Well, nothing is something."

"It is?"

"Sure. It's what makes 'things,' you know … things."

"You lost me."

"Oh, but think what we might find."

"What is that?"

"Do you have the flashlight with you? Give it to me."

Marsha turned it on. "Well look at that," she said. "I expected it to look like the inside of a papaya. Why didn't we look before?"

"Because everyone else was looking and going crazy. We were afraid."

Why didn't we realize … Do you mind?"

"No."

Marsha took her shoes off and, using her hands to pull herself up, climbed into the hole.

Doug sat and waited. He watched a couple of TV shows and ate some of the Fluff on a Ritz cracker. It was really good.

He thought about having to get up and go to the office in the morning and all the rewording acquisitions waiting for him to enter. The hell with that, he said to himself.

He turned off the TV, gathered up the jar of Fluff and the box of crackers and climbed into the hole.

There's Always a Monkey

Once there was a witch that lived in a small condo in a rapidly gentrifying neighborhood in Brooklyn. Her husband had worked very hard for very little money and died young. She had a son who moved into the city after he graduated from college. He called her once a week and took her out to lunch about once a month.

Her father had taught her a great deal of magic but she'd managed to forget it all. Her husband and son weren't aware of this. They always believed in her. So it was that when magic occurred anywhere near her, she took credit for it. If the sky cleared just as she walked out of the building, she took credit. (Though she told them very sternly that it was not always possible to manipulate weather.) When a neighbor who had been rude to them stumbled in the street, she took credit. When a dish fell but didn't break, she took credit and occasionally caught it in midair. (She cautioned that this wasn't always possible either.) Her husband, rest his soul, knew that anytime he lost his glasses or anything else, she'd find them – unless a counter-curse had been issued by a hostile.

The witch's name was Bernie and she was living a lie.

How bad could it be to live a lie if you don't actually harm anyone, she wondered? How stupid of me to have lost my witch powers, she lamented. Surely, they'll return when I need them. But she couldn't be sure of this.

She wondered if the loss had been caused by years of living in the city. After all, she'd been born in the country and grew up there. Perhaps she was meant to have stayed put. She'd done her best to ignore all the trees and flowers and wildlife around her when she was young, in favor of frivolous books, daydreams and long summer days floating in the cool river. Maybe it was arrogant of her to have moved to a city and lived there all this time. Maybe it was all the paper she used up scribbling thoughts and ideas for incantations that she never finished, the dust she'd swept under the carpets, the hours she'd wasted being unproductive, for weren't all her neighbors busybusybusy all the time, rushing off early and getting home late? Maybe it was all the ice cream she'd consumed in her lifetime, mounds of ice cream, enough to clog up the psychic arteries that had connected her to the cache of magic that congealed in dark corners of the universe.

Bernie had known for a long time that she no longer had the right to call herself a witch, that she was just a ... just a ... housewitch, a witchfrau! And not a very good one at that. Now that she was alone, she'd lost all connection to magic for sure.

She hoped no one would find her out.

But just when she thought she'd adjusted to her loss, she found herself in a situation that called for magic.

Her neighbor Rose, cute funny Rose, practically her best friend, got divorced and fell under a curse. Rose had been married to Mel for nineteen years when he ran off with a twenty-six year old blond prodigy who'd just joined his law firm. What chance did Rose have against two powerful lawyers? Because their daughter Noreen had just left for college, it seemed Mel had waited until Rose would end up completely alone before he struck the final blow. Then there was the curse. Marne was cursed to repeat one story endlessly, the story of how at the age of twenty-four, weighing sixty pounds less than she did now, she'd rejected the advances of a handsome businessman who'd become uberwealthy, died, and left his wife three billion dollars (the rest went to various charities).

"But if you had married him, you'd be alone now anyway," Bernie told her.

"Yea, but at least I'd be rich."

Rose was devastated and no amount of spa treatments or girl's nights out seemed to help her, not that Bernie could afford to take her out much and Rose had barely enough money to pay the rent even though she'd moved to a studio apartment on the second floor. Mr. Terriski, who owned the Good of Eats Deli let Rose work there occasionally but she wasn't capable of holding down a real job.

The diabolical Mel had moved to a better building on the next block with his new love and Bernie ran into him many times on the street cavorting openly with Miss Stiletto Heel (she and Rose called Mel and his mistress, the Two Heels).

It didn't take six months till the landlord threw Rose out for being behind on her rent and she had to go back to Donora Pennsylvania and live with her dying father, with whom she'd never gotten along. She had no computer to communicate with, and phone calls were futile as they always deteriorated into the same old story about the rich dead guy.

Bernie was furious with Mel, Miss Stiletto, and the landlord. She was not pleased with Mr. Terriski at the Good of Eats either as he'd raised all his prices in the last year. Bernie was so preoccupied with the troubles of others that she often forgot things she needed to get at Fairway and had to run to the Good of Eats where things cost twice as much. Nor was she pleased about the wealthy families that were moving into the neighborhood and crowding the sidewalks with huge baby strollers. They'd begun edging out the "mom and pop" stores in favor of fancy boutiques, which was why Mr. Terriski raised his prices, put in a new front door, realigned his shelves for wider isles and built a ramp for the fancy strollers.

The old residents had petitioned and protested to no avail. Bernie's budget was stretched beyond bounds. Something had to be done.

Bernie climbed up the ladder to the top shelf of the hall closet, where she kept her old magic paraphernalia, and took the cardboard box down from the back of the top shelf. It was dusty and smelled of mildew. Her wand was scratched, her cape was ragged and the books had begun to flake. She spread everything out on her coffee table, turned on the TV for company, and opened the Book of Spells. The dust made her sneeze.

There were spells to turn aside ill-luck and evil; spells to banish malignant spirits, spells to bind the magical powers of other witches and sorcerers, but no spell to reestablish a changed neighborhood and restore a friend's life. There was a spell to bring back the dead, but it was only temporary and way too tricky for an out-of-practice witch to attempt, not to mention a long shot that the guy would suddenly give up his wife and run back to Rose.

Bernie would have to come up with her own spell to amend the situation she found herself in.

She worked for three weeks studying possible ingredients and their optimal proportions. She spent another six days writing the perfect incantation. Then she headed down to Mrs. Reedworth's apothecary in the East Village for the proper herbs and talismans.

Mrs. Reedworth had a good supply of frankincense, dragon's blood, mugwert and Dogon incense. She had some beautiful northern horsetail for stirring, though it was rather expensive. But she had no fairy fungus, larchwort, or knotted roc bladder. Nor did she have any mocker bone.

"There's just no call for those things anymore," she said. "These days they only want love potions, good fortune spells, and Saint Joseph statues to bury so they can sell their real estate. There's no creativity left. The neighborhood's changed."

"Mine has too," Bernie fingered the dried salamander skins.

"You might try Chinatown, or Mr. Beisnerbon in Long Island City."

"Beisnerbon, is he still around? I wouldn't buy from him if he had the last Wild Ginger in the hemisphere."

"Amen to that, sister."

Bernie found the fairy fungus (hard to miss the smell) and mocker bone in Chinatown but substitutions had to be considered, adjustments made. She came across some mushroom-y things growing around the back door of a Thai restaurant in the neighborhood and settled for wings off of water bugs she collected from the laundry room. In a perfect world (Ha!) she'd like to finish the potion off with some hair of the urmahlullu, but she didn't know anyone who might be likely to travel to Mesopotamia in order to retrieve this exotic material for her, or even if Mesopotamia still existed, and lord knows how much urmahlullu might cost these days. The exotic properties would certainly enhance her spell but it appeared to be out of the question. There was, however, a housekeeper who worked for a family in the building, a Mrs. Sanchez, who claimed that the charm she wore around her neck was the talon of a Mayan vision serpent given to her grandmother on her wedding day. The problem would be getting her to give it up.

A secondary spell would have to be designed.

The project was becoming more complicated than Bernie had bargained for and it was giving her a headache. She had to lay down in a dark room for an entire afternoon, but in the end she decided she'd gone too far already and spent too much time and money to quit now.

That evening she called her friend Rose for support and encouragement but Rose was shocked.

"What kind of talk is that?" She said. "For god's sake! Water bugs! Dragon's blood! I never! You sound like a heathen."

Bernie was offended to find out her friend was such a bigot, a witchist!

"I'm putting papa into a home," Rose said. "Then I can move to Florida. Come with me. We'll play golf."

Bernie thought, if she thinks my spells are ungodly wait till she gets on a golf course with its voodoo: nine plus nine and numbered clubs; the fusion of elements: water, air, iron (a curious choice of metal), wood (Did they know the effects of different kinds?). How does she think people get suckered into it so easily, hypnotized into spending days in the hot sun hitting a ball into a hole? That's profane enchantment for you.

But all she said was, "I don't think so."

Bernie had to admit that Rose might be beyond help. But Bernie had gone to a lot of trouble and it was too late to turn back now. You never know till you try, she told herself.

The next day she spun a consent-inducing web-spell about her, doused herself in a modified topaz potion and waited for Mrs. Sanchez in the hallway.

"I'd like to make you a deal for the ornament you wear," Bernie whispered. "This old thing?" Mrs. Sanchez said. "You can have it. It just gets in the way when I clean the tub. I'm feeling guilty every time I try to put it in the trash but if I give it to someone who wants it, no guilt." The string that held it broke easily in her hands and she handed it to Bernie, who was speechless. "What do you want it for, eh?"

"I'm creating a spell."

"*Mi dios*, not dangerous, I hope."

"Oh, no, something I hope will benefit the whole neighborhood."

"Maybe you could conjure up a cold beer?" Mrs. Sanchez asked.

"Of course."

"Call me Clara."

Bernie sat with Clara Sanchez while she drank two Bud Lites that the super had left in Bernie's fridge ten months ago. Clara complained about the woman she worked for who left make-up streaked all over her bathroom, threw wet towels on the floor and never cleaned the tub after she used it. She complained about how much food they wasted and she had to throw away because "The Mrs." wouldn't let her take it home. She complained about the smell of cigarette smoke and the dirty underwear she was expected to wash by hand.

Bernie was worn out listening to her. She wondered if she might put something in her spell to help Clara and she remembered that if the neighborhood went back to where it was, Clara's situation would change for the worse when there was no one rich enough to pay for a housekeeper.

Three days later, on the night of the full moon, Bernie drew her spell. The smell of burning substances wafted out her open windows, through the neighborhood in an oddly-pigmented haze. Thirteen people reported it to the EPA, but nothing was done. Bernie got so nauseous that she called her son, Alfie, and asked if she could spend the night at his apartment. He hedged a bit but agreed.

"If you don't like the neighborhood anymore, why don't you sell your apartment? You'd make a mint and you could move somewhere … "

"Like Florida?" She asked.

Alfie laughed. "There's a lot of people that love Florida, but I can't see you there, Ma. Hoboken's supposed to be nice."

"I like my apartment. I like the view. I'm comfortable on the F train. I have friends, a life."

"I thought your friend moved."

"I have others." Bernie was thinking of how Clara sat in the laundry room with her and brought Subway sandwiches to share on the stoop. She thought of Sy Weinstein, downstairs who needed her to call out of her window and remind him that he was wandering down the middle of the street. She thought of Mr. Terriski at the deli who, despite his inflated prices, needed someone to talk politics with in the afternoons. The new people never had time for old residents.

Alfie took her out to dinner and she cleaned his kitchen for him. In the morning she took the train back.

The neighborhood smelled better but looked pretty much the same. Bernie noticed a gentle wind and looked up. From the roof of number 27, a swarm of time-flies swooped down and through the streets. The pumping of their tiny wings made a sound like thousands of ticking watches, the kind of vague white-noise that nobody notices except a trained witch. Bernie could feel the people on the street reacting unconsciously. Some quickened their step, pushed people out of their way, but some slowed or even stopped and looked up at the sky until the swarm forced their focus back to original objectives. Mothers looked down at their babies and spoke to them, words of instruction, words of encouragement. Bernie was pleased.

I must call Rose, she thought.

"Rose, you can come back. The time-flies ... "

"It certainly does. My arthritis ... If only I had married Danny. Did I tell you about him?"

"Yes, but there's a swarm of time-flies and things have changed."

"Things have changed everywhere." Rose sighed. "Oh, he was so handsome, wealthy, and he loved me. I was thinking about him just last night. Where were you? I tried to call."

"I was at Alfie's, but when I came back ... "

"Isn't that nice. How is the boy? My Danny had hair like him, soulful dark eyes like ... "

"Rose, for heaven's sake, the TIME-FLIES!"

"Yes, my Danny's gone 34 years."

The spell, odorous as it had been, hadn't reached Denora Pennsylvania and hadn't affected Rose. It didn't look like Bernie could get her back to where she might be influenced by it so she just let Rose ramble on. Maybe it was time for new friends. You shouldn't give up on friends that were in turmoil but Rose seemed comfortable in her situation. Who was Bernie to judge?

Two hours later the phone rang. Alfie was in a state, breathless and excited. "Mom, you did it again!"

"What's that, dear? You'll have to slow down."

"The spell! I went on that last interview with RSF&PGR this

morning. I got the job! I got my dream job! They're paying me big bucks too! You haven't lost your touch."

"Well, congratulations. But I think it's R-and-P-whatever that got the good deal. Slow down and tell me all about it."

Alfie couldn't slow down. He talked and talked. Bernie didn't understand a word he said. It was some kind of internet thing that entailed a lot of cyber-jargon, digital-doings, web-based watchamacallits. E-this and dot-that. Did he say emulations? Gateways? It sounded insanely complicated and futuristic but Alfie's enthusiasm was contagious. She was flattered he'd given her credit, humbled that he'd think she might understand what he was talking about.

When she hung up she had a craving for Chunky Monkey ice cream. It was a good excuse to go down to the deli and tell Mr. Terriski the news. On the way she ran into Clara Sanchez.

"How did your little project turn out, chica?" Clara asked.

"Fine, I think." and Bernie told her about Alfie, as best she could, and explained that magic is not an exact science; changes had been made.

"*Mi dios*," Clara said. "Listen, I have a little job for you. The Mrs. has a crush on a jeweler and she asked me what she could do to … you know … get him a little more interested. I told her I knew someone who might be able to help. She got more money than brain, this one. I figure you could use the extra cash."

"That would be nice. I guess I could make up a little potion … maybe a candle."

The "Mrs." hooked up with the jeweler long enough to accumulate some showy baubles and win the admiration of her husband who thought she'd become a sly negotiator. Word went around the neighborhood. Soon Bernie had more business than she could handle and a friend and partner in Clara Sanchez. All potions and talisman came with the usual caveats that left Bernie free of responsibility when they failed and when they worked, she was a hero. The new residents thought they were into something funky and cool; Bernie and Clara could afford to live in the neighborhood. Life was good.

It got even better when Mr. DeMott reopened his pizza parlor (renovated and a bit more pricy) and three ice cream "emporiums" opened. Bernie loved ice cream.

Alfie made his mother a website. His co-workers got interested and some of them became customers. Clara quit her job with the Mrs. to work with Bernie. They had more work than they could handle and often had to rely on Mrs. Reedworth for ready-made potions. Suddenly, Bernie had no time to do her laundry or get a haircut. She barely got through the week's mail on a Sunday afternoon when suddenly it was Thursday. The time-flies reeked havoc in the park, swarming around garbage bins and killing shrubs. The only thing that kept the population at bay was their tendency to fly into windows and shiny objects at speeds strong enough to kill themselves, and the young mother's of the neighborhood who were dedicated bug spraying.

Rose moved to Florida and fell under the golf-spell, spending hours and days watching matches on TV. The curse, while still in effect, had altered. Instead of her lost love, now she talked incessantly about golf. (Apparently this is a common feature of the "golf spell.")

Another spell was in order to straighten things out. Bernie knew it, Clara knew it, Alfie wasn't so sure about it. But we know that never happened, don't we?

Oh, and what about the monkey? The truth is, there isn't always a monkey – unless you count the people rushing around like howlers and the ones who just sit scratching themselves and picking the time-flies out of their hair.

The Backward Man

The Backward Man owns the Carney Motel in Repose, Fla., but it's the Alligator Girl that runs it as it's difficult for the Backward Man to maneuver. The Backward Man practices turning his head in the direction his body is pointed, but can't sustain it for long. His shins are bruised from running into objects. He often steps in things. He misses his mother who always held his hand when he went out, though his friends are very good about helping him. He can not go to the movies and eating is awkward, as is going to the bathroom.

He can not kiss and make love at the same time except with the Rubber Girl.

In the past people paid a great deal of money to see him and watch his strange ways of doing everyday tasks. They often laughed and even ridiculed him. He is sad for them; he does not envy their easy, mundane, stay-at-home lives. He's been around the world, met royalty and had famous scientists study him in the way all the wonders of the universe are studied. How sad, he thinks, to always be faced in the direction of what's immediately before you. He sees it as a life without mystery.

The Backwards Man believes in God because he knows many of His most wondrous and creative creatures personally. Even though he faces what is past, he does not dwell upon it; he knows that his feet will always propel him in the opposite direction.

It Takes a Universe

Millard Wurf led a perfectly organized life. He rose each morning at six-fifteen, did twenty minutes of exercise, showered, dressed, and left the house at seven-thirty exactly. He carried with him half a corn muffin with plain tofu spread and a bottle of cranberry juice. On Saturday mornings he had one poached egg and a multi-grain English muffin after which he walked to Alkaterina's bakery and bought three corn muffins and a loaf of rye bread for the week ahead. Don't ask about his Starbuck's order. I could go on …

His office, Alkaterina's bakery, Ki's Fruit and Vegie, and the drugstore were within six blocks of his apartment. He only left the neighborhood twice a year to go to a men's clothing store in Midtown that was run by a Mr. Mellquist and his two sons. Millard Wurf bought one new winter suit each October and one summer suit in late March after which he went home and threw away the suit he'd bought six years previously. His theory being that, with good care, fine tailored garments in a classic style last exactly seven years. He bought shirts, socks and underwear from Mr. Mellquist as needed and I don't have to tell you they were all the same – the suits were brown, grey and navy (lighter versions for summer), two of each. The shirts were white, pale blue, and tan. His shoes were sturdy brogues from Florsheim.

Millard Wurf's life had always been orderly and became only slightly less so after his father died at the age of 81 on Millard's forty-second birthday, which was orderly of him. Perfect order was disturbed only occasionally but enough to cause Millard Wurf great agony and disruption of his bowel movements. (What killed his father was the replacement of Dan Dusha, a local news radio personality, by a woman. His heart gave out with the disruption.)

I won't go into Millard's relationship with his father but you can imagine what the old man expected of his son. Your wildest assumptions are not too farfetched. Millard's mother died young in a state of frenzy. The incident made Millard feel helpless and fearful that something similar would happen to him if he didn't keep order in his own life and this he'd done long after his father's demands were silenced.

On the morning it all began, Millard Wurf donned his Tuesday suit and shirt, packed his corn muffin, locked his door and walked to the elevator. There in the middle of the hallway, on the pristinely carpeted hallway, lay an object. Millard Wurf cleaned his glasses with a disposable cloth marketed for that specific purpose, as he couldn't believe what he saw. He replaced his glasses and stooped to examine what appeared to be a substance from a living organism. His heart pounded, his bowels churned.

He considered employing the used glass-wipe to dispose of it but decided he paid an exorbitant maintenance fee for just such amenities as a clean, litter-free hallway and atrium. It was his duty to report inadequacies and lapses in service.

He seized his cell phone and dialed the office secretary. "I'll be a little late," he said.

"I suppose that means five minutes," she said.

"It may take considerably longer," he said. "There's a crisis at my apartment building."

"Oh! Are you all right? Is anyone hurt?"

"It's possible," he said. "Thank you for your concern. I believe I can rectify the situation."

"Be careful Mr. Wurf."

"Thank you Alice."

Millard Wurf was pleased to see Hans at the door. Hans was a neat and properly respectful fellow, always on the alert to be helpful.

"Morning Mr. Wurf," he said.

"Good morning Hans. It's imperative that I speak to Mr. Soto immediately."

"What is it Mr. Wurf?" said Soto who was right behind him.

Millard Wurf suppressed the instinct to shriek in alarm. Soto was an excellent super in that he ran the building like clockwork and could fix just about anything, but he was slovenly in appearance and casual in his demeanor, traits that irritated Millard Wurf and made him itch, especially since he had no real grounds on which to complain.

Despite the shock and his disapproval of the man, Millard Wurf pulled himself together quickly, something he'd practiced since his father's death.

"A very large, disturbingly filthy fingernail has been discovered in the hallway of floor number nine."

"A fingernail!" Hans said.

"That's what it appears to be. It's quite disconcerting."

"Are you sure?" Hans asked.

It was obvious that Hans understood the gravity of the situation but Wurf was not a man to deal with underlings. Soto looked him in the eye as if he was studying his intent but Wurf stood his ground.

"What did you do with it?" Soto asked him.

"Me? It's not my place to maintain the hallways."

"Of course not. I'll have Sam see to it." Sam was the fellow who collected garbage and recycling and put it out on the street. He vacuumed, dusted, and mopped the public spaces.

Hans proceeded to call Sam on the walkie talkie and ran to open the door for Mrs. Kentshire.

"Is there something else?" Soto asked.

"No, I … where do you think a thing like that came from?" Millard Wurf asked.

"Oh, probably a woman or a kid playing with a toy. "

But there were no children on the ninth floor and it didn't look like a woman's nail, certainly not a woman in this building as they were all well manicured. Perhaps one of the maids …

"It was very large," Wurf mumbled.

"A dog then. I have to be going Mr. Wurf. Thank you for alerting us."

As much as he didn't want to admit it, Millard Wurf was very unsettled about the incident. He kept seeing the fingernail all the way to his office and once there, was unable to eat his corn muffin.

Alice asked if he was sick and if he didn't think he should go home, a thought he rejected until lunch time when he still couldn't make himself eat and realized he hadn't gotten any work done. By two o'clock he'd lost his train of thought regarding an important contract he was working on and decided time off might do him good after all, recharge his batteries as Alice had told him. So he went home.

As it was before three, Hans was still on duty. "Did Sam remove the 'thing' from the ninth floor hallway?" Wurf asked him.

"Oh, yes, sir. The hallway's been vacuumed."

"Fine. You might mention carpet cleaning to Mr. Soto. The concept of discarded body parts is not only offensive, but unsanitary."

Indeed, the ninth floor hallway appeared to be spotless. An ordinary person wouldn't suspect the corruption that had been perpetrated earlier but Millard Wurf could feel it in his bowels.

After close inspection, Wurf entered his apartment and was able to consume a slice of rye bread spread with a thin layer of cream cheese and a cup of rose hips tea. Millard Wurf's culinary repertoire consisted of exactly thirty-three items of which rye bread, cream cheese and rose hips were three.

The next morning, resplendent in his blue Wednesday suit, Millard Wurf discovered a tuft of coarse hair the size (and color) of an avocado in the hallway. He found hair particularly repellent and kept his cut no longer than a quarter of an inch and often went to Lingenfield Barbers for a shave to avoid having to swab the tiny hairs out of his own sink. He insisted that all men and women in his office have neatly shorn hair or that women with longish hair pull it back tightly with no offensive locks escaping.

He retreated back to his apartment, bowels in turmoil. He called Hans. He called Soto. "I can not possibly leave my house until the situation is rectified," he told them.

Within the hour there was a soft knock at his door and Sam pronounced the hallway free of debris.

"What's happening?" He asked Sam.

"Donno, Sir."

"Someone on this floor must have a pet of some kind. I hate to think."

"Could be." Sam was a man of few words.

"You must have seen something. You're in people's apartments fixing things all the time. Pets are illegal in this building, you know."

Sam shrugged and turned to leave. "I gotta go, Mr. W. Leak in 3-B."

There was no use calling him back. Sam wasn't a talker.

Millard Wurf hurried off to work trying not to look about and telling himself that all was well now. His bowels were not convinced.

Alice and the girls in the office were concerned. He was forty-nine minutes late and he forgot to call. He thanked them for their interest, assured them he was fine and sunk himself into his work making certain he made up the forty-nine minutes at the end of the day.

He couldn't help but notice the odor in the hallway when he got home and it was more than his unsettled bowels could handle.

"Someone cooking," Mr. Soto told him. "What do you want me to do? Tell them they can't cook in their own home?"

But it wasn't like any cooking odor he'd ever come across and this was a multicultural city. Maybe he didn't leave his neighborhood these days but he certainly had when he was younger. He rode his bike to school, visited friends, went on class trips. He had one hundred, fifty-five diaries to prove it as his father insisted he record every nuance of his life. Millard Wurf had given up chronicling his life when the old man died, his one rebellion.

There was no other conclusion except that someone (something?) strange had moved on to the ninth floor. That weekend Millard Wurf set up a surveillance center beneath the peek hole at his front door which consisted of the tall chair he used at the kitchen counter augmented by Speck's Expanded & Unabridged Dictionary, a pot of rose hips, a new box of bite-sized shredded wheat, and a notepad to record his findings. Most anyone else would have included some form of reading material with which to pass the time, but Wurf was afraid that it might compromise his vigilance, so he sat on his chair contemplating the situation.

There were only five apartments on the floor. It was certainly not the Weihe's in A, a quiet middle-aged couple dedicated to their careers (of which he had no clue). The Weihe's left each morning at 7:30 burdened with computer bags and overstuffed briefcases. They often didn't return till after ten or eleven in the evening and worked most weekends. It couldn't be old Mr. Hartman in C who lived with a series of male nurses and took the air in his walker only occasionally. It might be the surgically-enhanced Ruth Mihaly in D who'd regaled him with meatloaf and cakes after his father died until he told her, in no uncertain terms, that he did not eat any food with more than three ingredients (not entirely true). Yes, she was the type that might sneak in one of those irritating little dogs, or a cat.

Then there was E. He couldn't remember thinking about E in a long time. Hadn't there been a couple named Polyblank that lived there for a while? Or had they been in A? He remembered being relieved to see them go as Mrs. Polyblank played the piano and he'd had to complain about her playing in the evenings and weekends. He didn't remember anyone moving in to E. They must have done it while he was at work. Was there a new name on the mailbox downstairs? He hadn't noticed. At least the new tenant was quiet. Then again, he'd never seen anyone going in or out of E.

A normal person might have asked about a new neighbor, but Millard Wurf was not the type to gossip or fraternize. He was a gentleman and a business executive; it would be unseemly to behave like a housefrau. Still, he had every right to know who he was living next to. He sat for nine hours and forty-three minutes on Saturday without seeing anyone go in or out of E and without going to the bathroom. He normally took a short constitutional on Saturday evening but there was a rainstorm. Though he owned a sturdy LL Bean raincoat and umbrella, as well as rubbers to go over his Florsheims, it was just too disagreeable to go out and deal with a mess when he didn't have to. So he spent the evening watching the hallway. Still nothing.

The next morning, dressed in his weekend khakis and blue shirt, he strolled casually, so he thought, downstairs. Albert was at the door. A gawky young man with problem skin who was working his way through refrigeration school, Albert was not his favorite doorman.

"Good morning Albert," Millard Wurf said.

"Mmmorning Mr … Mr … "

"Wurf, 9-B."

"Mr. Wurf. I'm not used to seeing you Sunday mornings. I mean, you're usually not out till … till."

"Four forty-five."

"Exactly."

"Well I've decided to take my Sunday constitutional early this week. The air's so clean after a rainstorm, don't you think?"

"Air? Yea, I guess. Gotta watch out for the puddles though."

Millard Wurf hadn't counted on puddles. He should go back for his rubbers but he was too anxious to find out about apartment E and this clueless young man would take less notice of his interest than Hans or Soto.

"I wonder if anyone's moved into the Polyblank apartment, 9-E? I haven't seen anyone and it's been a while since they moved out."

"Polyblank? 9-E?"

"Yes, yes. Ninth floor, piano playing ..."

"I don't know. I don't remember any Polyblanks, don't remember anyone moving in or out. Nobody's said anything to me."

"And would they normally? Say something to you?"

"People introduce themselves. Soto fills us in. We put their name on the mailbox, their package cubby. I haven't seen a name ... I could ask Mr. Soto."

"That won't be necessary. I was just passing the time. Good day." There was nothing to do but keep walking, no turning back.

"Passing time? " Albert swallowed hard and looked at him strangely. Millard Wurf ignored him.

On the street, Millard Wurf wandered aimlessly around the neighborhood for twenty minutes, too shaken to take his usual afternoon route. He noticed an ice cream store next to the dry cleaner, a new building going up at the end of the block. Someone had planted shrubbery and flowers in a space between two buildings. These were things he'd never seen before as his schedule and purpose didn't permit dawdling.

When he thought enough time had passed, he went back, nodded curtly to Albert and ducked into the mailroom. He couldn't find 9-E's box.

Back on his own floor, he noticed something in the hallway. He hesitated only a moment when the door to E swung open and a huge hairy fellow, with enormous ears and eyebrows swept up to his hairline, stepped out. Before Millard Wurf realized what was happening, this person swooped down, grabbed the "thing" from the carpet and stuffed it in his pocket. It looked like, but it couldn't have been, a flap of flesh – the size of a hand.

"Mr. Wurf, I presume," he said with a toothy grin. "I'm Ardweek, your neighbor. You've been asking about me, I understand. Very neighborly of you."

Millard Wurf was shocked speechless. He presented his hand to be shaken before he could think about what it might have just held. "I didn't … I mean I certainly … "

"Oh, don't worry about it. Curiosity is a charming human trait." Ardweek went on to discuss, in length: the intricacies of the city transit system, local politics, the Chinese restaurant around the block, the wonder of public access TV and a number of other things Millard Wurf knew very little about. Normally he would've excused himself from such a frivolous conversation but the fellow didn't give him a chance. It was as if he never had to stop and take a breath.

"I can see I'm holding you up," Ardweek said. "We can have this talk another time, maybe over a beer at that bar up the block."

"I don't drink beer," Millard Wurf said.

"Of course you do. It's a date. See you tomorrow evening."

"I'm afraid I can't … "

"Sure you can. Later, neighbor."

Back in his apartment, Millard Wurf noted that he'd have to make time to purchase a new pair of Florsheims next week as his spare pair was now irreparably damaged by the puddles. He was terribly confused and found himself watching a public access show that consisted of two brightly-clothed Caribbean women interviewing a Caribbean gentleman with a completely incomprehensible accent. After he turned it off in frustration, he read the local section of the Sunday paper, something he'd never done before: school meetings, letters complaining of potholes, amateur art shows, photos of ladies in community gardens – what was the use of it? This was an expensive building. The tenants were well-to-do and serious of purpose. They didn't chitchat about trivialities. Why would this person be interested in such things. Was his name "Ardvark?"

True to his word, Ardweek was at his door the next evening and badgered him until he agreed to go to a bar. (Had he actually agreed?) And though Millard Wurf was sure he'd ordered a glass of seltzer with lemon, a bottle of Corona was delivered to him. Ardweek was rambling on about beer in ancient Egypt and Mesopotamia, alcoholic consumption in Germanic and Celtic tribes. In his effort to keep up and figure out what the devil Ardweek was up to, Millard Wurf neglected to bring the mistake to the waiters notice. He was surprised to find, after some time, that he'd sipped half of it.

When Ardweek stopped talking to take a long pull of his beer, Wurf asked, "What is it you do Ardweek? For a living that is."

"I travel. I observe."

"An anthropologist?"

"Yes."

"How interesting. I suppose you've been to some dicey places."

"I have, indeed."

"Have you written books then? Made films?"

"Certainly, but not on this … continent."

"Fascinating." Millard Wurf was finding the beer refreshing in a bitter sort of way.

"But enough about me," Ardweek said. "Tell me about yourself."

Millard Wurf proceeded to give him a detailed account of his schedule and list his preferred brands of clothing, food and personal care products.

"What about your childhood, your interests?"

Wurf could list names, dates, educational details but he found himself getting bored. Had a second beer arrived? A third?

"You are the strangest human I've ever met, not that they aren't all strange – but usually in a … well, a different way."

What could he possibly mean by that?

The next day, Millard Wurf woke with a headache; he spilled coffee on his Tuesday tie and had to wear his Wednesday. When he noticed that only one of his Sunday socks was in the hamper he made a thorough search that was not only futile but made him fifty-six minutes late for the office. He'd heard people talk of socks going missing but never expected it to happen to him.

His life began to change rapidly. Ardweek insisted on taking him to a movie full of car chases and women with protruding breasts and long hair. He ate popcorn! They went to a Chinese restaurant, a hockey game, the Museum of Natural History, and had sushi. Millard Wurf hated the sushi. "Well, you're not going to like everything on the first try," Ardweek told him.

Then there was Rebecca, a woman he'd sat near at the corner bar. She never would've given him a second look if it hadn't been for Ardweek. He was so engaging. He was downright hypnotic and Millard Wurf, by affiliation, seemed the same to her. Suddenly the disruptions he'd worked so hard to avoid, seemed full of intriguing possibility.

Ardweek and Wurf went to the Chinatown Ice Cream Factory and to Ace hardware where Ardweek insisted Millard run his hands through a bin of lug nuts just to feel the sensation.

Target was the place Millard Wurf finally went crazy. He bought wine glasses, shorts, yellow bed sheets, and a cart load of pens, pencils and notebooks he didn't need. It was the stationary that did it, that made him give up trying to understand and bring his world back into line, that made him surrender to the chaos. Stationary was what he'd liked best about the diaries his father made him keep. It was what he'd always secretly coveted, red pens and blue, fancy notebooks and folders. Index cards! In different colors! Envelopes of all sizes and tints!

"My work here is done," Ardweek announced.

What did he mean by that?

"I mean that I must be moving on. You may have noticed that I'm losing my pieces. This climate is very bad for my constitution."

"Oh, dear."

"But I want you to fill those notebooks."

Millard Wurf hadn't thought about that aspect of stationary. His heart sank. He didn't want to keep diaries again; his life was so boring – or it had been before Ardweek. "Oh" He said.

"Write poetry, draw things, scribble. Write me letters."

"What about lists and schedules?"

"Certainly not! Nothing sensible."

"All right. I'll write you letters, and I could call … "

"Oh, there won't be coverage where I'm going."

"I suppose a visit is out then."

"We can talk about that sometime. There's one other thing I want you to do – for me. Here's the phone number for Rebecca, the woman we met the other night. I want you to call her."

"Oh, I couldn't … "

"Yes, you can. She likes you. I want you to make sure she's OK. For me."

"Well, I suppose … "

"That's my boy."

There were no sappy good-byes, just one more riotous evening and then nothing. The ninth floor was quiet again, no odd smells, no body parts on the carpet. In the months that Ardweek had been there, Ruth Mihaley moved to Boca Raton and a family with three children moved in. Suddenly there was no trace of apartment E. Had the family taken both apartments D and E? Walled up the entrance to E while Millard Wurf was at work?

Millard Wurf wrote letters to Ardweek and sent them to the address he left: 23372j4h system yy7, visk Ardnem, 6kf. Some kind of corporate code, Millard Wurf decided.

Rebecca became a fixture in his life – the only fixture as things continued to change rapidly and "fun" was his new favorite word. Millard Wurf wrote books on organization and he and Rebecca broke all the rules he wrote about.

He didn't hear from Ardweek often but knew he got the letters because he turned up at Millard and Rebecca's wedding, though Millard didn't get to speak to him much. You know how weddings are …

Precious Hairpin

In the early mornings, before the household was up and about, Precious Hairpin would lie in her bed and feel the pangs of old age. Some mornings it was her hip or her legs that ached, sometimes her shoulder or neck. In the winter she often woke with a sore throat; in the spring her congested head would pound and in the summer it was her stomach. The aches in her body were the most faint in autumn, which left her to turn her thoughts to pleasant and not so pleasant memories. That autumn she began her 108th year.

She could barely see and her hearing was selective, though not at her own command. Long ago, she'd given herself over to the whims of the universe and the mythical forces that decided what she should hear and how much she should see. She understood that her perception of the world was distorted but had experienced this as a common human condition and one not necessarily worsened by advanced age. Her strength was that she could still laugh at herself.

She lived with her granddaughter, Fragrant Mist who was not young either, and told everyone her grandmother was like Peng-zu who knew the secret of immortality and lived 800 years. Precious Hairpin scolded her granddaughter for spreading this rumor as she often caught glints of Death hiding in the bamboo trees outside her bedchamber, and heard Death's seductive voice in the wind. Perhaps it was her great and great-great grandchildren who snuck their friends into the courtyard to see the old woman. Still, she'd watched people around her fall like petals, and her own branches had been shaky for a very long time.

In her youth, Precious Hairpin had been a great beauty and some people thought she was still beautiful in the manner of the Jade Mountains or the mythological cinnamon tree in the courtyard of the Palace of the Moon. She'd outlived her six children and four husbands. She'd seen many wars. Sometimes she thought she might outlive the world itself – but she'd never admit this to Fragrant Mist.

Her first husband, chosen by her father, was a scholar and businessman who was a good provider but died young from strain and overwork. She barely knew him as he'd been consumed with business affairs, off on trips to monitor foreign ventures and generally obsessed with concerns outside of the family. Her second husband, chosen by her mother and dowager aunt, was a powerful warlord. Precious Hairpin was relieved when he was killed in battle because he was a cruel man – not so much to her, but to the peasants and his own soldiers. She hated to think what he did to his enemies. The town made her pay for a statue of him to be erected in the public gardens. After it was unveiled, she ran off with the artist who created it. She was happy with him for many years, until he succumbed to drink and died in her arms. She thought she'd live alone after that, her children grown, but she met Lui Luang on the road to the market one morning. Lui Luang was a Qi Gong master who'd only begun to teach her ways of sustaining her health when he dove in front of an ox cart in order to save a child, and was killed. (The child was saved.)

It was after this that Precious Hairpin relinquished any attempt to control her own destiny and gave in to the will of the universe. When Fragrant Mist brought food, she ate. When Fragrant Mist brought tea, she drank. When the servants came she let them dress her and accompany her out to the garden or courtyard to take in the warmth of the sun and the perfume of peach blossom, peony and magnolia. When Fragrant Mist's Second Grandson played the flute, Precious Hairpin sat close and smiled at the notes she was able to hear (which wasn't all of them).

Even though it was Precious Hairpin's house and her money that sustained them, she was grateful for Fragrant Mist's care. Fragrant

Mist's husband had earned a pittance tutoring a miserly lord's daughter in poetic composition even though he understood poetry in a purely mechanical and intellectual way. He died from eating a poison plum meant for the Lord's youngest wife. Fragrant Mist not only had the responsibility of caring for Precious Hairpin but also her own Second Grandson and, on occasion (more often than not) her other four grandchildren, as well as various greats and grands of her siblings. However, Fragrant Mist thrived in her position as caregiver and martyr. Her preferred mode of conversation was complaint about her situation − which she'd never consider changing.

"Here's your tea, old woman," she'd say. "I hope you're feeling well. My back is killing me and head hurts from that boy's flute playing. I have so much to do today I don't know where to start."

"Yes, dear." Precious Hairpin never complained about her own aches. All she heard was, "feeling well," "flute playing," and "today."

"You'll want to get out to the garden this morning before the children get here. I'm getting four of them so the parents can take in the full moon at the imperial palace. When do I get my invitation to the imperial palace, I ask you? Will I ever … ?"

"Yes, dear." Precious Hairpin heard "children" and "full moon." She smiled.

"Where are those lazy servants? I have to do everything myself. Have some more tea while I find them."

"Thank you, dear." Precious Hairpin knew that Fragrant Mist was particularly pleased with herself when she was so busy.

One morning Fragrant Mist limped into Precious Hairpin's bedchamber with a bandage around her ankle.

"I fell," she said. "And I have no time to rest. I'll probably limp for the rest of my life. Did you want to go out to the garden today?"

"Oh, yes, dear." Precious Hairpin heard "garden," and she could see that it was a lovely autumn day. It would soon be too cold to do anything other than take a short stroll on painful legs or freeze rice and cream in the snow for a treat (this was a winter activity she looked forward to).

"Well, the servants are busy fixing the loose paving I tripped over so I'll have to dress you. Come then."

"Yes, dear." Precious Hairpin could see that Fragrant Mist was doing her best to be patient and gentle but Precious Hairpin was having a hard time getting her arms and legs to do what they were supposed to do in order to get into her robes as quickly as Fragrant Mist expected.

"Now where is that slipper?"

Precious Hairpin heard "slipper." She bowed her head in order to scan the floor but was unable to get down on her knees to look under the bed. Second Grandson had to be called in and he had a hard time finding the slipper, which had tangled itself in a blanket thrown across a chair in the corner. By the time Precious Hairpin was ready, it had started to drizzle and they had to sit her under the eaves in the courtyard, but not before Fragrant Mist stepped in mud and Second Grandson broke a jar containing a rare trembling orchid, the type that do not survive trauma.

"What is happening?" Fragrant Mist asked. "Yesterday there was a dead magpie in the well and ants in the pantry."

Second Grandson shrugged and Precious Hairpin shook her head. She knew there were problems and that as much as Fragrant Mist liked to be busy, she hated mishaps. She prided herself on competence and perfection. She liked having control; she hadn't given herself over to the whims of the universe yet.

"It must be the work of a hungry ghost," Fragrant Mist announced. "We'll have to make offerings and do without our turtle elixir this month."

Precious Hairpin heard "do without" and "elixir." She was not unhappy as she hated drinking the concoction made of turtle blood that Fragrant Mist insisted everyone take each month to keep their chi strong.

Precious Hairpin watched in amusement as Fragrant Mist made offerings to her own and her husband's ancestors, the ancestors of her in-laws and some of her neighbors, even to those of servants who'd been particularly conscientious in their work. Still when the autumn rains came, leaks sprung in the roof, two of the servants were stricken with fever and lost their senses. More offerings were made including Second Grandson's hat (he hid his flute). He was relegated to wearing a pot on his head when he went out into the rain. In fact, there were so few pots left that meals could not be cooked when Second Grandson was out.

Instead of being appeased, the offerings had the effect of attracting unattached ghosts: washer women as ugly as Lord Chia, mangled warriors, fish-headed scholars, diplomats brandishing phantom flywhisks, acrobats, butterflies, cats, a monkey and a white tiger. The house was a spectral menagerie.

At first Precious Hairpin dreaded running into one (or all) of her husbands, but the visiting ghosts seemed to be strangers, unfamiliar entities who'd wandered the earth without descendants to make offerings. Once she got used to them, Precious Hairpin was thrilled to be at the center of a circus every day and set about wandering through the busy house with the support of two sticks. The consequence of this was that her legs got stronger and her balance better.

Fragrant Mist went about spitting on the ghosts to get rid of them but it only caused more to appear.

A Taoist wizard was called in.

Precious Hairpin, who was sitting in the courtyard when he came, was impressed by his scarlet mantle and tall yellow hat. In all her years she'd never seen such a person. Precious Hairpin could not imagine how he'd been found; she was amazed at Fragrant Mist's resourcefulness and desperation. She decided to get close so she could see his face as her eyes were not good. She pulled herself up out of the chair and toddled after him. He was surveying the room with an amazed look on his face when he turned toward her. Just then a phantom monkey grabbed his hat. The wizard called to the monkey and stamped his foot but monkey and hat disappeared out the door.

Precious Hairpin stepped closer and squinted to get a clearer view of him. "Young Cho," she said. "Is it you?"

"It is." Young Cho, who was nearing the end of his 70th decade, bowed stiffly.

"You? A Taoist Wizard?"

"Well, I have studied … "

"Studied, you say?" Precious Hairpin moved nearer so she could hear better. "I thought you were a pig farmer. Can you read?"

"A little. Some. They say I have a gift."

"Ah, and what is that?"

Cho looked embarrassed. "My pigs thrive and are the tastiest in the province."

"Eh?" She stepped even closer as she was always interested in hearing about tasty pigs and didn't know what connection they might have to magical talent.

"And I can talk to them. They talk to me."

"That's it?"

"Pigs are very spiritual animals."

"But your pigs live in this world, do they not?"

Cho hung his head and didn't have a chance to answer before Fragrant Mist came dashing into the room. She looked about expecting the ghosts to be gone. "Allow the wizard to do his work," she said to Precious Hairpin.

Cho proceeded to burn incense, chant and wave his arms. The ghosts formed and reformed in the smoke, danced to his chants and lifted his mantle exposing his scrawny legs. He was forced to forgo magical gestures and use his hands to hold his robes down.

"What kind of wizard are you?" Fragrant Mist asked.

When Cho said nothing, Precious Hairpin patted his shoulder and said, "I'm afraid your wizard is a pig farmer."

"What?" Fragrant Mist screamed. "Give me back my money!"

"I'm sorry," he said as he reached for his purse. "I tried. I really did."

"It's all right," Precious Hairpin told him. "Keep some of the coins and bring us one of your fine pigs for supper."

Fragrant Mist glared at her and grudgingly took what coins Cho offered. The monkey felt sorry for him and brought his hat back before he left.

"I know you enjoy this," Fragrant Mist said to Precious Hairpin. "But I can't live like this and it's no way for a boy to grow up."

Precious Hairpin tottered back to her chair. She'd heard enough of what was said to understand the problem. The boy seemed perfectly happy; the ghosts weren't vengeful or salacious. On the contrary, they were often entertaining. But a boy should be surrounded by real people and creatures if he was to learn how to live in this world. Fragrant Mist had a kind heart, you wouldn't think she'd be bothered by orphaned phantoms. But it meant more beings to look after. She was thinking of the boy. What could be done?

Precious Hairpin banged her walking sticks until servants came to help her back into bed where she stayed for three days pondering the situation. Of course, she asked Second Grandson to bring some pig to the bedchamber for her supper. And it was the most succulent pig she'd ever eaten.

Someone would have to lead the ghosts to the Western Heaven where the goddess could welcome them back to the Afterlife and convince them to stay. Someone would have to do it before that foolish woman turned all their money and household goods into offerings, or spent it on another inept wizard. She took a deep sigh, for after all, she was the most likely candidate, and the issue of aches and pains would be solved in the Afterlife. Surely there would be flute players and gardens and succulent pigs ... All that was left was to prepare herself up to meet the spirits of her ancestors. After all, Precious Hairpin had given herself up the will of the universe; she couldn't be expected to take her own life.

The next morning, instead of laying in bed, she rotated her ankles and stretched her arms. She rolled up to a seated position and swung her legs over the edge. Then she planted her feet firmly on the floor, took a deep breath and began the motions of Chi Gong as her fourth husband had taught her. It was the only way she knew to connect to the universe and prepare for her fate. The ghosts gathered about her chattering softly but she didn't hear a thing as she was so concentrated on her exercise. When she finished, she dressed herself and hobbled out to the courtyard where she proceeded to practice Tai Chi, something she hadn't done in a long time. The familiar movements were a bit wobbly but comfortable, and she felt the energy of the earth ascending through the bubbling well of her foot. The ghosts gathered around in stunned silence. This was a fine way to end her life, becoming a part of the universe and allowing it to draw her gently up into the heavens with a ghostly entourage following.

Meanwhile, Fragrant Mist was bustling around furiously as she'd slept longer than normal and, as usual, there was much to be done. Before she woke the old woman she had to wash and dress herself in a refined manner and powder her face, set the servants to work, make offerings. Perhaps she was elated that she was not surrounded by bothersome ghosts that morning, or perhaps she was horrified to discover Precious Hairpin's bed empty, or shocked to see her leading the ghosts in Tai Chi forms. Who knows what prompted her to run out to the courtyard with her weakened ankle, trip over the lintel, fall against the wall so forcefully as to loosen a heavy roof tile which fell on her head and killed her instantly. Her own spirit, knocked loose by the blow, ricocheted into the courtyard and sailed out among the assembly of ghosts. It was so startled, it raced off to the heavens with a piercing screech that disrupted the monks who were meditating in the Jade Mountains.

Precious Hairpin ceased movement and the ghosts took flight thinking a demon had escaped from the body of Fragrant Mist and would be back to lead them to the Ten Hells for judgment.

Servants surrounded the remains of Fragrant Mist and Second Grandson wept into the voluminous robes of Precious Hairpin.

"There, there, boy," she said. "The Goddess is in need of someone to look after hungry ghosts that roam the earth, and Fragrant Mist is such a good caregiver that she's been chosen for the job. It's a great honor. You must pull yourself together and go to the pig farmer to buy a succulent pig for the funeral banquet. It's not everyday a family member is chosen by the Goddess. Perhaps after the mourning period is over we can hire some real acrobats and bring in trained monkeys to raise our spirits. Perhaps for your birthday, we'll go to the cricket fights." (Something Fragrant Mist had strongly disapproved of.) "Would you like that?" There are some things you can control and some things you cannot.

Second Grandson, being an obedient boy, did as Precious Hairpin asked. Fragrant Mist was given a fine burial and an elaborate feast.

Precious Hairpin lived to choose a wife for the boy, an exquisitely beautiful acrobat with a loving heart and a talent for cooking. She lived to meet eight more grandchildren, thirteen great-greats, and nine ggg-grandchildren before the Goddess chose to take her. Had she not heeded the will of the universe that day and taken her own life, who knows what would have happened, how the imbalance might have spread under the management of Fragrant Mist.

Each morning for the next fifty years, Precious Hairpin lay in bed feeling her body, taking inventory of the aches and pains to make sure she was still alive. Occasionally, she thought she could hear a word of complaint in the breeze that blew through the bamboo trees outside her bedchamber, but she was too deaf to make it out completely. She didn't live as long as Peng-zu but that was not her decision.

Icon

After the death of Brother Icilius, noises were heard in the lower cellar. No one other than Brother Icilius had been down there for centuries, so novices were sent to investigate. Three young men spent half a day sifting through dusty wine bottles, arcane apparatus, broken swag from the belfry, ancient flaking texts, forgotten religious paraphernalia, and cobwebs. Rats nests were gently removed to Tonymy Forest on the outskirts of the village Belleprey. It was the unruly boy Chion, quiet and disheveled, that discovered the icon in a dusty corner.

Chion carried it up the worn limestone stairs and out into the sunny courtyard where he could see it better. He was careful not to trip over his ill-fitting sandals which he kicked off in order to scurry out to the scriptorium for a soft cloth, to the kitchen for a cup of spring water, and began a careful cleansing. He was intrigued by the intricate carving and inlaid stones on the casing. The faded colors gave the impression of having been carefully appointed and composed of substances he couldn't readily identify even though he was the most promising apprentice of brother Xavien who prepared the novices for the job of copying intricate illuminated manuscripts. The golden hinges and hasp were of a style Chion didn't recognize and when he opened the doors, which were about the height of his forearm, the image was obscured by dust and mold. Undaunted, he lovingly swabbed the inner panels. It was reasonable to assume that such a fine piece of work would be undertaken in honor of a great goddess. He hoped it might yield the sacred image of the Blood Mother.

Chion worked on the icon for days under brother Xavien's supervision. Xavien was pleased that Chion had finally found a suitable project he could devote himself to. He instructed Chion in the use of a particular alchemical mixture that removed dust and soil, particle by particle without harming paint or gilding. The image Chion uncovered was a ghostly outline, more of an essence than a true figure, an impression of spirit, mesmerizing in its depth. It was as if the artist had recreated the aura of his subject and disregarded its corporal body.

When the icon was brought to the chapter-house, the monks viewed it with awe. No one had ever seen anything like it, nor could they guess the sacred personage it represented. Brother Xavien had refused to comment, so Chion asked the Abbot, "Is it the Blood Mother?"

The Abbot looked to the Prior who's head wobbled uncertainly. "I shall have to meditate upon it, my son." the Abbot said. "Until it's decided we'll keep it in the Sacristy, away from villagers who might be overwhelmed by such a powerful relic."

It was true the villagers of Belleprey were easily agitated. Some were hardworking, some were unwholesome. They were all ineffectual and bewildered despite the monks many acts of charity and attempts at educating the young. So many tragedies had befallen Belleprey that the people no longer hoped. They were thankful to survive each day of toil or deviousness and each night of unrestful sleep. As appalling as life in the village was they feared the outside world more, even though they had almost no contact with it.

After evening vespers, the Abbot retired to the Sacristy to meditate upon the icon.

The next morning the verger found him wandering about the grounds in delirium. He was taken to the infirmary and given various herbs and potions while the monks prayed over him. Though the treatments quieted him, he never fully regained his senses and spent the rest of his days on a bench in the cloister, alternating laughter and tears but utterly speechless.

The Prior became the new Abbot and he was a much more worldly man. Previously a villainous swindler, he'd entered the monastery after he killed a woman. As she lay dying, the woman cursed him with a hideous skin disease of seeping tumors, now barely concealed by his robes. Not only was his body disfigured, but the pusy liquid that seeped from the wounds soaked through his clothing and issued a foul stench.

Because he couldn't sit, his method of meditation was to pace before the icon for hours. Young Chion watched him in secret.

On the second day of this restless meditation, Chion noticed that the Abbot's robes were dry but the smell had worsened. On the third day, he saw the Abbot sit before the icon and murmur a name that Chion did not wish to repeat. But when the Abbot threw off his robes and rode out of the monastery on their only mare, Chion was forced to report the name to the other monks.

"Mother Birthwort."

"Nonsense, boy," brother Xavien told him. "No one would dare create an image of the Evil One, let alone spend so much time and effort on it. We must search the monastery records for documentation pertaining to this icon."

A new Abbot and Prior were chosen and they decided that whatever secrets the previous Abbots might have concealed would have come to light of themselves eventually, for guilt, like water, wears away even the strongest defenses in the end. They agreed that no earthly creation should be feared by pious men. Monks were encouraged to go to the Sacristy to view the icon and offer their opinions.

The monks found a multitude of excuses to avoid doing this, for don't we all harbor some shameful secrets that we hope will remain hidden? It was only Chion who lingered nearby, dusting and repositioning the icon while waiting for someone to view it. This didn't occur until the village woman who brought bread for the monks every week, wandered into the Sacristy and was hypnotized by the open icon. Chion watched her quietly from behind a damaged pulpit.

Brother Asum noticed her as he passed by and led her out to the garden. "Who is that saint?" she asked. "It could be me dead father working his carving knife. May his spirit watch over us all."

The baker woman was a tireless worker whose catalog of tragedies left her hunched and nearly hairless. She'd taken care of her frail father all her life with no help from her worthless husband and nine children. She was most certainly not a liar, nor was she given to daydreaming.

Brother Asum told her that they hadn't ascertained the identity of the depicted, and assured her that when they had, he would inform her straightaway so she might claim the curious personage as her patron saint.

When she left, Brother Asum, burning with curiosity, faced the icon. Later Chion overheard him report to the new Abbot that the image seemed to vibrate for a time and then resolve itself into a likeness of his departed sister with whom he shared a special bond. He was hesitant to describe this relationship in detail but he seemed neither overly disturbed nor rapturous about the revelation, which was a great relief to the other monks.

One by one, they slipped into the Sacristy to view the image. Though Chion was occupied with the task of searching records for mention of the icon, nothing in the monastery went unreported. The monks saw lost family members, beloved and loathed. Brother Enonis saw a griffon, Brother Lindeaus a loon. The verger saw a giant Salvinia. An elderly deacon saw the ship his father had sailed away on sixty years before. And one of the schoolboys saw himself as an old man. He went home and told villagers about the mysterious sacred object that the monks had found.

The curious villagers began to approach the monastery in small groups. The monks tried to discourage them but the Abbot relented and allowed them to view the icon singly and in pairs. "How could the experience be worse than the multitude of misfortunes that have already befallen the people of Belleprey?" He said.

There was no consensus about what was depicted, no way to predict what someone would see in the murky portrayal, why they saw what they saw, or their reaction to it. For this reason, it was determined that the depicted was most likely St. Mnemon and that his image stirred lost memories both real and illusionary – for memory is closely tied to imagination. Most of the pilgrims were not inordinately disturbed by the experience since imagination tends to atrophy under conditions of continual misfortune. Those stricken by fear weren't held suspect as tragic memories were commonplace in the village of Belleprey.

Still, imagination plays unaccountable tricks and we're not meant to remember everything – to do so is bittersweet and even cruel for some people. You'd think this would be especially true for these villagers, but they were so used to distress that they were, if not immune, at least numbed. The new Abbot held that memory was impossible to restrain even without an icon and people were better off facing their demons.

In contemplating its effects, the pious monks wondered how an artist might achieve such a stunning feat. They considered the paradox of artist and icon that inspired memory, being consigned to oblivion. But, they reasoned, this is how memory works, sporadically, selectively and unreliably.

When the unscrupulous Lord Mayor arrived with his toadys, Chion knew there would be trouble. The Lord Mayor stood before the icon stiffly. He fondled his closely trimmed chin hair with one hand while he grasped his ceremonial sash with the other. "A fortune," he said finally. "I see a fortune for our village."

Chion knew that any such fortune would more likely end up in the Lord Mayor's personal coffer than in the treasury of Belleprey.

The Mayor called his guard to retrieve the icon.

"No!" Chion called out.

Everyone – monks, Mayor, guard and villagers – turned to him.

"It's too delicate to be moved," he said.

Brother Xavien spoke up. "The boy's right. It's very fragile and still needs a great deal of attention. It's quite ancient. Without proper restoration, it could disintegrate before we unlock its secrets."

The Abbot nodded in agreement.

"Fine," the Lord Mayor said. "I'll leave it in your capable hands. When can I send my men to retrieve it?"

"Well," Xavien began. "A special pavilion will have to be built for it."

"Done," said the Mayor.

"It won't be simple," Xavien continued. "The icon's origins and purpose must be discerned: we're still searching the libraries ... an astrological chart will have to be drawn to resolve what materials, orientation, and decoration are suitable for its safekeeping. Proper chants must be divined, a program for rituals and maintenance drawn up ... We don't want to take any risks with such an artifact."

"How long will all this take?"

"Oh, it's an ongoing process. We'll advise you periodically by a team responsible for carrying out proper procedures. Even so, we can't promise longevity in the village; the atmosphere is stifling down there as compared to the mountain air at the monastery. You're more prone to fire and flooding."

"I suppose you could care for it here?"

"That would be simpler, but do as you wish."

"Fine. You may keep it but I hold you personally responsible for its preservation. Strict accounts are to be kept regarding pilgrims and fees. I'll give you detailed parameters in a few days."

"Please take your time. We have much to do."

When they left, the Abbot called Xavien to his office and Xavien insisted that Chion accompany him.

Chion looked down at his feet, afraid to face the Abbot's scrutiny.

"Do we know what we're dealing with?" The Abbot asked.

"In regard to the Lord Mayor?" Xavien ventured. "I don't trust him,"

"Of course we can't trust the Mayor. Everyone knows that. It's the icon I'm talking about."

"We know it's something that evokes strayed memories, something powerful. A relic created with this much care and mastery had to have had deeply sacred inspiration. I believe this boy has a connection to it and will eventually unlock its mysteries."

Chion cringed. He hoped Xavien wasn't mistaken but he wasn't sure he had a connection to anything, let alone something as sacred as the mysterious icon.

The Abbot glared at him. "Do you mean to tell me that we must depend on a novice to unlock the mystery of this relic?"

"He's the one who found it. He cleaned it and he's kept watch on it up until now."

Chion hadn't realized that brother Xavien had taken notice of his interest.

"Are you up to the job?" The Abbot asked the boy.

"I'll try, sir."

"That's all we ask," brother Xavien said.

"Well, then at least clean him up," said the Abbot.

Chion got a new robe, and sandals that actually fit. He trimmed his nails and bathed. Brother Aver cut his unruly hair, a process he'd all but given up as Chion's hair grew in an extremely haphazard way.

Xavien told Chion he looked "quite human," and at evening vespers the Abbot actually smiled and nodded to him. Chion was both humbled and frightened.

The next morning, the Deputy Mayor arrived at the monastery to announce that the Lord Mayor had arranged for a group of high officials from the capital city to view the icon in one month's time. He expected all preparations to have been made by then or the town of Belleprey would assume patronage of the artifact and it would be relocated to a pavilion in the marketplace. Extended regulations to follow.

Those days, the village of Belleprey, never without tragedy, was experiencing a plague of fugits. At random hours of the day and night, these birds swarmed about the villagers and their domestic animals causing long intervals of incessant chitter that made teeth ache and turned goat milk green. A slimy guano had begun to coat houses and affect roads previously so dusty that when sheep herds passed by, the town disappeared in a grey cloud. The fact that the Lord Mayor could conceive of bringing the icon into such a situation illustrated his foolishness. That he could entice outside officials to make the pilgrimage to Belleprey at any time was impossible to imagine.

"Still," Xavien told Chion, "as there seems to be no record of this icon or instructions regarding it, if we're to have any recourse against the Lord Mayor's demands, we'll need your help to learn how we should proceed."

"Me?" Chion croaked. "How can I do that?"

"Meditation, my boy. It's the only way."

Chion didn't know what to say. He was much more of a daydreamer than a serious meditator, though he'd never admitted this to anyone. During morning prayers he dreamed of finding his mother living in a castle in the warm south, possibly by the sea, where she'd welcome him with an elaborate feast of gemfruit, a delicacy Chion had only read about. When he worked in the scriptorium under the scrutiny of brother Xavien he thought of the bread-maker's daughter, a chubby girl, given to giggling and humming. When he walked along the Cloister he dreamed of taming the sphinx, fighting a three-headed chimera, capturing a mantid owl, riding the Whistling Leviathan. He dreamt of gravy in the refectory (his dreams were not all elaborate) and at night in the dorter, while the other monks slept, he dreamed of the world outside the monastery, a transgression he could never own up to.

Although Chion seemed dedicated and conscientious to the other monks, he couldn't turn off these thoughts. Neither monks nor villagers understood or respected the workings of imagination. They were resigned to misery, oblivious regarding possibility. How could he admit such a thing to anyone?

Chion dutifully sat before the icon in a pose of meditation but, alas, his dreams continued and turned dark. He imagined the monastery going up in flames, the monks scattered or dead. He thought the fugits were invading the granary, the gardens, his robe. The figure in the icon became in turn the Abbot, brother Icilius, the distorted body of the old Prior, and a monstrous three-headed version of the Lord Mayor.

Each day the Mayor's assistant came to announce one less day to complete the preparatory measures, carrying more edicts from the Lord Mayor. Chion could hear the impatience in the Abbot's footsteps. He could feel the despondency when Xavien patted his shoulder. He could smell the pity and despair emanating from the other monks who looked in on him periodically.

Fourteen more days, twelve more days, ten ...

Chion was exhausted from his daily "meditations." He sat, he stood, he paced, and when his mind wouldn't clear, he tried to think. He knew it would be no use to try and talk the Abbot and Xavien into relieving him and he became angry that they'd placed this burden on him. Why should he be the one to have such a responsibility?

On the morning the Mayor's assistant announced "five more days," Xavien told Chion that if he wanted to take a rest or even give up, it would be understood, but Chion couldn't make himself move from in front of the icon. It's hard to admit failure at a young age, even if you know it's looming. Chion couldn't bear to appear at supper or to retire to the dorter, despite appeals from the Abbot, Xavien and the other monks.

As he sat late into the night, his mind finally began to shut down. His unruly hair had grown out at an alarming rate and occasionally he felt a tingling come through it to his head and limbs. He twitched and shivered.

Moonlight gave the image a glow. Two ambiguous dark spots resolved themselves into a pair of sad eyes. The misty figure wavered and the wind outside blew a low sigh. Or was it Chion lamenting the painful memories of Belleprey? Though it didn't seem particularly loud, the mournful sound carried down the mountain to the village. Fugits began to swarm. Waves of chitting and screeching were carried on wind currents caused by the frantic flapping of tiny wings. Guano flowed. The turmoil drove villagers up the mountain to the monastery. Manic birds and confused domestic beasts fell into the slime, disintegrated and expanded it. Several villagers, including the Lord Mayor, slipped on the secretions and fell victim to it's mordant properties.

By the time Chion had the presence of mind to close the doors of the icon and subdue the moaning, the fugits were gone and the village was flooded with a noxious mixture of slime and marrow. It took six days for it to harden into a substance they used to pave their streets and tile their roofs. The valley crops had been consumed by the swarm of fugits so all the villagers had to eat that winter was hop-rice and junk weed that grew on the sides of the mountain. But the newly paved streets kept the invasive grey dust (that had previously covered everything) down, the tiled roofs kept the winter rains and mold out of the houses, and the fugits that had caused havoc and devastation as they multiplied wildly, were gone.

The monks and villagers argued over wether the incident had been grievous or fortunate but it was never satisfactorily decided, for don't most events have aspects of both? It was agreed that the icon was gaining power from being exposed and that it might be prudent to dispose of it and avoid risking future episodes.

Chion watched with a sinking heart as villagers tried to smash the icon, paint over it, burn it. But it wouldn't be destroyed. They were reluctant to put it in the river, their main source of water, since they didn't know how water would be affected or if their undisclosed memories would be carried downstream and into the hands of unscrupulous sorcerers. (Didn't they have enough problems already?) They finally buried it in the windward side of the mountain.

But mountains have long memories and a flood of nightmares was unleashed upon the villagers. Miners began to see ghosts. The mountain writhed. Chion knew there'd always been ghosts and that the mountain had been sporadically unstable. He still couldn't believe that an exquisitely worked relic harbored evil (Chion was very naive), but he suspected the villagers were not prepared for the storm of re-membrances the mountain might spew over them. He felt that their lives were miserable enough without having to flounder in a sea of wayward memories and he couldn't bear to think of that magnificent artifact rotting under the earth. So, one moonless night he retrieved the icon and returned it to its dark, but safe, corner in the lower cellar to await a day when memory could foster a favorable change for the people of Belleprey.

Alas, the village of Belleprey has not yet flourished but plods on from one tragedy to the next as it's always done. The plague of fugits never reoccured but the paved streets and tiled roofs have crumbled and the thick dingy dust reappeared. Other plagues come and go. However, this can't be attributed to Chion's action for certain, nor to the icon. Fortune is as unreliable and unpredictable as memory, and destiny is not easily changed by unruly boys, imposing artifacts or lowly fowls. Be grateful for the imagination you've been blessed with, guard your memories and beware of what you deem true, or holy.

And what happens to a boy with imagination and mettle who finds himself in an inapt situation? Perhaps he moves on to seek his fortune in the world beyond. Perhaps he remains in the monastery to tend to the memories of a wretched town. Or perhaps he marries the baker's daughter and raises sheep and children.

Meeting the Dog Girls

Every Saturday morning the Dog Girls met at Ory's Diner for an early breakfast. They told rambling stories and laughed a lot. They talked about hard times, tedious husbands, weather, crops and how to take care of day to day stuff.

"For that kind of nicker, I'd check the carburetor," one of them said once – they took good care of their cars and trucks.

"You don't get much benefit out of medicine if it tastes good."

"How often do you give that old dog Pepto Bismol?"

"Men are best at being grandfathers and brothers."

"Ain't it the truth," I'd say as I set their plates down in front of them. "Fellas around here treat you like you was dirt one minute and then expect you to sleep with them the next."

They talked about their animals a lot. They treated them like people, with respect and affection, and treated people like children, with patience and kindness toward the nice ones, and sternness toward others. Some folks, like Sam Ralston, they totally ignored. Sam is a local trucker and he was always trying to hit on the Dog Girls, but they acted as if he wasn't there. Sam didn't actually notice because he really wasn't all there anyway. They openly flirted with Ory's boy, Alfie, a shy 15 year old who came in to bus for us on the weekends. The flirting was all very innocent, meant to give Alfie some confidence. Everyone admires Dog Girls and all men desire them, whether they admit it or not, so it sure gave Alfie a reason to hold his head up.

I have to say that they gave my soul a flutter also, feeling swallowed up by them hills and like I was never gonna see anything of the world outside before the Dog Girls come into Ory's. I am the youngest waitress at Ory's, just 25 last birthday. I got the job when Lully Kemp ran off with that trucker from Kiski. It was the biggest scandal around here since Millard Harden shot his wife and boy on Easter Sunday 1975 down by Hedgy's Run.

Dog Girls wore combat boots with a hole drilled in the heel through which they threaded their laces. Waitresses, like me, wear light comfortable shoes – sneakers or old oxfords. We wear support hose and still get spider veins (or worse) by middle age. I admired the Dog Girls so much that I went out and bought myself a pair of combat boots to wear on my days off when I went to help my grandpa.

"Look at them boots," he said to me the first day I wore them. "You could walk through a swamp in a thundersquall in them things."

I loved the confident whomp they made on his wood floor. I was so much more substantial in them.

I take care of my grandpa because he took care of me after my folks died when I was seven. They hit a patch of black ice in an old Chevy and flew off Three Mile Hill like a eagle with headlights. Actually, grandpa took care of me a lot before the accident too. He made my pair of shoes every Easter. He put vinegar on my bruises. He tried to teach me how to juggle.

At first, folks around here said that Grandpa was unequipped, set in his ways, too dogged to raise a child. He was always early and his stuff was always redd up, whereas I'm late a lot and naturally messy, my bra strap shows, my hems come out. Grandpa was very strict with himself, but not so much with me. I tried hard to live up to his standards, but I'm not much like him. He loves me anyway. Folks finally came to see that, and left us alone.

Sometimes the Dog Girls wore caps that said, "John Deere" or "Detroit," but mostly they didn't bother to cover their heads at all. In the winter they came with snow in their hair. It sparkled in the florescent light. With the whoosh of cold air that ushered them in, it gave them a look of what grandpa would call "festooned fairyfolk." After they sat for a while in the warm diner, the snow would melt and leave their hair dripping till they'd give it a good shake. Once I saw them in the parking lot cutting each other's hair. They snipped off the back, then held their heads down and cut an oval in front so they could see and hair wouldn't get in their faces when they put their heads down. Dog Girls are very practical.

One thing I have is hair, scads of it. When I was little, grandpa used to get neighbor ladies to cut it short; he's a fiend for neatness and simplicity. But it grows like hellfire, so I gave up on it when I moved out of his house. I didn't know anyone to cut it and I'm not big on beauty parlors. I try to keep it pulled back or braided out of my face, but it has a mind of its own and tends to pop out every which way. Francine, who works the night shift at Ory's and has medium length "big" hair, spends two hours in Gaynell's Beauty Nook every Wednesday – and that's when she's not getting her roots touched up!

The dog Girls never messed with themselves like Francine and other women. By this I mean they didn't tweeze, shave, paint, dye, pierce, tattoo, squeeze in, pad or push-up any parts of themselves. Men admired them anyway (even Alfie, who's pretty much afraid of girls). I, personally, never had the knack for any of that stuff even though Francine has tried hard to teach me.

I would stand at the diner window on Saturday mornings, posting specials and watching for them to come down the mountain in the predawn fog. The Dog Girls were excellent drivers and never went slow. They drove four-wheel vehicles with their heads hanging out the window, hair blowing and rock 'n roll blasting out of the radio. I always loved the feel of wind in my hair. Grandpa didn't like to get his little bit of hair mussed up. He'd open the windows for me though, because he knew how happy it made me. "Tarnation, girl," he'd say. "Ya look teched with that hair all over the place." Then we'd both laugh.

He never liked the radio on when he was in the car, though he didn't mind "lite FM" played real low. Grandpa really hated rock 'n roll. I didn't much put the radio on, because I knew he tolerated it just to make me happy and it's kind of irritating not to be able to hear the words to the songs when it's so low. For me, Dog Girls were a truly glorious sight coming down the interstate with hair blowing and radios blaring.

Ory admired Dog Girls as much as anyone, but frowned when he saw them coming. He was always afraid they'd scare the other customers away. Usually, they came very early in the morning, five or six a.m., and were gone before the real tetchy breakfast crowd got here. Folks who came at that hour were too hung over or sleepy or drawn up in their own worries to pay much attention to Dog Girls. Once in a while the Dog Girls would linger over coffee until folks came in and stared at them. A few people were frightened so Ory would seat them at the other end of the diner. I think grandpa would have liked the Dog Girls even though they were messy and sassy, but by the time they started coming to Ory's, he didn't get out all that much.

The waitresses never minded Dog Girls lingering because they left big tips and were always kind and patient, even when the orders were screwed-up. Ory's waitresses don't usually screw-up because we're experienced and the place never gets too busy. When they do, you can bet something really horrible is happening in their lives, and Dog Girls have sympathy for folks in troubled times.

The Dog Girls loved meat and ate a lot of bacon. They put it on everything, even ice cream! They drank coffee or soda pop, and never fruit juice; they weren't big on sweets. My Grandpa loved his sweets, until Doc Keener told him he had diabetes. Grandpa took the pills Doc gave him and stayed on the diabetes diet. He never cheated by even one bite. That's how he was. After grandma died twenty years ago, he never looked at another woman even though the church widows hounded him to death for years.

Dog Girls loved napkins and used them to wave around and shred as they shared blood-and-thunder stories, to wipe their faces and clean their combat boots, write lists on and draw maps. But they loved snow best. Snow was certainly their best setting, despite the trying road conditions. Whenever it snowed you could bet that Dog Girls would be out in it, marking up the whiteness with footprints and angels, throwing it at each other and laughing. They were always talking about how much they loved it. Dog Girls always sleep with their socks on, since their feet and hands are very susceptible to the cold. This is why they always wear boots, even in the summer. Around here it is less cold when it snows; perhaps that's why they love snow so much. Even so, they put cayenne pepper in their shoes to keep their feet warm.

I saw them playing in the snow on a back road off the pike once, and I knew I was a kindred spirit. I'm not overly fond of the cold, but I have always loved snow. Rain makes me sad. Thunder storms are okay if I'm in the car or the house, but sometimes they give me earaches. Too much heat slows me down and makes me dizzy, which is okay when you don't have to work. But snow makes me laugh out loud, just like the Dog Girls.

Hunched over coffee at Ory's one morning, the Dog Girls decided they should drive to Mexico together. Lavitta had told them long-spun stories about the Mexicans and their humble country.

Lavitta was the oldest Dog Girl. She was a shade under 50 in people years. Her hair was dull brown and gray, but long and soft. The others called on her for advice, though she rarely gave any. Mostly, she told stories. Although the younger Dog Girls had been to more places and done more things, it was Lavitta who had the best imagination and knew a story to match every situation. She told the other Dog Girls about Mexican volcanoes, lost lagoons, deserts, tropical forests, feathered serpents, swarms of butterflies, and the place "where the sky was born." She knew how to make *huevos a la Mexicana*. The Dog Girls were downright inspired.

Once they made The Decision, they began saving their money and collecting maps. I watched and listened, and brought them maps and books from my grandpa's house. (He told me to take them. "I won't be going nowhere any time soon," he said.) I served the dog Girls their bacon and coffee, cleared off the table, and felt the excitement build week after week until I couldn't stand it any longer. My insides churned like the milkshake machines at the Shake and Twist every time I heard them talk. I hadn't ever been further than Hunker but for listening to the Dog Girl's stories. I hadn't ever seen a real living breathing flamingo, or an ocean, or eaten a tamale. It all sounded so openhearted and full of promise. Finally, I asked if I could go along.

They were surprised; I must have seemed a kind of stick figure next to their sturdiness. They said there wouldn't be enough room in the car.

"I don't take up much room," I reminded them. "And I don't have much stuff to take along neither."

"Goin' on the road is hard," Landy said. "And Mexico is a real different from West Virginia. You ever been anywhere? Wheeling? Pittsburgh?"

Landy was the blonde one. She didn't seem to have a home, though she pretty much stuck around these parts. She said that she lived with her boyfriend over to Three-Mile Hill, but she was always hitching a ride to someplace else. She carried her stuff around with her in a huge backpack. She ate crab apples and still cried when she thought of her dead mother.

I could only shake my head at her questions. One time Francine asked me to drive up to Morgantown, to see her boyfriend play in a band. When I told grandpa about it he said, "That there's a big crazy place up to Morgantown. Yer liable to git hurt, girl." I told him that I knew how to take care of myself, that he'd taught me everything I needed to know. But Francine broke up with the guy next day so we didn't go after all.

Doxie and Peer looked sympathetic. Doxie patted my hand and said, "You got your whole life here, girl." (This was true if I considered my whole life to be grandpa, which it pretty much was – and wasn't that a reason to get myself out of Hunker? I could get Mz. Ritter to look in on him, and Francine. Alfie could do the heavy chores.)

Doxie and Peer were mother and daughter, though they don't look very much alike. It happened like that in some litters. Doxie's hair was motley brown, worn and scraggly and often matted in spots; while Peer's was blackblackblack, medium long and thick and silky. Peer had one gray eye; it made her look exotic. Doxie threw her no-good husband, Tellis, out years ago. Tellis had a good heart when he was sober, but he couldn't stop drinking and he was a mean drunk. Doxie didn't mind him fighting with her; hell, she sometimes enjoyed a good fight. But the night he hit Peer in the face with his fist – and Peer only ten (people) years old – she knew he had to go. "Mostly it's good to be loyal," she said. "But there are times when you just gotta git!"

Doxie couldn't believe how pleasant her life was without him. He came to visit once in a while, and sent them money when he got union work. For the last year or so, he claimed to be sober, but Doxie found empty Jack Daniel's bottles in his truck.

I was sure that it was my "time to git," as Doxie put it. I was determined to go, and set about convincing them to take me along. I put away every spare penny and stole food from the diner when I could, or ate peanut butter and bananas, or went without. I even went to the library, over to Supple, and boned up on my Spanish. *Tengo hambre*; I am hungry. *Despacio, por favor*; go slow, please. *Hagame favor de decirme donde esta verdad;* please direct me to Truth. *Quisiera volar*; I would like to fly.

I didn't tell grandpa, knowing that he would agree with the Dog Girls that I wasn't ready to go out into the world. Hell, grandpa didn't think there was a reason for anyone to leave this hollow ever, least of all me. A contrary old critter like him could do without me for a while, couldn't he?

Landy said the Mexican Indians revered Dog Girls and coveted blessings from them. She said that she'd never wanted to go to a place that favored her kind above others before but since she'd lived with "that scrapper" (what she called her boyfriend), she looked forward to being appreciated. One day I heard her say that Mexico was a place of vibrant colors, where nothing was black or white. Even the shadows were tinted in shades of chocolate. I used to think of this when I laid down to sleep in my tiny room on Bump Street. My bed was so hard that it made my bones ache. I knew I should either gain padding over my bones, or buy a softer mattress for the bed. Neither was possible once I began saving money for Mexico. When I closed my eyes real tight, I could see Mexican colors swirl around like confetti, and I couldn't feel my bones scrape on the hard bed. I was determined to get them to take me along.

I began to swim in the river to make my body strong, and watch sunsets to enrich my spirit. I discovered that the river did as much for my spirit as the sunsets. I told this to Lavitta, and the Dog Girls decided to go swimming with me one Saturday afternoon.

We left our towels on the bank and climbed the railroad bridge. One by one we jumped into the river, hootin' and hollerin'. Peer hollered the loudest. It didn't really matter because there was no one within miles to hear us. Dog Girls are very strong swimmers, but I was easily able to keep up because I am much better in water than I am on land. (Water's the best place to be when you want to cry without anyone knowing and I done a lot a crying after my folks died.) I taught them how to twirl in the air when they jumped, and spit out water like a fountain. We washed our hair in the rapids and ate Turkey Jerky that we'd bought out of machines at Riley's Texaco. We watched the sun set and the stars come out. I showed them my personal constellations – the umbrella, the harmonica in the milkweeds, the three-legged eyeball.

They still weren't convinced I should go with them.

I wished them "*buenas dias*" every time they came in, and "*adios*" when they left. They smiled and answered "*gracias*" but didn't change their minds.

One morning Landy asked me, "What were you and Alfie doing down by the river last night? Trying to set the woods on fire?"

"Shhhhhh!" I knelt down beside the table. "Please don't say nothing to Ory. Alfie's dog Becca died and he wanted to give her a Viking funeral is all. If Ory finds out, he'll tell Alfie's mama and she'll make him go to 'Boot Camp for Heaven' all summer. She found Jesus down to the Glorious Name Fellowship last year and there's no talking to the woman. Ory wanted to put Becca in the garbage! Alfie and that old dog grew up together; he's got a right to send her off the way he wants."

"Was she a good dog?" Peer asked.

"As good as they come. She fought a fox off a the boy when he was six and slept with him ever since. Woke them all up in the middle of the night when Alfie got sick and chased the old turd that sells dope away from the school. Ory knows it too, but he won't stand up to her since she started preachin'. Says he don't cross no woman with Hellfire in her heart. We told him that Becca musta gone off to die."

Landy was the only one who didn't look sympathetic. "What the Hell is a Viking funeral?" she asked.

"You know, like in that old movie when Kirk Douglas died and they put him on a boat and shoot flaming arrows into it."

"Hail, Ragnor," Lavitta said.

"Exactly." I said. "I think Janet Leigh picked the wrong guy in that one."

"I hear that," said Lavitta.

"We won't tell," Peer said.

Before they left, Lavitta told Alfie a story about a dog she knew when she was a child. Doxie and Peer hugged him and Landy patted him on the back and told him to "be brave."

Not long after that, Doxie said that maybe I could go to Mexico with them. The others agreed and for the first time in my life, I felt as if I belonged, as if I was a person of consequence. It was like walking in my boots on grandpa's floor all the time.

The next day my grandpa took sick and I had to move out of the room on Bump Street to take care of him. At first I thought he would be okay after a little pampering, good food and fresh clean clothes. There was nothing serious wrong with him, just a lot of little things. His ancient body was filling up with fear, a fear that comes of worn sheets debased with nightmares, dishes tainted with memory, solitary moments caught in dim corners. I tried to chase the fear away with my boots. I sang into the dingy corners and replaced the mustiness with the fragrance of pie spices, bread baking and *café con leche*.

Grandpa had to be kept on a special diet of deference and low sodium. I'd had my room on Bump Street for six years and now I wondered how he'd lived alone for so long. He had no concept of what was good for him. He sat outside in the cold with his shoes off and ate red meat and white bread at every meal because they weren't on the diabetes list. I did what I could, but his skin grew knobby and dry, and often he was too weak to sit up. His eyes became so watery that it was as if they were melting.

The closer someone gets to death, the less real this world seems to them, and grandpa began to focus on that other world more and more. Sometimes he thought I was grandma and other times he didn't even know I was there. When this happened, I tried to think of the chocolate shadows in Mexico.

When I was little, grandpa used to take me for walks to watch the rust wash out of the factory pipes into the creek. We'd swirl the reddish-brown ooze around with sticks and make shiny designs in the oily water. He told me adventure stories from the Bible without ever nagging me to get saved, and took splinters out of my knees. He bought me frozen shrimp, made ice cream out of snow, and cooked potatoes in campfires.

So I couldn't leave him.

I finally told the Dog Girls this, and they said they would wait for a while. "Maybe he'll get better," they said. I shook my head and told them they should go on without me. I was all grandpa had in this world.

We sat by the side of the road above Iron Bridge drinking warm IC Lite and watching the sun set behind Bartsel's Deer Processing Plant. None of the Dog Girls could remember their own Grandpas. "Short life span, I suppose," Doxie mumbled.

"All the more reason for you to go on without me," I told her.

Peer let out a low howl.

"Hey," Landy said, "we'll send you postcards from everywhere we go. You can come meet us after … "

"I guess that would be okay," I said. "He has some stuff I could sell when he's gone to Glory … " I was sorry I'd said this because I didn't really want him to die.

I wanted him to tell me stories and take me for walks, but he just slept and stared into space and squeezed my hand when I sat with him.

Nobody said anything for a long time. We watched the stars come out one by one. I figured it just wasn't my time to "git" after all. Like Doxie always said, "Mostly it's best to be loyal." And I owed my loyalty to grandpa.

"By the time you git there, we'll be able to show you the ropes. You got to pay for what you git, honey, if not in money, then in tears and sweat."

They left for Mexico at full moon. "Better to travel at night," they said. "Less traffic." Alfie and I opened the diner to feed them and make sandwiches for the trip.

I guess facing death makes you less fearful about things in this world because a few days ago grandpa said, "When I'm gone I think it'd be good fer ya to git out an see some a the world. Wished I'da did it."

"Well, you get yourself fixed up and we'll go together," I told him. He just nodded and smiled.

Lavitta told me before they left that many miracles occur in Mexico. She thought it had something to do with the spirituality of the people, and the heat. "Reality hates heat," she said.

I gave them my old Girl Scout compass and a dozen Manx scones made from my dead grandmother's recipe.

Yesterday I got a postcard. It said: "*El milagro! Esta nevando.*"

When I close my eyes tight, I can see vibrant Mexican snow swirling about like a giant kaleidoscope let loose on the world. I can see the Dog Girls rolling around in it and hear them calling out to me. I can imagine the huge pyramids and see Indians bringing offerings to them. I can feel the blessings of the Dog Girls shower over us all like a blizzard. I have taught Grandpa the trick of seeing colored snow. He claims he can do it with his eyes open even though color has abandoned him. The strange thing is that Grandpa has become his own snowstorm. His puny old frame is flaking off in small pieces that I collect in an old Cheerios box. A box that I will take with me on the long bus ride to Mexico to meet up with the dog Girls. Each day I brush the tiny flakes that accumulate about him as he grows smaller and smaller.

The General's Tears

In his old age, the general loved his ornate bed-chamber and the crisp embroidered sheets on his hand-carved bed. He loved the gold braid and shiny buttons stamped with campaign insignia that embellished his dress uniforms. He delighted in each ribbon and metal that military officials had rewarded him with, and he had his wives polish all four hundred and sixteen of them each week. But his most prized possession was the heart of his first kill, a Carthusian dove, its species long extinct. He kept it in a velvet-lined coffer in the drawer of his nightstand. It had rested there since he was a child. On his ninetieth birthday the shriveled heart had been no bigger than a raisin and as hard as a stone.

On the morning of his one-hundredth birthday he opened the coffer to find only the smallest grain of matter resting on the fragile velvet. The General pounded his fist on the nightstand so forcefully that the house shook. The mice in the walls ceased their scrambling and resident spiders discontinued their weaving. A marbled egret in the gemfruit tree that stood in the courtyard huddled over her eggs as the wind seemed to stop. The General's wives cowered in the cooking shed.

The remains of the heart bounced out of the coffer and into his demitasse cup. The coffer fell to the floor and shattered. The General, who had been looking up at the heavens when this happened, was distraught in the belief that this last remnant was missing. He slid off the bed on to his arthritic knees, gulped his coffee, and crouched, searching for the treasure that he believed to have fallen to the floor.

But something happened when that tiny heart entered his system awash in his morning coffee.

He began to weep.

The General hadn't wept since he left his mother's arms. He hadn't wept when she died, or when his father and brothers died. He hadn't wept for his own children or wives who'd departed this life before him. He hadn't wept for the men he'd killed in war (nor the women or children). He hadn't wept for the men who were slain while under his command. But his stubborn body had retained one tear for each of them and those tears flowed relentlessly now. They seeped through the floorboards and into the parlor. The Aubusson carpet swelled sponge-like, and still tears flowed out on to the veranda. They washed down the front steps, through the courtyard and into the region beyond, turning the well-manicured grounds into a swamp and drowning the ornamental shrubs, Reaper anemones, Philippi heathers and Gatling lilies. An adventurous mold-like substance oozed over the yarrows and Dunkirk oak. The entire kitchen garden was lost.

In time, the General's wives waded out of the cooking shed searching the sky for clouds, but the sky was a perfectly bright aquamarine. As the flood seemed to be coming from the house, they ventured inside together. The youngest wife (barely twenty, taken by the General to repay her father's debt) held a palm out to catch the drips from the ceiling, lifted it to her tongue, and declared it salty. There was a collective gasp as each wife perceived the undoing of the General at the same moment. The oldest instructed the others to take the carpet out and hang it on the clothesline in hopes of salvaging it.

"What of the General?" Asked the wife who smelled like the jasmine flower tea he had sent to them from the Huang-dao valley twice a year.

The oldest just shook her head and waved them out. She thought of going to him but knew he wouldn't want anyone to see him in such a state. In any case, his tears were seeping through the rickety stairs as well as the ancient ceiling; it would be unsafe to try and get to him.

The wives removed what they could from the ground floor before the situation became perilous, then they sat on the dining room chairs a good distance away and watched the house crumble into the mud. The children played quietly, making pies and castles from the ooze.

"This is what comes of men and their wars." The oldest sighed.

"What do we do now?" Asked the wife who smelled like the sweet cinnamon bread the General's mother had baked on winter mornings.

"We gather what dry wood we can find and build a fire. Then we'll bake the mud into bricks and build a house that can withstand what comes next."

And so they did – even though the mud was corrupted and there were more men about to make war.

When they melted the General's metals down it was discovered that that they weren't gold, but a corrupt alloy that wouldn't even make good cooking utensils, which was what they'd planned to do with them. They fashioned them into gardening tools instead, wrapping the handles with fabric from the Generals old uniforms, fabric that had taken three days to dry out in the hot sun.

Of the General himself, they found nothing.

The swamp became overrun with milk toads, whose sonorous croaking in the evenings soothed the surviving members of the household. The children fed the toads Heffer beetles and roundelays until they were large enough to eat.

When the Brigadier and Honor Guard arrived to collect the Generals remains, they were shocked by the situation of wives and children living at the edge of the swamp, existing on milk toads and wolf-weed. Though the Brigadier offered no help, some of the young soldiers in the Honor Guard left coins. They took the General's spiked helmet to lay at rest in the Warrior's Cemetery and promised to have a statue of the General erected in the town square.

"What good will that do us?" asked the wife who smelled like the Spring rain on the day the General's first born had come into the world.

"It will give you stature in the community." the Brigadier told her.

The wives just stood there. They knew that these things were important to men.

When the soldiers left, the wife that smelled of cinnamon said, "I hope we won't be expected to polish this statue."

"I hope we won't be expected to contribute to it," said the oldest. But of course they were.

And since they had nothing else, they offered bones from the milk toads to be ground into the mortar of the base.

The General's daughter whose freckles were sprinkled on her shoulders like brown sugar on pippin-seed cakes was enamored of a young soldier in the Honor Guard, but her mother told her. "When he goes off to war, he'll change."

"But who else is there for me to marry?" the girl cried. "All the young men who want to make something of themselves become soldiers."

"There are merchants and craftsmen," the mother told her.

"Merchants are arrogant. They'd never take a poor girl with no dowry. And craftsmen are always in debt." The girl hadn't really known her father, the General, as he was rarely home until he was very old and then the wives kept him in his bedchamber, or on the small balcony outside of it as they believed his decrepit appearance to be too frightening for children to be around. The girl only remembered whimsical trinkets he brought them from his travels.

She couldn't be dissuaded from running off with the young soldier.

Soon another daughter fell in love with a soldier, and another, and another.

The circumstance of the General's tears had discouraged his sons from becoming soldiers but, unfortunately, they had no recourse but to go to war for if they didn't, they and their widowed mothers might starve.

Vagrants and dogs settled beneath the General's statue.

"There is honor in soldiering," the wife who smelled of jasmine sighed.

The others barely looked up from their milk toads.

Grasping The Bird's Tail

Feng Yi was a master of disguises. One day he would be a young man in a bright costume with spring in his step; the next, he was an old sage stooped to the earth and balanced on the threshold of eternity. He was highly respected for his imitations of women: the young nun contemplating her place in the universe, the spoiled princess shuffling about on bound feet. He was most famous, however, for his study of children at play in the open meadow of Infinity.

He had been chosen by the August Personage Theater Troupe at the age of six, some thirty years ago. In that time he'd been a diligent student of Madam Wu, the matriarch of the troupe.

When their labors at the Theater were finished, the other actors would usually go into the nearest town and find a friendly wine shop where they would spend hours laughing and sipping, telling stories and secrets. Feng Yi, however, had taken up the study of T'ai chi Ch'uan and spent his spare time in solitude, practicing his forms. His unswerving inner purpose distanced him from his colleagues, as well as others, because of the strain they placed upon his higher nature.

It was because of this, that he was the last to attend Madam Wu in her deathbed.

"Please forgive me, Madam," said Feng Yi. "I was practicing my forms in the meadow beyond the moongate. Alas, I was so engrossed in an effort to match my inner stillness to the perfect stillness of twi-light that I did not hear them call."

The frail old woman waved her delicate hand to stop his excuses. Paper lanterns made eerie shadows across her face and the aromatic powders of the doctor made Feng Yi feel weak. Madam Wu was the only person to whom he'd ever formed any attachment in his life.

"Come closer, my boy," she said. "For you I have a personal me-mento." She held up a small silk feng-huang bird. It was embroidered in many colors and stuffed with the soft batting of an old winter jacket.

Feng Yi took it and held it up to the light. "It is beautiful," he said.

"With it comes a last lesson to my most ardent pupil."

The other actors, who had been murmuring prayers and compos-ing couplets at the other end of the room, paused to hear what the great lady had to say.

"You have sought to become many things and accomplished much in your young life. Now you must seek Feng Yi."

Feng Yi's heart pounded. "I do not understand."

"I was afraid of that. You have a solitary nature and somewhat perverse spirit." The old woman reached lovingly for his wrist. "I am loath to leave you at this stage of your learning." There was a faint gurgle in her chest. "We always think we have more time than we do … " Another ominous gurgle. "Do not betray your heart … "

The gurgle changed to a low rumbling and Feng Yi looked down, for only a second. When he looked up again, the spirit had left the old woman's body.

What was she talking about? Seek Feng Yi? Why hadn't she been given enough time to explain? A wave of anguish tarnished the dim lantern light.

Suddenly Feng Yi felt the weight of attention from the other ac-tors in the room. He wished he'd been close enough with just one of them to share his grief and confusion.

Instead, he clutched the silk bird and backed out of the room as smoothly as a disappearing fire's shadow.

Feng Yi attended the simple funeral service. The other actors watched him with solemn eyes but only one of the younger ones dared approach. "Will you take over the management of the troupe now, Master?"

"I cannot," answered Feng Yi fearfully. "My studies are not over. I must make a journey."

"Where will you go?"

"I will return to the Valley of Black Pebbles in the Mountains of Dispassion, beneath the Northern Heaven. That is where I began, where my brother still lives. Perhaps it is where I will find that of which Madam Wu spoke."

"Excuse me, Master, but are not some quests attainable intrinsically? Perhaps you can find what you seek right here with the August Personage Theater Troupe?"

An icy mist ascended Feng Yi's spine. Suppose the fellow was right?

At that moment a disturbance to the left made the young actor look away for a moment. When he turned back, Feng Yi had disguised himself as part of the crowd.

"Master, please," the young actor called. "We would like to be your friends … "

But Feng Yi had disappeared.

And so began the journey of Feng Yi, which he knew in his heart was to avoid the last lesson of his beloved teacher, Madam Wu. He told himself, however, that the journey was a period of mourning, after which he would face the demons and spirits in his own mind, in his birthplace. Only then could he return and take his place in the August Personage Theater Troupe, perhaps by the spring presentation of "The Cloud Wanderer and the Bamboo Sage."

The first part of the journey took seventeen months.

From the birthplace of the Emperor's Third Concubine (where the august Personage Theater Troupe was camped), two weeks along the silk route, to the Passage of the First Origin, to the Trail of Careless Youth, along the River of My Lord Thunder, across a treacherous catwalk through the Ox-Head Mountains, through the Province of Transmigration, to the detour known as Bronze Rhinoceros, along the Fields of Poppy.

Throughout his travels, he was acknowledged as a great actor. He was invited to perform at elaborate banquets in the homes of princes and magistrates, and in the caravans of great merchants. For these short entertainments, Feng Yi received food and a warm place to sleep for the night. The journey was not unpleasant.

Several times a host asked Feng Yi to stay with him and start a theater troupe under a wealthy protectorate. Feng Yi would murmur something about obligation to his dead teacher and commitment to a quest. Then he would disappear quickly so as not to sound like one of those bumbling Zen monks.

Finally, Feng Yi reached the Mountains of Dispassion where he wandered alone for many months. It would have been enough to dishearten most men, but Feng Yi was not unhappy. Each morning he performed T'ai Chi Ch'uan and each twilight he paused for his meditations. In between, he survived on mushrooms, herbs, and other wild plants. He drank the cool water from springs and rivulets that meandered through the mountains. In the evening he would throw his worn saffron cloak over himself and sleep disguised as a patch of poisonous mushrooms. He met no other human in these months.

As the sun lifted itself from the Lake of Solitude on the plateau to the east, so Feng Yi lifted his arms against the pull of gravity. Elbows bent, wrists curved, knees obedient. Soon he had achieved the form "Grasping the Bird's Tail." He thought of Madam Wu's gift for only a moment and then became attendant to the movement of the Tai Chi forms that followed in the long succession of the exercise. The lack of distraction permitted a new degree of perfection.

Time and motion flowed harmoniously. He was concentrated on the perfect movements of the form called "Cloud Arms." Indeed, an early-rising family of wood ticks had paused on the back of a cinnamon tree to discuss whether he might be an indolent cloud that had gotten caught on a ledge of the Mountains of Dispassion.

By the time Feng Yi had reached "Parting the Wild Horse's Mane", two herons, a frog and a company of cicadas had come to bask in his shadow, thinking he was an illusion borne by some disposed wind from the Northern Heaven. Many of the younger creatures had never seen a man.

When he reached the quick fist movement of the "Warrior Form," the startled creatures withdrew except for a sleepy butterfly that had dozed off for that moment. His form completed, Feng Yi settled beneath a venerable cedar to breakfast on tree-fungus before continuing his journey.

After he finished his meal, Feng Yi thought he saw a small cloud of smoke from a campfire. He crept toward it and saw a ghost who had set about burning an accumulation of memories. Feng Yi watched from behind a clump of bamboo and became disheartened. Surely this harmless ghost had appeared in his path to direct him to the Valley of Black Pebbles, and yet Feng Yi had hoped that his Destiny would lie in the Mountains of Dispassion as an ascetic. Hadn't his T'ai Chi forms reached unprecedented perfection in these mountains? Hadn't he begun the search for his true nature without the press of civilization?

He held up the embroidered bird. Birds are a symbol of flight, he told himself. But some part of him was not satisfied with excuses anymore and whispered that this bird was more likely meant to be a symbol of his higher nature. Perhaps my period of mourning is over and the real journey is about to begin, he thought. Sadly, he watched the ghost throw memories into the flame.

Perhaps, he thought with glee, this ghost is so fearful of men that he does not know the way to the Valley of Black Pebbles. And before he could change his mind again, he disguised himself as a tree spirit and addressed the ghost.

"Do you know the way to the Valley of Black Pebbles?'

"That is a place where only men dwell," said the ghost.

"I know," answered Feng Yi. "Unfortunately, I have business with men."

"Please do not tell me about business with men; I am seeking exoneration and entry into the Northern Heaven. Do you see that patch of iris in the ravine?"

"Yes."

"Beyond it is a small stream. Follow it to the Valley of Black Pebbles."

"Thank you. I will contribute a spell to your sacrifice." Feng Yi spat into the small fire and the flames disappeared because they too were ghosts and ghosts cannot exist in conjunction with men's saliva. The ghost never suspected Feng Yi to be a man so he believed the spell that put out the fire would hasten his exoneration.

"Thank you, Tree Spirit."

"Thank you, ghost," Feng Yi called over his shoulder.

The encounter with the ghost had not gone as expected and Feng Yi followed the stream reluctantly. He wished he was back with the August Personage Theater Troupe playing a harmless character in a classical play instead of following this trickle of water to his Destiny.

It was not a difficult passage but it took him three days to traverse the length of the narrow channel. Feng Yi saw it as a reprieve. Finally, he stood on a precipice above the Valley of Black Pebbles. Here he spent the night, and in the morning his mind gave new weight to the form known as "Carrying the Tiger to the Mountain." He was unable to leave his emotions behind as the form implied and he began to question his other abilities.

"What can I possibly learn here?" He thought from his vantage point. "It takes all my energies to discipline myself and keep my own mind and body in harmony without the emotional strain of others around. Why did I come? Maybe I should go back."

"You can always trick them as you did me."

It was the ghost Feng Yi had met in the mountains.

"I am sorry." Feng Yi hung his head. "I only wanted directions and I didn't want to frighten you."

"I suppose I did learn a lesson. I could seek revenge, but that would not get me the exoneration I desire. Seeing your torment over this journey, I think I shall let you go on."

"I see," said an unwilling Feng Yi.

"Well then, go. Leave these mountains and meet your miserable Destiny."

Feng Yi's clothes were tattered from the journey so he appeared in the village disguised as a beggar. He hobbled into the square with the help of two crooked sticks and lowered himself before the shrine of the founding ancestor. A small girl approached carrying fruit.

"Please, Young Mistress, I am hungry," he croaked.

"How did you get here?" she said in surprise. "Do your begging somewhere else." She threw a rotten plum at his chest.

"Have you no charity for one who seeks absolution under the eyes of the Immortals?" He begged.

But the little girl just laughed and continued on her errand.

A group of village boys were playing a game in a courtyard nearby and heard the conversation. They left their game and came out to jeer at the crippled beggar, for they knew there was something dubious about him.

"You are a pitiful heap of viscera," they chanted.

"You could not have been born, but must have escaped from the bowels of a monster," they called.

Feng Yi shook his head, for children are expected to be cruel.

Soon an old peasant woman hobbled past. She looked at him and began screaming. "Harmful emanations! Save me! Protect me!" She stumbled past him screaming and waving her hands.

Soon others wandered out to the square.

"Where did he come from?"

"Why don't you take your weary flesh to some other village," someone called.

"Find your Tao elsewhere," they taunted.

One kicked dry earth at him. Another threw a stone. Soon others bent down to search for more stones.

Feng Yi jumped and began to shout. "It is I, Feng Yi!"

But this seemed to scare the people more and he was forced to run away from the Shrine of the Founding Ancestor, out to the Square of Eternal Wisdom, and into the courtyard of the local magistrate who was visiting his concubine at the time.

Still the crowd chased him.

Feng Yi entered the Celestial Pavilion and ran down the Corridor of Perfect Knowledge into the Court of Eternity. Here he hid behind a pile of embroidered brocades.

Feng Yi disguised himself as a shadow and dozed until the afternoon mealtime. When the Pavilion was quiet at last, he was able to achieve his escape. "I do not belong here anymore; these people are cruel and heartless," he said to himself. "I will depart quietly."

Near the gates, however, he ran into the old woman again and she gasped loudly.

"Be silent, old woman," said a young girl spinning silk in a disheveled courtyard nearby. "Go home to your mistress." And the old woman scuttled away.

"Thank you, Young Miss. I am Feng Yi, the actor."

"I am known as Red Orchid," she said.

She had been quite plain until Feng Yi smiled and called her "Young Miss," then a warm blush illuminated her face.

"Are you a spirit?" she asked. "Not many men come through the Mountains of Dispassion to this village. That is why the villagers are so fearful."

"I was born here. I have a brother; he is known as Linking Rings.

Do you know of him?"

"You are brother to the illusionist?"

"When I left, he was a child performing magic tricks."

"I will take you to him; his wives are my friends."

Feng Yi wished he had kept his mouth shut and pursued his plan to leave. However, he followed the girl, who was not so much of a girl and more of a woman when she stood up. It seemed that the loom kept only her fingers and eyes nimble.

She led him through many courtyards to a very large household with children playing everywhere. When Feng Yi saw the children he became fearful and disguised himself as a tiger. Red Orchid only laughed, her face illuminated again, but the children ran away. Inside, on a huge teak chair, a man in a blue-green robe embroidered with bats was lecturing his wives on the etiquette of vegetables.

"One must approach a mushroom slowly from the shadows, and pluck it at the appropriate time or it will disappear."

With that all the mushrooms in the lacquer bowel in front of him went up in a puff of crimson smoke. The wives sighed.

"Whereas leeks appreciate boldness … "

As he drew closer, Feng Yi could see the man's face clearly and it was amazingly similar to his own.

"Ah," he said in shock.

The wives began to scream and hid behind the chair.

"It is not a tiger," Red Orchid called.

Linking Rings stared intently without moving. "Of course not, it is my brother, Feng Yi," he pronounced finally. "Fetch tea." Then, "never mind, I will entertain him. You take your rest, my lovelies." And the wives scampered away with Red Orchid to weave tapestries and gossip.

Feng Yi was thankful for the stillness.

"It is as I had foreseen," said Linking Rings. "You have not changed a bit. If you would be pleased to relinquish your disguise … "

"Thank you, brother. It is good to see you well."

"I trust your journey was not too difficult?"

"Actually, the journey was much more pleasant than the arrival," said Feng Yi. "That is, before meeting Red Orchid. I had remembered this as such a delightfully isolated little village."

"Red Orchid is quite perceptive to have seen the implication of your situation. Our village has been found by few traders, but we are quite civilized," said Linking Rings.

"A pity," Feng Yi mumbled.

"Oh, I think not," said Linking Rings. "But how inconsiderate of me, you must rest from your journey."

After a delightful tea and exchange of old memories, Feng Yi attended a performance of magic that Linking Rings had prepared for his seventeen children and their friends. Feng Yi did his best to accustom himself to the children. After the performance, Linking Rings had a huge banquet prepared. All of this excitement made Feng Yi so tired that he missed his evening meditations and could barely find his sleeping rooms.

In the morning, after green tea and sweetmeats, Linking rings took him on a tour of the village. Feng Yi was so caught up in the bustle of the large household that he did not take time out for his T'ai Chi.

They had an audience at the House of Twelve Ornaments with the local magistrate and visited Flying Geese, the oldest man in the village. In the marketplace Linking Rings was quite well known.

"Do you always make tea for guests and do the shopping?" Feng Yi asked. "Surely this is an odd household?"

"Nonsense," said Linking Rings. "My wives are very industrious weavers. They and Red Orchid are responsible for almost all the silks, brocades, gauzes and tapestries in the village. They make quite a good living."

"How scandalous," said Feng Yi.

"Not at all. The arrangement is very pleasant for all of us."

They visited the Golden Mang Teahouse and Feng Yi disguised himself as the East wind. The women of the Golden Mang closed the door on him; Linking Rings had to persuade him to enter as a man.

"Surely these painted women are Evil?" Feng Yi whispered.

"Actually, I think you will find them very pleasant and kind." And indeed they were, for Linking Rings had a hard time convincing his brother to leave.

After a pleasurable lunch, they visited the silk worm farm and many shrines. Linking Rings pointed out the Endless Knot Buddhist Temple, the Musical Stone of Jade Confucian Temple, and the Flower Basket Taoist Temple.

"There must be much disharmony between the many religions,"

said Feng Yi.

"Actually not," his brother responded. "Life in our little village is quite harmonious."

"Do you feel that you have reached enlightenment, brother?" Feng Yi asked finally.

"I have certainly reached a state of contentment, and yet I still strive daily for perfection." Linking Rings laughed.

"And what of me, brother? I have come here seeking Feng Yi. You knew me as a child and you see me now; what do you think?"

"Have you ever seen the paper-tearing trick?" his brother asked.

"Yes. Please do not avoid my question."

"I am only using your method of facing life."

"But I ask for friendship and you offer illusion."

"Exactly. Can you not grasp what is inside yourself?"

"Within myself there is a master of disguises and an enlightened practitioner of T'ai Chi Ch'uan."

"Really," said Linking Rings. "Indeed you are a skillful actor, but where did your disguise get you in the Golden Mang Teahouse? Where did it get you that first day at the shrine of the founding ancestor? Or with the children? You are just as you were as a child, disguising yourself in order to avoid confrontation. Feng Yi is confined within himself. It has troubled me for thirty years."

Feng Yi was embarrassed and threw his cape over him and assumed the disguise of a rock in a patch of pigweed, but he knew what his brother said was true. He could not betray what had been in his heart for the whole journey.

"Allow me to offer you this one trick," Linking rings called to the rock that was Feng Yi. "Have you ever seen the illusion after which I was named?"

Linking Rings then produced five silver rings from his jacket. One at a time he tapped them on the cloak of Feng Yi to demonstrate that they were solid. One at a time he allowed the tenant farmers who sold taro and ginger to inspect them.

"They appear to be separate and independent." Linking rings held them in two hands.

"But they are not." Suddenly he dropped four of them. The rings hung in the air connected to the ring he still held.

"They are joined, as you can see." He held them up to the gathering crowd and spun them around.

" ... Bound to each other as we all are." Linking rings gathered the rings in both hands again and with a flick of his wrist, they fell in a chain, each one entwined with another.

"You see, we are bound to each other." He handed the joined rings to a farmer who demonstrated to his friends that they could not be disconnected.

Feng Yi peeked out from under his cloak to watch. "But I am an enlightened practitioner of T'ai Chi Ch'uan," he mumbled.

His brother stumbled about the square in vexation. "That can be just another method of curling up inside yourself. It is easy to be enlightened when you wander alone through the Mountains of Dispassion without the pressure of humanity at your back."

Linking Rings paused for a moment to watch a colorful fennghuang bird land on the rock that was Feng Yi. He was drawn closer to it as he spoke. "Enlightenment entails constant vigil; it takes all our efforts. And I personally think it is sometimes a bit selfish." With that Linking Rings stubbed his toe on the rock. At the same moment Feng Yi grabbed at the long tail feathers of the bird.

Feng Yi thought for an eternal moment before relinquishing the bird and helping Linking Rings up. "You are right, brother. I could have wandered through the Mountains of Dispassion happily forever, but I would not have conquered my fear. I have run away long enough. I shall stay in this village without a disguise and I shall take on students of T'ai Chi Ch'uan."

"I would be honored to become your first pupil," said Linking Rings, rubbing his bruised toe.

"We can begin now," said Feng Yi. "Perhaps you could call Red Orchid also; it is not enough for only eyes and fingers to be nimble."

Soon Feng Yi was leading a group of students in his own courtyard much to the confusion of local woodticks. He made many friends and confined his disguises to occasional dramatic presentations. His marriage to Red Orchid was blessed with several children and many exquisite tapestries. And all through the Valley of Black Pebbles and across the Mountains of Dispassion he was known thereafter as Grasper of the Bird's Tail.

The Ustek Cloudy

Among players and collectors of marbles, there exists the legend of the "Ustek Cloudy." The Ustek is said to have come from a village in Czechoslovakia that lies midway between Prague and Dresden. It is an area of undistinguished artisans and negligible childhood diversions. In antiquity, this area attracted many masterful magicians who were expelled from more civilized regions of the world. It is whispered that some of these accomplished sorcerers may have discovered the elixir vitae that allowed them to survive to more recent eras, and that they may have created the Ustek Cloudy as a refuge in the event of future persecutions. Nevertheless, we have no concrete evidence to connect these magicians with the Ustek, nor do we have any other explanation for its existence.

The Ustek may have arrived in this country in the mid-1800's by way of the Spanish vessel "Desear" out of Cadiz. The captain's log mentions "la sefera fantastica," in the possession of an anonymous young passenger. He writes briefly of "reflections of an erotic miniature landscape" he views in this tiny sphere. There is no way of knowing for sure if this is the Ustek Cloudy, but it seems likely as the legend states emphatically that there is only one such marble in existence.

The first definitive mention of the Ustek comes from a young man named Mac Spiner in Ossning, New York. Spiner won the Ustek

Cloudy in a game of ringtaw in 1927. He was apparently not advised of its qualities, and discovered them himself that night. His diary describes it as follows:

" ... orange in color, it looks like a regular cloudy. But hold it up to your eye and you can see a whole world in there – trees, flowers, grass and a little stream. I think I'll give it to my teacher Miss Figuroa, maybe she'll let me stay to clean the boards ... "

Spiner did give the Ustek to his beloved teacher. Miss Figuroa's diary gives a more detailed description:

" ... a most amazing object, salmon in color with varying shades of delicate iridescence. When held up to the light, one can see inside a miniature landscape, so sublime as to entrance. The fantastic foliage seems to shimmer about a spill of crystal water. A glittery fog somewhat obscures this unpredictable view – I assume this is why our Mac insists on calling it a 'Cloudy.' He was told it was called the 'Ustek Cloudy,' a very ostentatious title for a child's toy, at least that's what I thought before I had the leasure of careful observation. Can it be birds that I see in there? Yes, there is some movement. And a stone bridge, perhaps a rainbow beyond. Studying it is a most tempting pastime; I can not seem to get enough."

There, Miss Figuroa's diary ends, somewhat abruptly as she seems to have disappeared. Her neighbors remembered her as a romantic young woman given to poetry and daydreaming. They thought she may have run off with a beau, though no one could name any recent suitors. Everyone agreed that she was unusually dedicated to her students, and it seemed unlikely that she would run off without making some arrangements for them. The local police presumed abduction, but no substantial clues were found, nor was there evidence of foul play.

The Ustek is said to have been in the possession of Ambrose Bierce early in 1913. Some aviation workers claim to have seen it in the cabin of the Lockheed Electra piloted by Amelia Earhart. It appeared next in 1946 in a curio shop in Aspire, Maine; in a moshie tournament in Kansas City, Mo. in 1948, and a few months later in the collection of a wealthy banker in Assembly, Wisconsin – but he could not be located for comment. It was seen by several young cadets at West Point in 1949, among the belongings of Richard Calvin Cox. Crew members of a Boeing 727 report that it was in the possession of the alleged D.B. Cooper just before he disappeared over Reno, Nevada. There is even one bazaar newspaper article from Skinny-Dip, Idaho, dated 1908 that states "an intricately cultivated child's marble on display at the county fair was swallowed by a passenger pigeon in full view of the Tea Garden Society."

A twelve-year-old girl in Hunker, West Virginia, reports being charmed by a monstrous marble in 1978. She stated that no sooner had she looked into it, than she found herself walking beneath lush overhanging foliage of a type unidentifiable. Despite this abundance of plant life, she felt that somewhere near there was a large population of both animals and people, mostly children. She advanced through a breech made by a tiny clear stream. In the stream she claims to have seen sparkling reddish fish whose scales reflected her a thousand fold and would have held her entranced had it not been for her mother's insistent calling. The mother was possessed by a disease the rustics call Cassandra's Fever, a symptom of which is an abnormality of the vocal chords causing a horrible shrilling of the voice. They, of course, would allow no outsider to examine either the girl, the marble or the mother.

Since then, there has been no definitive sightings of the Ustek Cloudy. However, there have been innumerable unexplained disappearances of children (and adults) in recent years. Researchers tend to attribute these disappearances to alien abductions. I believe there is a much more sinister power at work here, a power that stretches through space and time to the ancient magicians of Ustek, traces of whom have all mysteriously disappeared.

OTHER BOOKS FROM NONSTOP PRESS

The Collected Stories of Carol Emshwiller

$34.95 Hardcover (ISBN: 978-1-933065-22-9; *ebook available in July 2011.*)

A MASSIVE NEW COLLECTION OF 88 STORIES. Emshwiller's fiction cuts a straight path through the landscape of American literary genres: mystery, speculative fiction, magic realism, western, slipstream, fantasy and of course science fiction. Arranged chronologically, this landmark collection, the first of two volumes, allows the reader to see Emshwiller's development as a writer and easily recognize her as a major voice in the literary landscape.

Musings and Meditations: Essays and Thoughts by Robert Silverberg

(trade paper $18.95 ISBN: 978-1-933065-20-5; *ebook available in August 2011*)

A NEW COLLECTION of essays from one of contemporary science fiction's most imaginative and acclaimed wordsmiths shows that Robert Silverberg's non-fiction is as witty and original as his fiction. No cultural icon escapes his scrutiny, including fellow writers such as Robert Heinlein, Arthur C. Clarke, H. P. Lovecraft, and Isaac Asimov.

Why New Yorkers Smoke edited by Luis Ortiz

(trade paper $14.95 ISBN: 978-1-933065-24-3; *ebook available in September 2011*)

Subtitled; *New Yorkers Have Many Things to Fear: Real and Imagined.* This collection of original stories answers the question "What is there to fear in New York City?," with creative responses from Paul di Filippo, Scott Edelman, Carol Emshwiller, Lawrence Greenberg, Gay Partington Terry, Don Webb, and Barry Malzberg, among others. The contributors represent a combination of New Yorkers, ex-New Yorkers, and wannabe New Yorkers, and their tales of fear all use the city as an ominous backdrop. Blending the genres of fantasy, science fiction, and horror, the stories in this anthology showcase work from up-and-coming writers as well as veterans of fantastical fiction.

101 Best Science Fiction Novels: 1985-2010

co-authored by Damien Broderick and Paul Di Filippo.

Inspired by David Pringle's landmark volume, SCIENCE FICTION: THE 100 BEST NOVELS, which appeared in 1985, this volume will supplement the earlier selection with the authors' choice of the best SF novels issued in English during the past quarter-century. David Pringle will provide a foreword, and publication will occur in early 2012.

Cult Magazines: From A to Z, A Compendium of Culturally Obsessive & Curiously Expressive Publications Edited by Earl Kemp & Luis Ortiz

$34.95 ISBN: 978-1-933065-14-4

Featuring full-color reproductions of hundreds of distinctive cult magazine cover images, this reference's backgrounds, histories, and essays offer a complete picture of a bygone era. Fully illustrated in color.

Other Spaces, Other Times: A Life Spent in the Future
by Robert Silverberg

$29.95 Hardcover (ISBN: 978-1-933065-12-0)

A collection of autobiographical writings. Fully illustrated, with color. sections.

The Day Of The Locust by Nathanael West

Art by Martos (ISBN 9781933065373; Trade paper, ebook, graphic novel, available in early 2012)

Library of Artists

Vol. 1: Arts Unknown: The Life & Art of Lee Brown Coye by Luis Ortiz; $39.95 hardcover. *Fully illustrated, in color.* ISBN: 978-1-933065-04-4

Vol. 2: Emshwiller: Infinity x Two
    The Art & Life of Ed & Carol Emshwiller by Luis Ortiz; $39.95
    hardcover ISBN: 978-1-933065-08-3

A 2008 Hugo Award nominee and Locus Award finalist. *Fully illustrated, in color.*

Vol. 3: Outermost: The Art + Life of Jack Gaughan by Luis Ortiz; $39.95 hardcover Fully illustrated, in color. ISBN: 978-1-933065-16-8

www.nonstop-press.com

Gay Terry has published stories in the *Fortean Bureau*, *Lady Churchill's Rosebud Wristlet*, *Twilight Zone Magazine*, *Full Spectrum 2,* and other publications. She lives in Brooklyn, New York.